THE

RUINATION

OF

ESSIE SPARKS

Wild Western Rogues Series

Book Two

Barbara Ankrum

Book design by eBook Prep
www.ebookprep.com

Cover design by The Killion Group Inc.
www.thekilliongroupinc.com

August, 2016
ISBN: 978-1-61417-866-8

ePublishing Works!
www.epublishingworks.com

DEDICATION

This book could not have happened without the support and love of several people. First and always, my husband, David, for his unwavering belief in me.

To Challee and Matt Garland, for everything and then some.

And to Julie Ganis for her expert editing skills and long friendship.

Thank you all so much!

THE
WILD WESTERN ROGUES
SERIES

The Lady Takes A Gunslinger
The Ruination of Essie Sparks

PROLOGUE

The Industrial School for Indian Children
Gallatin River Valley, Montana Territory
June, 1888

The door to The Wages of Sin creaked opened with a rusty-hinged sound that woke thirteen-year-old Little Wolf from his fevered dream. Disoriented, he cracked open a swollen eye and an arrow of sunlight blinded him. Greedily, he inhaled the fresh air that rushed in past the suffocating morning heat.

Had he spent three days or four inside Wages? He'd lost count of the moons that had cooled the oven-like wooden shed at night. All he knew was one more day baking under the sun, and his dead father—who at first had only visited him in his dreams, but now sat in the corner of the box, waiting, watching—might do as he'd promised and take him to walk beside him in the world of his ancestors.

All the things his father had once taught him were fading from his memory. The true language of the People had been ground out of him and the comforting echo of his mother's voice was nearly disappeared. But he wasn't ready yet to leave this world or to greet Maheo, the Great Spirit, or the angry God that Reverend Dooley always threatened him with.

Ah, how he missed his parents. How he longed to feel his

mother's arms around him again, even though he was too old to want or need such things. Two years in this place had forced him to be as the willow and not the oak, as his grandfather had taught him.

So, if they pushed that watery, pig-slop, *vého'e* soup through the door again, he would drink it down. If they beat him, he would not let them kill him. And if they let him go, he would let his anger heal him, and then he would do the thing he'd decided to do.

"Dead or alive?" a man's voice asked from outside the shed.

His skin crawled at the hopefulness in the guard's question. It would be less trouble for the one they called Sergeant Laddner if he was dead. Then they could put him under the ground with the other Cheyenne children buried behind the school. The ones they'd helped to kill or those who'd died of *vé'ho'e's* sickness, or the ones whose hearts had broken.

But *he* wouldn't be less trouble. He would be more. Much more.

The *Tsitsistas* had a word for the one called Laddner— who wasn't really a soldier anymore at all, but a hired guard here—but that word, like so many others, had been scrubbed from his memory. Coward, the whites might call him, if they were not so afraid of him. Perhaps the wolverine was his spirit animal, because nothing else could account for the viciousness of a man who took such pleasure in hurting the children of the People.

"Alive," another guard said, dragging him out of the box to curl on the hard dirt at the door. He tipped something over Little Wolf's head. A bucketful of cool water slapped him hard, like an open hand.

He gasped, but turned his face up to catch the water with his tongue, his thirst a wild thing. He brought his hand to his mouth and licked his muddy fingers.

Five feet away sat a tin cup full of water. Out of reach. Beside it was the book he'd taken, the one written by that man about that *vé'ho'e* boy named Huckleberry. Beyond that, small islands of children huddled together, watching to see if the guards had killed him. They didn't dare come any closer.

Little Wolf's focus was on that cup full of water. It shamed him to crawl on all fours toward the thing like a weak bobcat toward its mother's teat, but he could not stand. His shaking arms fought him.

The other guard picked up the book. "Is this what you want, boy-o? This stupid book you stole?"

He shook his head, gritting his teeth. *Books cannot not be stupid. Only men like you who cannot read them.*

Laddner picked up the cup of water, held it just out of his reach. "I'm gonna give you this water when you tell me you've learned your lesson, Daniel. Have you?"

Little Wolf's mouth was too dry to speak. A frog-like croak came out instead. *My. Name. Is. Not. Daniel.*

The other guard laughed at him. Laddner just shook his head. "What was that? I didn't quite hear you."

If the hatred he felt for this man could pierce his white, soldier skin, cut through his ribs and stab his heart like an arrow, then the soldier-pretender would be dead now. One day, Little Wolf would count coup on him, like his father before him had done to his enemies, before peeling off Laddner's scalp and leaving him to soak this Cheyenne earth with his blood.

"All right," Laddner went on, "the reason you've been in there so long is because you were warned once before about the books. And you disobeyed the rules. You tell me you understand that, Daniel, and I'll give you this water."

Little Wolf heard the distant shout of a woman, shoving through the crowds of children, calling for them to stop. He didn't need to look up to know which woman it was.

"Leave him be!" Her voice came suddenly from nearby and he felt her drop down beside him. Mrs. Sparks put her hands tenderly on his shoulders. "Daniel?"

"You are not helpin' his cause, Essie," Laddner said.

"His time in there is up. You have no right."

"No *right*? When I was a boy, my daddy used to take a leather strap or a...strong piece of wood to me when I did wrong. Taught me well. This?" He pointed to Wages. "This is easy time. What the boy needs is a firm hand. A hand of discipline. All of these children need discipline. And I've been tasked with giving them some by Reverend Dooley and by the Almighty himself."

"The Almighty, is it? Careful, sergeant," she said, sending him a dark look. "Your piousness is showing."

Laddner's face flattened with distaste. "Glass houses, Mrs. Sparks."

His partner guffawed until she pinned him with a withering look. The man stopped laughing and cleared his throat.

Brushing her red curls from her eyes, she glared up at him. "Oh, please spare me your concern, sergeant. And don't think I won't take up your treatment of Daniel with Reverend Dooley."

Little Wolf collapsed against her and she held him with his back against her chest as he watched the man warily. The sergeant was yellow-haired with eyes the color of the cold, deep water. But when he smiled down at Mrs. Sparks, his eyes were full of lies.

"I imagine you will mention it, rebel that you are. But standing in righteousness is firm footing. We are lifting these children up from the heathens that birthed them, Mrs. Sparks. And that does not come without a price. The reverend would agree. Just look. He's up in his window, watchin' even now."

Indeed, the headmaster was at his office window. He stepped back into the shadows as they looked. Maybe, Little Wolf thought, I'll have the good reverend's scalp, too.

"The reverend has no patience for thieves. Nor for those who protect the wrongdoers. It doesn't bode well for this boy's future or yours, by association, if you catch my meaning."

But Mrs. Sparks didn't seem concerned with his meaning. She pressed the backs of her pale fingers to his hot cheek. Her touch felt cool.

"You've nearly killed him in this heat. Give me that water. Now."

The sergeant handed the cup to her with a level smile. "You should think twice before issuin' orders. Choosing sides against the reverend can be dangerous. He's got his eye on you. So you'd best mind your P's and Q's and start acting like a proper schoolmarm, or you're like to find yourself outside these gates with nowhere to go."

"*Proper*?" She tipped the cup against Little Wolf's lips and he guzzled down the water in gulps. Her palm flattened against his hot forehead. "And who taught you about proper, Sergeant Laddner? The wolves that raised you?"

A snicker of laughter from one of the clusters of children drew his slow, hard gaze. The other guard feigned an empty-handed thrust at them and they scattered like scared cats.

He'd seen the way Laddner looked at Mrs. Sparks, the way he sniffed after her when she wasn't watching. But all the men acted like fools around her, with her wild-colored hair and those blue-green eyes that seemed to look right inside a person.

"We can be friends or enemies, Essie," Laddner said. "And I'm not an enemy you'd care to have."

"Or there's a third choice," she said, pulling Little Wolf to his feet and bracing her shoulder under his arm, "which is that you are nothing to me. And call me Mrs. Sparks or call me nothing at all."

As they shuffled off toward the dormitory, Little Wolf smiled darkly. He loved her for speaking the very words he wanted to say.

"Have it your way, then," Laddner shouted after them, a smile in his words. "But I wouldn't be throwing rocks if I was you. *Mrs. Sparks.*"

She *would* throw rocks, Little Wolf guessed. She mostly always did, when it came to the children. But something about that man's words echoed in his head like an omen.

He would live. He had survived the Wages of Sin and he'd never go back. He would be a good, pretend white boy for as long as it took to get his strength back.

Because now he had a plan.

CHAPTER 1

August, 1888

Standing rigidly before the half circle of five school board members who'd gathered for an emergency meeting called by the Reverend Dooley, Essie Sparks ignored the painful kink in her shoulders. The knot had evolved from a night of tossing and turning at the prospect of this meeting. Not that she had any doubt as to its outcome.

She clutched the thick-chained gold locket at her throat, rubbing it between her fingers out of long habit, taking solace from it. Silly. There was no solace inside this locket, only painful memories. But somehow she felt less alone, standing before these five, with the locket close to her heart.

They had chosen the church sanctuary for their inquisition. Knowing what was coming, she'd dressed contrarily in a sunny gold calico, though she supposed the irony of such a small defiance would be lost on them. Her fingers played with the locket in the sweltering room as she waited for the Reverend Dooley to finish reading his prepared statement. She hardly listened. Blood was rushing in her ears, making it impossible to concentrate. And what did it matter? She was well acquainted with the list of complaints against her.

Instead, she let her gaze drift over the faces of her

accusers who, except for Reverend Dooley, avoided making eye contact with her. Rufus Chanley folded and refolded his hands. His wife, Elda, stared out the window behind Essie's head, looking sour. The Deek brothers, both pious ranchers in their fifties, alternately checked their watches and twisted their beards. All good, upstanding members of the church that sponsored this school, as well as school board members. And not one of them would meet her eye.

Hypocrites.

"...and so it is the determination of this school board that your teaching contract is hereby terminated. You will have two days to pack your things and vacate the premises." Dooley removed his wire-rimmed glasses and folded them carefully on the table.

That small action—the putting down of his glasses—seemed like some final punctuation mark on the downward spiral of her life. But all the same, she asked, "There is no redress? You will not hear my side? I am simply to be dismissed?"

"We already know your side, Mrs. Sparks. We have seen it in action often enough. We do not traffic with subversives. We will, of course, provide you with a train ticket back home—"

"*Home?*" She felt her cheeks flame with heat as she searched the faces of the others. "The reverend knows well that I have no home to go back to."

"Where you settle yourself after the termination of your contract is of no concern to us, madam," Dooley told her flatly, shuffling papers before him, aligning the edges in irritation.

"A contract that was to last for an entire year," she pointed out. "It's been just over six months since I arrived."

Dooley drummed his sausage-fingers on the table with impatience. "This board can terminate any teacher's contract as it deems necessary. Your subversive tactics and your—"

"Yes, you said that word, subversive. In what way was I

subversive? By caring for these children? By teaching them to read and do arithmetic? By allowing them hope?"

The other board members looked to Dooley to explain, preferring not to get in the middle of what was clearly his fight.

"*Hope*?" Dooley scoffed. "Mrs. Sparks. Need I remind you of the purpose of this school? That our mission is to drum the savage from these poor, godless heathens given to our care? Instill decent, civilized Christian values upon their lost souls? We have been tasked with teaching them the error of their ways, not to give them false hopes. Not to encourage them to imagine they can rise above their stations, or to expect higher education where none exists for them. Not to justify open rebellion or—"

"Of course, you're referring to Daniel. The boy you nearly killed in Wages last month."

That got the attention of the others. Dooley narrowed a look at her. "Killed? That's an exaggeration of the worst kind. He was punished for stealing a book. And mark me, outside these walls, such a crime is punishable by much, much worse."

"You say stealing, I say borrowed. But that's just semantics, isn't it? Where the children are concerned, the benefit of the doubt always falls your way."

"Why would you ever think it would be otherwise, Mrs. Sparks? I am the headmaster of this school, in case that hasn't been made perfectly clear."

"Oh, yes. Quite. And shall I assume," she continued, "that Sergeant Laddner had something to do with this decision? Since he is your right hand in all things, including the withholding of water and decent food to those children you punish in that box?"

"That is not true. And Sergeant Laddner had nothing to—"

"And who has threatened me, personally, on numerous occasions, if I do not fawn over his inappropriate and disgusting attentions?"

A rumble of whispers broke out in the semicircle of board members.

Dooley's face clouded up and he shoved to his feet. "Be careful what you imply here, Mrs. Sparks. You are the focus of this meeting. As for that boy, he is an incorrigible troublemaker who was merely taught a lesson after a few days in Wages."

"*He wanted to read a book*. That was his only crime. How can you deny a child—"

"Deny?" Dooley repeated incredulously. "Look around you, Mrs. Sparks. These children are fed, clothed, educated and redeemed. They are not starving on the reservation like their indolent relatives. They should be grateful for everything we've done for them, not biting the hand that feeds them! *Deny*? It is by our grace that they even live now."

Essie panned the small gathering with her gaze. "It's you who have it wrong, Reverend Dooley."

Dooley gathered up his papers. "This meeting is adjourned." The others began to rise, but she spoke over them.

"There is no us and them. They *are* us. Human beings, with feelings and hopes and dreams. Not inanimate clay to be molded into what you want them to be, stripped of everything dear to them, even their names, their language, their families. They are children, just like yours, Reverend Dooley and yours, Mrs. Chanley. If you spent any time with them at all you'd see—"

"We've said our peace," Matthias Deek said in sharp warning.

Dooley stalked out of the room. The Deek brothers followed. Mr. Chanley tugged on his wife's arm, but the salt-and-pepper-haired woman hesitated, turning back to Essie.

"They were born into savagery and that is all they will ever know, but for the skills we give them here, Mrs. Sparks. Surely you must see that. They are the lucky ones. But you? You do not fit here. You must move on with your life. I pray that God lights your path."

And with that they filed out, leaving her standing alone in

the rough-hewn sanctuary.

Feeling suddenly dizzy in the sweltering chapel, Essie braced one hand on the backless pew beside her and sat down. *God?*

An irrational laugh bubbled up in her. No. No God would miraculously show up to care about her now when He'd so clearly forsaken her and these children so completely. No, she was on her own now. And somehow, she would have to manage. Six months had not been anywhere near enough time to save the money she would need to survive on her own.

But she had her wits. And a ticket. That ticket would take her to some new life that she couldn't even imagine just now. It wouldn't be Maryland, though. She wouldn't go back there. Everyone she'd once loved there was gone.

But she would get as far away from this place as possible. With winter coming, she should head south to the warmth. She might take that train to North Dakota, then cash in the rest of her ticket and head down the Mississippi, perhaps. Look for work? But who would hire her without letters of referral?

Panic crept up her throat, along with the very real possibility that she had just thrown away her future.

And who would protect Daniel now and the others? Would they understand her abandoning them this way? Would he? She'd never planned on involving her heart here at this school, but she had, nonetheless. Now, it felt broken.

Abigail Gallinder, a sweet-faced teacher who was three years younger than her own twenty-six, appeared at the chapel doorway. Abby tucked a nervous hand against her pinned-up chestnut-colored hair when she saw Essie, and her expression fell.

"They've done it, haven't they? They've let you go."

Essie held back the tears that suddenly threatened. "I'm afraid it's come to that, yes."

She crossed the distance between them and sat down beside Essie. "I'm so sorry. It's not right. It's not fair."

A lump formed in her throat at the thought of leaving

Abby, too, who'd become a good friend. A fellow subversive, she was much better at editing her thoughts and feelings, instead quietly doing what needed to be done to help the children. Illicit late nights of girl talk in Essie's room had solidified their friendship, and together they'd planned some of the subversive activities of which Essie had been accused, like teaching the children baseball with sticks and balls made of rolled-up stockings, and listening to their prayers in their native tongue. Abigail knew most of her secrets and had kept them all. A truer friend could not be found.

"What will you do now?" she asked, her eyes welling. "Where will you go?"

Essie took her hand. "Don't worry about me. I'll find my way."

"I do, though. Worry. You must promise to write me. Promise."

"Of course I will. How could I forget you?"

Abby studied her. "It won't be the same without you here. If I had half a nerve, I'd go with you. Get out of this place for good." She touched a knuckle beneath her nose and pressed it there. "But I...I can't go. Not until they kick me out. Like you, I'm...entangled with these children now. I don't know how you'll manage to leave."

Nor did she. But in two days' time, leave she would.

Rubbing the precious gold locket between her fingers, she cast a look at the stack of bibles on the pew beside her. If she were still a believer, she might just blame their vengeful God for ripping away every child—or more accurately, every *person*—she'd ever allowed herself to love. But it was some comfort that the failings of her life were hers alone.

Somehow, she would survive this and rebuild her life. Pull her inner strength around her to protect her from any more pain. From now on, it would be just her and her alone. No more love. No more risking her heart. She consoled herself that she still had her dignity, and that at least this place was too remote for them to smear her good name wherever she was going.

She hoped. After all, what more could they take from her?

Two nights later, as the Rutting Moon started its slow descent in the sky toward dawn, the man the Cheyenne called Black Thorn inhaled a quick breath of night air, sensing that something was wrong. He tugged the Winchester rifle slung across his back by its leather strap over his head and settled his grip along the wooden stock. Exactly what triggered the hair on the back of his neck to rise as he lingered at the edge of the nearby pines, he could not say. He could not detect any scent of smoke or carbine. No loud voices or any outward signs of trouble. Instead, what he heard was dead silence. And that was unusual.

He had come here two nights running to make sure his plan would work. He had watched the boy go into his dormitory at night and knew, by the position of the moon, when he left that place just before dawn to tend to the horses. He should have been out by now.

As the thick clouds pulled away from the moon, he pushed his long hair aside, his gaze narrowing.

Horses. That's what was missing.

There were no horses in the outside pen as there had been every other night. Not a single one. In the dead of the Montana winter, they would put the horses up, he supposed, but not in the heat of summer.

He waited until the clouds swept back into place before urging his horse, Náhkohe, and the smaller pony he'd brought for the boy out of the shelter of the pines and headed toward the empty paddock. He dismounted silently and ground-tied the two horses. Listening to the silence within the barn, he guessed there were no horses inside either. The stable had been emptied, the gate at the back side of the corral left open. And the stockman he'd seen every night was nowhere in sight. If the two guards in the nearby towers knew the animals were gone, they'd sounded no alarm. In fact, he guessed they were asleep at their posts as they had been the previous night he'd come to survey the best way to grab Little Wolf.

A bad feeling crawled through him, making the urgency to get the boy stronger. He had sworn an oath to his mother's dying younger sister, White Owl, to bring the boy to her and he meant to keep it.

But where is he?

He found the stockman a minute later, lying on the stable floor, out cold. There was a gag around his mouth, his hands and feet were bound and blood caked around a still-leaking wound to his head.

Black Thorn hovered in the shadows, trying to puzzle out what had happened here. For all he knew, Little Wolf might be locked in that box they kept at the center of the compound. He could be sick or even dead. But someone had let the stock loose and disabled the only man blocking the path of escape. Logic told him one of the children had done this.

Was it Little Wolf? No. Impossible that the boy would run just as he was coming for him. Unless...

Had the boy heard of his mother's illness? But how? News of family was systematically kept from the children. Just as families were denied visits with their children.

For the hundredth time tonight, he wished he had taken the boy yesterday when he had him in his sights. But he'd wanted a peaceful exit. None of them could afford violence.

But if wishes were horses, his father used to say, *the Cheyenne would win.*

From the shadows outside the stable, he looked up at the two-story dormitory. Only one light glimmered through a window at the corner of the second floor. A shadow—a woman—paced back and forth in front of the lace curtain, illuminated from behind. She was undressing, he saw now, removing one garment after another, then braiding her long, curly hair. Odd, that she'd decided to undress when dawn was nearly breaking. Now and then she stopped and stared through the curtain as if she were searching the darkness for something. Or someone. Why, he wondered, when the rest of the world slept, was she awake? Was she part of what was happening here tonight?

Then the light extinguished and the schoolyard fell into utter darkness.

But for a long moment, she stood at the window in her underthings, like a ghostly watcher. Would she see him if he moved? Had she seen him somehow already?

A moment later, she disappeared from the window and did not come back.

For the next few minutes, he waited for her to rise again. He listened to the blood rush in his ears and felt it pulse against his throat. Sweat slicked his skin, despite the still cool night air. From the sheath at his side, he pulled his hunting knife, counting the windows from the left side of the building. He needed help finding the boy and had no time to waste hunting for him.

Despite her vow to face morning on her own terms, she must have fallen asleep, because she'd been dreaming of Aaron. About his tiny fingers curled around hers. His rosebud mouth curved up into a smile. Toothless gums, bright blue eyes. She imagined they would have stayed blue, had he lived. Not the ice-blue of his father's eyes, but a warm, deep, ocean blue.

In her dream, she was holding him against her, walking on a verdant field, the chime of a milk cow's bell clinking in the distance. All around them birds were fluttering, mingling, cooing. So many that she had to step around them as they scattered in her path, their wings brushing against her, their feathers floating in the air. Aaron reached out his small hand to catch one and as he did, he spoke to her, some whisper of warning as the entire flock rose at once and lifted into the sky, their wings battering her face until—

She woke with a start at the pressure of something over her mouth.

With a muffled scream, she opened her eyes to find the

dark shadow of a man above her, his hand over her mouth! She thrashed against him, clawing him with her fingernails, but he forced her still with both his weight and the blade of a knife she felt nick the tender skin of her throat.

Panic took hold of her.

She could see nothing in the thick blackness, but against her ear, he hissed a word.

"*He'kotoo'estse!*" His long, dark hair curtained against her cheek.

Her mind froze along with the rest of her. *Renegade. Cheyenne? Are there others? Am I being taken?* She made a squeak of terror against his palm and shook her head, indicating she didn't understand him.

I'm dreaming. This is just a dream. Wake up!

"Scream and I will kill you." This time, shockingly, he spoke in perfect English. "Understand?"

CHAPTER 2

With a desperate nod of her head, Essie prayed he would know she meant to cooperate. She would *not* scream. She would *not* die here tonight. She would *not* let him kill her.

He was built like an anvil, and tall, she realized as she became aware of his long body pressing against her. His arms and chest were bare and strongly muscled. The eyes that stared down at her, once hers adjusted to the dim light, were a silvery gray. Not black. Nor was his long hair as black as the children's, but closer to the dark color of roasted chestnuts.

Half-breed? That would explain the English.

And how had he gotten in? Past the guards?

He pressed the blade harder against her throat. "I am going to take my hand away," he said in a voice so low she had to strain to hear him.

She swallowed against the blade. Her whole body shook and she gasped for air as he lifted his hand away.

"Little Wolf," he demanded between gritted teeth. "Where is he?"

She shook her head. "Little...Wolf?"

"*Daniel*." The word was a whispered snarl. "The name you gave him when you stole his. Where is his bed?"

Cheyenne, then. A Cheyenne renegade who spoke perfect English. "Down the hall. Let me up and I...I'll show you."

"And why would I trust you to do that?"

"You have the knife. I—I won't scream."

He had no apparent answer for that. He glanced around the room, then, searching for what, she couldn't imagine. Perhaps deciding whether to kill her, gag her or knock her senseless. But he must have believed her, because he lifted his weight from her and stood, keeping the knife at her throat. "Get up. *Slow.*"

Shaking, she did. Her legs felt like quicksilver and a rush of fear charged through her. The floor was cold on her bare feet. Dressed in only her unmentionables—her white, cotton one-piece chemise and drawers, her loosened corset and several tucked and gathered petticoats and the soft bustle she'd chosen for traveling—she felt near naked standing before him. His gaze raked down her there in the dark, but she sensed he could see all of her.

She'd stood on this precipice once before, looking down over the edge between life and death. After Aaron. But the decision she'd made then still pulsed through her now and warned her to fight. To think. To clear her mind of fear. Slowly, she reached for a dark blue paisley shawl she'd left lying at the end of her bed and showed him she only meant to wrap it around herself.

He lifted his chin, giving her permission, before moving behind her to curl an arm around her shoulders and poise the knife back at her throat. "One sound…" he warned.

She nodded and he opened the door to the hallway. Nearly dark as her room, the corridor was illuminated only by a small oil lamp at the end, near the stairwell. At the doorway, she gestured with a nod to their left and he tugged her toward the room where Daniel and three other boys slept.

Their door was open slightly, since Micah, the seven-year-old who slept in the bunk above Daniel's, had night terrors and could not abide the dark. Essie pushed the portal and stared into the room. Micah, Joseph and Samuel were all asleep in their beds in various states of sprawl, their dark, cherubic faces upturned, carefree in sleep.

Daniel lay burrowed under his thin wool blanket.

She pointed to that bed and her captor pulled her with him to lower the blanket from the boy's face. But when he did, nothing but a pillow lay where Daniel's head should be. He yanked the rest of the blanket downward to find clothing, wrapped in bundles under his covers.

Her stomach sank and her mind went momentarily blank. *Impossible.*

But then she remembered the look in his eyes that day she'd taken him from Wages. And ever since then, he hadn't been the same boy. Now, with her dismissal, she might have underestimated his anger with her, too. His sense of abandonment. He had looked to her for protection. And she was leaving. *Oh, Daniel...what have you done?*

If one could feel fury, it practically rolled off the man beside her. He started to jerk her back out of the room, but she stopped him.

"Wait!" she whispered, reaching for the boy's bed.

She lifted up the thin straw-filled mattress and searched the hidden slit in the middle.

Empty. Her heart sank.

The knife tightened at her throat again and the man jerked her back out of the room and down the hall. She nearly fell as he pulled her along and she felt the sharp prick of the blade draw blood again. But except for a hiss of pain, she made no sound until he'd stopped with her in the stairwell at the end of the hall.

There, the thin light from the oil lamp illuminated his face as he tugged her around and pinioned her to the wall with his arm. She inhaled sharply at her first good look at him. It was the scar that caught her breath, a slashing, flat red line that cut from the top of his left cheek to nearly his mouth. It was the only flaw in an otherwise shockingly handsome face that indeed branded him not as a full-blooded Cheyenne, but at least half white.

He jerked her upward and grated close to her ear, "Where is he?"

She shook her head. "I don't know. I think he's run away."

His hand tightened on her arm. "No one runs away from this place."

"No one *escapes* from this place," she corrected.

"What were you looking for in there? Under his bed?"

"His medicine bag. He smuggled it in when he came here. The mattress was a secret hiding spot."

"A secret he told *you*?" He snorted his disbelief.

"Yes."

His gaze slid away from her, in the direction of the stairwell below them and down the hallway they'd left. Clearly he didn't believe her.

It could only help her cause to convince him. "It was a...he said it was a gift from his cousin or uncle. Someone named Black...Black Thorn. Do you know him?"

His eyes narrowed with a little flinch of surprise, but the look disappeared so quickly she might have imagined it. "Tell me where he's gone."

"I already told you," she repeated, leaning away from the knife blade. "I don't—"

"*Séaa*—" he hissed back, then spat out a handful of words in Cheyenne she didn't understand.

"If he's run, you're wasting time here with me," she said, cutting him off. "I've told you the truth. Just let me go and I promise I won't make a sound. Go and find him. He will be in terrible trouble if he's caught."

He loomed over her, raking a look down her as if he were assessing her ability to fight him should he choose to squash her like a bug. She supposed he enjoyed peeling her naked with his eyes, as a way to intimidate her.

Leaning close to her ear, he said, "How simple your life must be, that you'd imagine I would trust you with mine." The blade dug deeper into her skin, slicing her, drawing a bead of blood that she felt trickle down her neck.

"Simple? Cut me again and I will show you how simple it is to scream. I have very little left to lose here myself. You can kill me, but then you'll never find him. Because you'll be dead by dawn."

His free hand moved to her jaw and he squeezed. "Not

before I slice open your throat."

"But you won't. Or you would have already." She turned her head and met his hard gaze with one of her own.

One side of his mouth lifted in something that was not a smile. "Are you sure, *vé'ho'á'e*?"

She knew that word. *Vé'ho'á'e*. It meant '*white woman*,' but, like all words that referred to her kind, it was a word mostly spat by the Cheyenne when the whites turned their backs. Strange, from a man whose blood clearly came from both worlds.

"Go on, then," she hissed back. "Do it. What are you waiting for?"

A small line formed between his eyes as he considered her words, and his nostrils flared with anger. Lifting the knife away from her throat, he kept the blade pointed near her side. "One sound—" he warned again and tugged her down the stairs beside him.

They made their way past the kitchen and the great room, and were almost out the side door when, from somewhere behind them, came the sound of glass shattering on the pine planked floor.

It was Abigail, standing in the hallway in her wrapper, staring at them in horror—a broken glass spreading a white pool of milk on the floor.

In the next instant, the girl screamed bloody murder.

He cursed and hauled her out the door into the dark. Essie could hear Abby screaming and screaming behind her and knew it was only a matter of moments before the whole place was up and after them.

Oh, Abby! Thank you!

She stumbled as they raced toward the barn but he refused to let her fall. He tugged her beside him so hard she couldn't get her feet under her enough to kick at him. Behind them, shouts of alarm sounded and lights came on in the dormitory.

With the moon half out, he yanked her into the tall shadows of the fort-like lodgepole pine walls that enclosed the yard, toward the barn. Of course, it would be the first and only place Daniel would go, to his beloved paint pony, Lalo. He pretended to hate the job of mucking stalls so they would be sure to keep him there.

"The horses are gone," her captor said as if reading her mind. "All of them."

She felt the blood leave her face. "What?" Running away was one thing. Stealing a dozen horses was something else altogether. They hung people for horse thievery here. That he was a Cheyenne boy would only go against him. "You must find him before they do."

He shot a surprised look back at her. Or it might have been hate. Yes, it probably was.

Far across the yard, she thought she caught the glint of rifles pointed in their direction.

Oh, no. No!

She flung herself at the man holding her and knocked him forward just as two bullets tore into the wood fence behind them with a splintering explosion.

He pulled her back to her feet as two more gunshots exploded nearby. Hauling her inside the barn, he yanked the doors shut behind them. Did she just…? No. She could barely put one foot in front of the other without falling.

What are you doing? Let her go, some vestige of his common sense warned. *Let her go and get out before they kill you.*

Another voice argued, *She could be useful. As a hostage. Or a distraction.*

But with his arms around the half-dressed woman, some baser instinct fought him. He told himself it had nothing to do with the fire in her eyes—no, that was hatred. Or the way the woman felt, flush against him—*irrelevant.*

Or almost irrelevant.

I have very little left to lose here myself, she'd said, *so kill me, but you won't get the boy.*

She was right. He wouldn't. Maybe either way, he was already dead.

The sound of voices and rifles cocking outside the far end

of the barn reached them at the same instant. They both jerked a look at the doors they'd come in. He heard her suck in a breath, but she didn't scream. With the roll of one shoulder, he pulled his Winchester rifle around on its strap from behind him and into his free hand.

He backed her toward the open doors at the other end of the aisle, where dawn was lightening the horizon, but before they could get out of sight, the far doors flew open. Two men with shouldered rifles spotted them and began to fire.

Bullets ripped at the wood beside his head and inches from hers. He shoved her outside and pushed her behind the wooden doors. She went flying, skidding across the dirt in her white camisole and petticoats with a small gasp as bullets tore into the ground near his feet.

He fired back, two, three, four rounds before diving outside beside her and crawling to his knees in the straw-littered dirt there.

Náhkohe, his Appaloosa, pranced—quivering—fifteen feet away as more bullets tore at the edges of the door. The pony he'd brought for Little Wolf had bolted from the paddock at a gallop and was already disappearing up the hill.

He grabbed the woman by the arm and pulled her to her feet. Terror filled her expression as he dragged her toward his horse.

"Please!" she cried, but he ignored her, turning back to fire another round behind him as he heard the men leave their cover in the barn and run toward the open doors.

He threw her up onto his horse and vaulted up behind her. Corralling her with his arms, he jammed his heels in Náhkohe's sides and the horse raced forward out the open corral gate at a flat-out run.

Two more bullets whizzed by him, close enough to feel as they screamed past his head. Shoving the woman down against the horse's neck, he fired blindly back. Maybe he hit one. Maybe he didn't. He didn't bother to look. Instead, he pulled his focus to the stand of pines a hundred yards ahead and closing.

He counted the distance in hoofbeats. Each ground-eating plunge of his horse's stride took them farther out of gun-range and expanded his odds of surviving this fiasco. Blood roared in his ears and suddenly throbbed in his left thigh.

Two more shots came close, but by the time they reached the trees the gunfire had faded in the distance. He didn't slow the horse. They plunged into the thick stand of white pine and aspen on some slender animal track that wound through it. Low-hanging branches slapped at them, slicing at their skin and ripping at her hair and shawl. Roughly, he shoved her head down against the horse's neck and bent over her, taking the brunt himself.

Aspen branches cut and stung his bare arms, but he didn't slow. After a few minutes, the aspen gave way to a thick stand of taller pines and he followed the hoofprints of the herd of horses Little Wolf had freed this morning.

This had all gone so wrong.

Options chased through his brain and he discarded each just as quickly. None of them were good. Most ended with him swinging at the end of a rope.

He cursed under his breath, knowing they had minutes— at most, hours—before their lead evaporated. Once those men located the escaped horses, his survival would all depend on his ability to disappear up in these wild mountains.

The woods grew thick and dark, and even he lost his sense of direction. The woman in front of him clung for dear life to the horse with her knees. She hadn't begged him to stop. Hadn't cried. Hadn't so much as spoken since they'd taken off. Probably scared spitless, being taken by a beast of a man like him. So be it.

He grimaced.

After a mile or so, they broke free of the woods and into a clearing that dipped down into a wide track of grassland. Náhkohe grunted with the effort of their combined weight. By now, they were deep into a wilderness where telling north from south was near impossible, except by the sun.

Another handful of minutes and he slowed at the sight of a gathering of horses grazing in the high summer grass. No doubt the ones from the school. At their approach, the horses herded up, watching nervously as he turned the Appaloosa abruptly in their direction. He shouldered his rifle again and fired over their heads.

The herd exploded into a run, pounding across the long, flat track of land ahead of them.

Following the path of the herd's churned-up ground over a hill, they veered abruptly—and dangerously—down a steep slope that led to the briskly running Buffalo Wallow Creek below. He cinched an arm around the girl's waist as they plunged down the slope, pulling her weight backward against him toward the animal's rump to counterbalance the near vertical drop.

Miraculously, they reached the mist-shrouded creek below without breaking their necks, turned the Appaloosa sharply upstream, and stopped as the other horses disappeared across the water and up the far slope. At the end of summer, the creek ran only at knee-height down the twenty-foot-wide, rock-strewn creek bed.

With his arms still around the woman, he paused at the edge of the water, indecision pulling at him. He'd wrestled with discarding her here or keeping her since they'd ridden away from the school, her extra weight already a strain on Náhkohe.

Common sense told him to throw her off the horse, right here, right now. Leave her here where the others could find her. Maybe they'd turn back then, leave him alone. Not likely. Especially if he'd managed to shoot one of them back there.

Then again, they were already miles from where they'd started. He'd brought her to the middle of nowhere. Leaving her here, alone…anything could happen to her. She could easily get lost trying to find her way back and die of exposure. Or be attacked by one of the predators—animal or otherwise—hunting these slopes.

On the other hand, why should he care?

On the other hand, he believed she knew where the boy was headed. And he would find out where.

Still breathing hard and hunched over the Appaloosa's neck, the woman looked like a battle survivor. Which, he supposed, she was. Her petticoat was ripped in a dozen places, her braid had torn loose from its moorings and her hair had exploded in a reddish tangle around her head.

He dismounted into the frigid water, snagging the reins over Náhkohe's head. A sharp pain ricocheted up his left leg that made him hiss in a breath. Glancing down at his leg, he guessed he had less time than he'd imagined. He waded into the strong current of the creek, dragging the horse behind him.

Essie gripped the saddle horn along with a hunk of the horse's mane as they started into the water. He wasn't crossing the creek. He was taking a path straight down the middle, putting the shoreline and possible salvation out of her reach. Anger, more than fear, washed over her. Anger at him for taking her, anger at Daniel for running away. Anger at herself for…for…

Everything.

The sun poked through the damp mist here and swathed him in a halo of light that sparkled across the water in a surreal way. She couldn't seem to take in what had happened, what *was* happening, to her.

The world flashed before her like a series of cards in a stereoscope. The mountains looming ahead, the deep gorge vanishing behind them in the mist, the muscles of her captor's arm, flexing and rippling as he tugged the reins at a run. The metallic gleam of the rifle slung across his back. The morning sun, opening the sky ahead, and the current, beating them backward.

Somehow, she'd been half expecting this for more than a year.

Not this exactly. Not even *she* could have imagined *this*. But some…explosion of her life, surely. Some…consequence. Some natural culmination of her life's slow crumble. Of her stumble into Dooley's desperate fiefdom, her own dreams denied, the grief she'd buried—all of these swirled inside her now as she watched her known world disappear behind her.

And against all imagining, being taken made her feel...*dangerous*.

Alive.

Here, on knife's edge of life or death, with her pulse ringing in her ears and this stranger dragging her into the wilderness, her future was suddenly not stretching out before her like an endless vacant prairie, but a like crossroad.

She reached for the locket that dangled from her neck and rubbed it between her cold fingers. Had it been a mere hour ago that she'd been sitting in the dark, waiting alone for morning? Wondering what would become of her? Well. The universe had answered that question for her. Now she knew. She'd become the hostage of...of—*him*.

She squeezed her eyes shut.

What if he meant to kill her? Or molest her? Could she fight him off?

For a moment back there on the shoreline, she'd thought he might drag her off the horse and leave her. But no. Apparently, he wasn't done with her.

Her gaze traveled from the rifle slung across his back to the large knife sheathed at his hip. She probably couldn't manage to steal his gun, but if need arose, she could kill him with that knife. Or wound him at the very least.

A look up at the mountains surrounding them reminded her that he could be taking her almost anywhere. Most of the Cheyenne had been moved onto their new reservation north of the Yellowstone, except for a small, irate contingent who'd escaped to the mountains. *Is he one of them?*

He seemed to belong more in their world than in hers, despite the color of his skin. She would never trust a man who had kidnapped her.

Over the rush of the water, she shouted, "Where are you

taking me?"

He ignored her as if she hadn't spoken and kept moving through the current.

"I know you can hear me. I insist that you let me go. I'm of no use to you. I can promise you that."

Nothing.

"Please?"

Now he muttered something in the Cheyenne tongue.

She straightened in the saddle. "Kidnapping me will only make things worse for you when they catch you."

Did he just laugh? He simply kept picking his way around stones and flood-wrenched saplings.

"They will hang you," she went on, feeling daring. "Make no mistake. But if you intend to molest me, things will get very ugly for you."

The spotted horse tossed its head as the man calmed him with a palm to the animal's jaw.

Her threats seemed to fall on deaf ears. "They'll find those horses, you know," she said. "And when they do, they'll come after me."

On this point, she had no confidence at all. They had washed their hands of her the day they'd dismissed her. But chasing an Indian who'd bested them was a different matter altogether.

Turning in the saddle to look back for the herd, she saw them disappearing over the far rise behind them. Who knew how long it would take the men from the school to find the missing horses and give chase? She tried to remember if she'd seen the paint, Lalo, amongst the others and realized she'd entirely forgotten to look.

Only the roar of the rushing water stretched between them.

He walked to the left of her, and now and then, his profile came into view as he guided the horse. From this side, one could almost forget the brutal scar on the other cheek. He was irritatingly good-looking.

"How is it you speak English so well?"

Silence.

The current shoved against him, making walking hard. Even the horse found it difficult to find purchase on the riverbed.

Her teeth chattered. Not from cold. From the shock, probably. She set her jaw hard against the sound and turned her thoughts to Daniel and the horse he'd stolen.

Think. Think. Did you see it?

She closed her eyes and pictured the herd tearing up the hillside, but couldn't spot the one she sought. No matter how hard she tried. Where had he gone? What was he thinking, running away? How far did he think he could go on his own?

He'd been so different since his stay in the Wages; she should have seen this coming. He'd fallen into bad habits. His schoolwork declined. He'd even stopped reading books. But who could blame him after that debacle with the copy of "Huckleberry Finn" that had gotten him into trouble. She'd catch him staring out the window or drawing pictures on his slate.

In the river, suddenly, her captor stumbled hard on a rock and righted himself, dropping the reins to catch his balance on a nearby boulder. The Appaloosa reared his head at the unexpected movement.

Seeing an opening, she kicked the horse hard in the sides and urged him ahead. The animal shrieked in surprise and shot forward, splashing in the water.

The man roared and lunged for the confused horse, who pranced sideways in the creek, half stumbling on the rocks below.

"*Hohtáhe!*" he yelled at the horse. "*Tó'hetanó!*"

"*No!*" She kicked her heels again, but she didn't have the reins and she couldn't steer an animal as strong as this one by sheer will.

And when he caught the reins and yanked them back to him, he looked killingly mad. "Now," he growled, reaching up to grab her, "you walk!"

She kicked at him. "Don't…you *touch* me!"

But she was no match for his strength. He yanked her off

the horse and into the creek, where she half fell into the knee-deep water before he shoved her upright. Her bare feet instantly sank in the muddy, frigid water and her petticoats soaked through to her knees.

"Ohhh!" she sputtered, spreading her arms wide to balance herself against the current, wishing she had the height to scratch his eyes out. But he didn't give her time to do more than stumble to a stop before he pulled a short piece of rope out of his saddlebag and tied her hands in front of her.

"No! Wait! I'm sorry! I didn't mean it. I won't do it again!"

Ignoring her protests, he dragged her by the arm behind him, alongside the horse.

The sharp rocks on the creek's bottom stabbed at her bare feet and she felt her way gingerly along behind him, occasionally stubbing her toes on hidden obstacles. "Wait! Ow!" she cried, splashing through the water after him and trying to gather her sodden petticoats at the same time, one handed. "I can't—! What do you want with me?"

Black Thorn stopped dead and whirled to face her, making her nearly collide with him. "I want you to stop talking so I can think!"

She narrowed a look at him. "The time to do your thinking was *before* you threw me on this horse and stole me away. Which you clearly didn't do. Just let me go and I'll…I'll forget your face. I swear. I'll…tell them not to chase you. I'll tell them anything you want me to tell them."

His fingers tightened angrily around her arm and he growled, "You're not from here, are you?"

She opened her mouth to ask what that had to do with anything, but he cut her off.

"If you were," he snapped, "you'd understand that nothing will stop them from coming after me. From killing me if they catch me. I lose them or I die."

"But…you must have known that could be the consequence. Why would you risk doing what you did?"

A look of disgust crossed his expression. "You

understand nothing."

"Maybe you're right. Maybe I don't. Why don't you explain it, then? You could have come and asked for the boy. They would have—"

"They would have *what*? Handed him over to me? When they are burying the People's children in those little graves out back of the school? Erasing family from the minds of the ones who survive? Cutting off their braids, taking their clothes and their true names and their memories until they've stolen everything that made them Cheyenne? I should have asked *those* people for him?"

Fury brimmed in his gray eyes, making her want to take a step back from him. But he held her fast with his big hand. She swallowed thickly and looked down.

"I'll only slow you down. Two of us on that one horse."

"Or you'll be the thing I bargain with," he retorted.

"If it's a hostage you want, you should have taken someone else. They have no use for me either."

He stared at her for a long heartbeat, as if trying to gauge whether she was lying or not, before shaking his head. "Move."

They waded up the creek, pushing through the foamy water that tumbled over hidden obstacles and tore at her petticoats like tugging hands. She lifted them in one arm as she struggled to stay upright and only managed because he kept her from falling. Occasionally, she'd look backward, hoping to see them coming. But all she saw were antelope, camouflaged in the aspen stands, and the occasional rabbit or beaver watching curiously from the safety of the shoreline.

She squinted up at him in the brightening light. "You will regret taking me."

His brows lowered and a muscle jumped in his jaw. "I should have let them shoot you," he said under his breath, pulling her behind him.

"Shoot *me*? They were shooting at *you*!"

He stopped again and leaned closer. A nasty grin parted his lips. "If it comforts you to think so."

Furious, she jerked her gaze away from him. "Nothing about this whole day comforts me! Not the least of which is being hauled off into the wilderness with a...a..."

Her gaze had fallen to the water between them and the curious cloud of red spreading in the foaming water. For a moment, she didn't understand what she was seeing. But she followed that red to a dark stain on the front of his leggings and the even darker hole where the stain began.

Shocked, her gaze rose to those silvery eyes of his to find him scowling at her, daring her to say one more word.

"Is that...blood?"

CHAPTER 3

He clapped a hand against the wound to cover the dark hole which was leaking badly.

"You were shot!"

"You're very quick," he said. "For a white girl."

She narrowed her eyes at him. "And you speak English very well for a *Cheyenne*." She pushed past him through the current. "Not that I care a whit what happens to you, but if that bullet is still in your leg, you'd best get it out. Or you will probably bleed to death."

"I am touched by your"—he stopped to think of the English word—"concern, *vé'ho'á'e*. You better hope I do bleed to death."

She was right about the bullet, but there was no time for his leg. He followed her without reply, then moved ahead of her. She only fought him for a moment this time, before conceding she had no hope of escape.

"Oh, I wouldn't waste hope on a man like you."

"A man like me?" He jerked her to a stop again with a half-amused look. "A half-breed, you mean?"

"A kidnapper of women, I mean. A man who cares for no one but himself."

She was right. He was already regretting taking her. He started moving again.

"Besides, if you die, who will find the boy? Whether you

believe me or not, I care for Daniel." She shook her head. "*Little Wolf.* I cannot wish ill upon his father."

"Then wish away. I am not his father."

She brushed the tangled hair from her eyes. "But…I thought…You're not—?"

The face of his aunt's husband, Running Elk, swirled in his memory. The man who less than two months ago had died of a combination of hunger and consumption. He was fairly certain Little Wolf didn't know he was about to become an orphan.

"Then who are you?" she asked.

He tugged on her arm, focusing on the pain in his leg to push him forward. How had this whole day gotten so out of his control? It had been more than a year since he'd had to use his father's language. Months on end with the tribe had him thinking in Cheyenne, even dreaming in it. More than that, he was known for his silences among the People. All this talk made his head hurt, not to mention the pain throbbing in his leg.

"All right," she said, stopping again. "Wait. Listen to me for a minute. I know you want to blame me for everything the school has done, but—"

"For stealing children?"

"I did not steal—" She stopped and glared at him. "No one stole them. Parents sent their children there. Voluntarily."

"No, they didn't. But if they had, it would have been because they were *starving* in the camps. What choice did they have? That place or death."

She flinched, then her expression flattened. "Look who's talking about stealing children! What exactly do you call what you were trying to do back there?"

With a disgusted look, he pressed on through the current.

"All right! Let's just say I understand you wanting to take Daniel away from that place. I might even understand not wanting to go through proper authorities."

"That is not his name."

"Little Wolf," she corrected, flustered. "Yes. But I knew

him as Daniel."

"You did not know him at all." Watching her prickle like a wild cactus pleased him in some perverse way.

"He's not the little boy you knew anymore, either, but trying to be a man. Did you know that when you came for him? No child would do what he did this morning."

"If you knew him so well, why didn't you try to stop him?" He stumbled on another rock in the water and grabbed her arm for balance. He hissed out a breath and clapped a hand over the wound. Blood had begun leaking alarmingly between his fingers.

He met her eyes and she lifted her chin.

"Maybe I'll be lucky," she said, "and they'll follow the trail of your blood like breadcrumbs. Right to the source."

He hated that she was right. Hated weakness of any kind. But his thoughts were muddied by the loss of blood and he ground his teeth together for a moment before he decided. There, in the middle of the rushing creek, he reached for the wet bottom of her petticoat.

She gasped in surprise and made a grab for it, but before she could stop him, he'd slipped his knife from its sheath and torn the bottom ruffle of her petticoat off. He brandished the knife under her nose again and shoved the long strip of sodden cotton into her hand. He took a handful of her tangled red hair in his fingers and tugged her head back so there'd be no mistaking his meaning. "Wrap it. Tight." With his other hand, he undid the leather lacing on his leggings and dropped them. "And touch nothing else."

She inhaled sharply and her eyes flashed at him in the morning sun, like the blue-green-colored turquoise that came from the nearby mountains. He felt her begin to shake. She turned her head, averting her eyes from his nakedness, and began wrapping the wound on his thigh.

"If you think you can disarm me by shocking me," she muttered, "you are mistaken." But that didn't stop her from sneaking looks at him.

No skin off his nose. He found himself staring down at her, as well. At the sweep of freckles dancing across her nose in the half-morning sunlight. At her skin, pale as the translucent petal of a spring flower. And that hair. That red hair that coiled in ringlets, escaping what had once been a confining braid. His urge to touch it not only caught him off guard, it maddened him. He wanted nothing to do with this woman except what was absolutely necessary to his survival. But despite the pain in his leg, his cock seemed to have a mind of its own about his indifference and stirred to life near her bent head.

Deliberately, he looked away and focused on the pain. "*Tighter.*"

Around and around she wound the cotton until she ripped one end and tied the two pieces together—*he sucked in a breath*—hard. His leg throbbed like it had been stuck with a hot poker.

"Enjoy that?" he asked when she'd finished. He yanked his deerskin trousers back up.

"You did say tight."

"Maybe you enjoyed the rest of the view."

Shock stained her cheeks red. "Oh! Maybe I do hope you bleed to death!"

He leaned close to her. "Better hope not, or you will be out here all alone."

Her eyes cut sideways at the forested woods beside them and the craggy mountains beyond as she considered his words. "I can think of worse things," she said. And then she stopped talking.

Finally.

It gave him some small satisfaction to hear her sharp tongue silenced for now. The foolish *vé'ho'á'e* had no idea how to be a prisoner.

Pulling her behind him again, they made slow progress as he kept an eye out for pursuers. If they were lucky, the men from the school would, at least for a while, chase the path of the horses in the other direction and lose their trail here in the creek. He watched the creek for a good place to exit, but the muddy banks were smooth and wet and would leave footprints and a plain trail to follow.

Behind him, the pain in his ass had gathered up her wet skirts in one arm to make walking easier. Grudgingly, he admired her for not whining about the cold. But he could hear her teeth chatter behind him. The sound made him smile.

The sun was fully up above the mountain in the distance before he spotted an outcrop of water-grooved limestone that sloped in a low, flat slab into the creek and would allow them to climb out on the right side, the same side they'd entered on, track-free. They'd come far enough and needed to make up time. They'd be looking for him on the far side, he hoped. Not here.

He led Náhkohe out, his hooves scraping against the slippery stone. Then the woman, who shrugged off his help, climbed out herself.

"Sit," he ordered.

Frowning, she collapsed in a sodden heap on the sun-warmed rock, breathing hard and watching him.

He lowered himself gingerly down and scooped up a few handfuls of water to quench his thirst. Turning back to her, he found her still watching him like some wild animal that both fascinated and frightened her at once.

Ignoring her, he crossed the rock to the bank beyond, which was bordered by a thick hedge of Juneberry bushes. *A good place to leave the creek behind.*

He took his knife out and sliced a small, thickly laden berry branch off the bush and handed it to her.

"Eat."

She turned her face away. "No, thank you."

"Suit yourself."

"For all I know, you'd try to poison me."

He ripped a berry off, popped the fruit in his mouth and chewed. "If I wanted you dead, which I am suddenly considering, I would not use berries." Shoving a berry toward her, he gestured to the small crown at the bottom tip, like every blueberry he'd ever seen. "This? Good. *Eat.* Bottom smooth? Bad. *Die.*" He proffered the branch once more and, reluctantly, she took it.

She watched as he cut a second branch for himself, feeling dizzy from blood loss, not hunger. He carried jerky and some other dried food in his saddlebags, but the fruit might strengthen his blood.

He let Náhkohe get a good drink of water before leading him back to the bank, where the woman was. She sat quietly, plucking berries and eating them without taking her eyes off him. Pulling a blue gingham shirt from his saddlebags, he slipped it on over his head before replacing the rifle around his shoulders and reaching a hand down to her. "Come."

She chewed a berry slowly, watching him. "What if I say no?"

"I wouldn't," he warned.

"You could just leave me. I'm no threat to you here."

Impatient now, he flicked a beckoning hand at her again. "No."

"They'll be coming for me soon." Still she didn't move off that rock.

"Do not make me throw you on that horse, woman."

She lifted her chin. "My *name* is Essie Sparks."

"Well, Essie Sparks, unless you want to ride tied to the back of my horse, face down, you better climb on. Because we are going up that mountain."

He grabbed her by the arm and hauled her to her feet.

"Fine! All right. Let go of me. I'll get on myself." With her hands still tied, she pulled herself up, astride the saddle. A moment later, he did the same, settling against the horse and her backside with a grunt of pain. He kicked Náhkohe into a trot up the winding track beside the stream that led up the mountain.

Essie had no idea where they were headed, but *up* couldn't be good. *Up* meant wilderness. *Up* meant farther away from the civilized world she knew. Away from rescue and hope and that train she should be boarding this morning to her new life.

Grassland turned to aspen groves, which gave way to

lodgepole pines farther up, and then the thick-barked ponderosa pines. As they picked their way through the forest on some animal track, she wondered if the men at the school had found the horses yet. If they even cared she'd been taken. If Mitchell Laddner was one of them, sent to find her, how hard would he look? He hated her and would probably be happy to see her gone. But if she knew him at all, he wouldn't feel the same about the renegade who'd taken her and bested him. That would never be tolerated by a man like Laddner.

"Are you going to tell me who you are to Danie—I mean, Little Wolf?" she asked as the sun broke through the morning clouds above them.

After a long pause, he answered, "That is none of your concern."

He kicked the horse into a lope, to discourage more talking, she supposed. And it worked. It was all she could do to focus on staying on the horse. She wasn't a rider, and except for the few times she'd been allowed to ride a ladylike sidesaddle at a slow walk, she'd never galloped on a horse before. Her full concentration went to gripping the animal with her legs and clutching the saddle horn. She thanked heaven for the small protection her bustle provided between them, until he jerked the horse to a stop and slid his knife from its sheath again.

She tensed, terrified he meant to kill her with it, but instead he sliced the ties to her exposed bustle and flung it into the bushes far off the trail, discarding the only measure of decent space between them.

She shot him a withering look before facing forward again. As if it wasn't humiliating enough to be pressed up against him in her undergarments with her arms bare and everything she owned practically on display, but now she hadn't even the comfort of the bustle separating her backside from…from *him*.

How many other pieces of clothing would he see fit to dispose of before this was over? She couldn't think about that now. She could only focus on surviving this insanity, one minute at a time.

They rode for hours in silence. Only the sound of the horse's hooves sliding on rocks underfoot and the sound of the morning wind whispering through the trees broke the monotony of their ride. She planned and discarded a hundred plots of escape as unworkable. An elbow to the injured leg? Too risky. A head butt backward to catch him off guard? Again, that might only infuriate him.

The farther they rode the more she felt him waver. In fact, twice, she could have sworn he jerked himself awake. Maybe he would faint and fall off the horse behind her with no effort on her part. But that wasn't likely.

At least he'd taken no liberties with her. She counted herself lucky that he was probably too weak to molest her. Anyway, if he intended to do so, wouldn't he have already? For all his threats and bluster, he wasn't as savage as he would have her believe. Instead, he spoke with intelligence. Education, even. Was it possible he'd been raised in the white world, only to end up in the Cheyenne world? If that were true, given his half-blood breeding, apparently the Cheyenne people must have been more welcoming than the whites to a man like him.

Her affection for the children at the school often made her wonder if, in fact, the Cheyenne were not the civilized ones, and whites the savages? As a group, they were not judgmental or even exclusionary as white children often were. Instead, despite the constant repression, they interacted with one another as siblings of a sort, being both protective and kind.

Essie closed her eyes at the thought of the children. Daniel, in particular. What would happen to him if they caught him? She couldn't bear to think of the punishment he'd face. How desperate he must have been to embark on such a daring, foolish plan. And what of all the others she'd left behind? They were on their own, just as she was now. Alone in a world that didn't seem to care what she wanted, and certainly not what they wanted either.

Their pace up the mountain was brutal, but every now

and then he would turn the horse to look back down the valley below to spot pursuers. For the most part, the mountain blocked their view. The guards had likely found the horses at least by noon and followed them, which gave her captor only a few hours lead.

At a vast, granite outcrop, he dismounted and dragged her off, too. They crossed the rock on foot, tugging the horse behind them. Such a place would likely make tracking them difficult for the men below, and when he wasn't watching, she secretly tore bits of lace edging from her petticoat to drop behind her as they trudged up the slope.

After a few minutes of climbing, the warm rock scraped and dug painfully into the soles of her tender bare feet. He pulled her along by the binding at her wrists. Finally, as she stumbled after him, she jammed her toe against a small ledge of rock and crumpled to her knees.

"*Ow*! Ohhh!"

As if he'd only just remembered she existed, he stopped and looked back at her. "You are hurt?"

"Yes! My toe!" She cradled her bare foot in her hand, not caring at all what he thought. "*Ow, ow*! I might have broken it, thanks to you! And look. I'm bleeding."

The cumulative effect of the rock on her bare feet had done her no favors. Indeed, there was a small cut on the bottom of her heel, covered with a smear of blood, and her toe throbbed. But if she exaggerated the damage, he deserved the delay for dragging her up here in the first place. She felt exhausted after their long ride and wanted nothing more than to stop for a moment to breathe.

Impatient, he glanced at the dome of blue Montana sky above them and the hawk circling overhead. It dipped and swirled in the air currents, unconcerned with them or their petty human problems. Nearby somewhere, the rush and roar of some cataract sounded and the horse's ears perked at the prospect of a drink.

Essie's gaze fell to her captor's bloodied leg and she felt suddenly guilty for her silly complaints. For the past hour, he'd been limping badly on it and she could only imagine his pain was much, much worse than anything she might whine about. Still, why should she feel sorry for him? It was his own fault he had a bullet in his—

Without so much as a by-your-leave, he bent down and picked her up, throwing her over one shoulder like a sack of grain.

She *gawped* as the air whooshed from her lungs and she thrashed against him. "Oh! Put me down! I mean it, put me down!"

Naturally, he ignored her and limped along toward the sound of the nearby water. He quelled her thrashing with a steely arm across her thighs and another planted, horrifyingly, on her rear end.

Clearly, she had underestimated him and his strength. Upside down, the view from the granite slope was disorienting and terrifying. Now, instead of pounding on his back, she gripped his shirt in fear. His cross-slung rifle jabbed painfully at her ribs. One slip down the bald face of this rock and they would both fall to their deaths. She squeezed her eyes shut to keep from being nauseous.

"Please don't drop me," she begged him, under her breath. If he heard her, he didn't reply. Instead, he just moved at a frightening clip—much faster than he'd moved with her in tow—toward the sound of the water.

Minutes later, with the blood rushing to her brain, and distracted by the humiliating familiarity of his hands on her thighs, she realized he'd asked her a question.

"Excuse me?"

"Your foot," he repeated. "How long was it bleeding?"

She frowned. "Long enough."

"*How long*?"

"If you must know, since shortly after you dragged me off the horse. Not that you would care."

He cursed under his breath. A white man's curse. She'd never heard a Cheyenne swear. In fact, she'd heard there was no such thing as a curse word in the Cheyenne tongue.

"If you'd cared, you would have let me get dressed before

dragging me off into the wilderness. Without *shoes*."

"Next time," he answered, "I'll make sure you're decent before they start shooting at us."

"At you. They were shooting at *you*. And believe me, there will be no next time."

"You're right. Because unlike those little pieces of lace you've been ripping off to leave like breadcrumbs for your friends, your trail of blood on that rock face will lead them right to us."

Essie's eyes widened. He'd caught her leaving the lace behind? Good God.

"If you saw me doing it, why didn't you stop me?"

He gestured out with a tip of his chin at the expanse of Montana that stretched before them. "Feel that?"

She felt nothing but the urge to kick him. That and the insistent tug of wind caressing the rock face.

"That breeze will scatter those bits to the four winds and will only confuse them more. That was more favor than risk."

Drat. He was probably right. *But the blood.* The blood was a different story. Maybe there was hope for her after all. And when they caught him…

Her gaze flicked to the rock face behind them. When they caught him, they would…hang him.

Or worse.

She pressed her lips together. No, that wasn't exactly what she wanted at all.

He swayed for a moment under her as if he'd nearly lost his balance and she gripped his shirt tighter. She felt a surge of shame for hoping they would catch him. He hadn't actually hurt her, after all, her foot aside. Oh, he'd scared her silly. But he could have done worse, much worse to her.

No, she didn't wish him dead. She simply wanted him gone. She wanted to be on that train right now back East to begin her new life, and not here on this mountain, slung over his shoulder like a bag of potatoes.

And while she might have saved *him* from the first

bullets fired at them, he might, indeed, have saved her from the ones that chased them out of the barn. Even if they hadn't been shooting *at* her, they hadn't taken care not to hit her either.

She thought of Mitchell Laddner and shuddered at the possibility that he might be the one who had come after them. He had no love for her either. How far would a man like him go?

She swallowed thickly.

As they moved toward the sound of the water, she stared at the rock face, thinking of the blood she'd left behind and suddenly wishing the wind would scrub that away too.

CHAPTER 4

On the banks of the creek, Mitchell Laddner scanned the muddy ground near the water from atop his bay horse. He had easily picked out the unshod pony's prints from the jumble of hoofprints before the other searchers had even decided which direction the rest of the herd had taken on the other side of the water. The trail of blood brought a smile to his lips. He thought he'd hit him, outside the barn. His gaze moved upstream, where he guessed the renegade he was after had gone with that woman, Essie Sparks.

He could not shake the image from his mind of the man's face that morning in the half-light of dawn as he'd taken a bead on him. That scar on his cheek, those silvery-gray eyes that didn't belong on any damned redskin he'd ever seen, save one.

A cold finger traced up him; cold as that day on the Powder River and the battle that had cut down his only true friend, Private Lorenzo Ayers, like an animal.

Twelve years had come and gone since that day under Colonel Reynolds' command. Laddner rarely spared so much as a thought anymore about that heathen squaw he'd shot, stumbling from her tepee in the chaos of that freezing cold March morning. And no one had actually seen him cut that woman down. No one but Gray Eyes, as he'd come to think of him. They'd both been practically boys then. But the government had pinned a medal on Laddner for his part in the charge, and for the killing of Whirlwind, one of the Northern Cheyenne warriors who'd come out shooting that morning.

There was only one reason that battle still haunted his dreams. It was the look in that scar-faced, half-breed's eyes that he'd never forgotten. Their eyes had met over the heads of the two small children he'd had in his arms. Laddner had raised his gun to shoot them, but that bastard had shouted at him in perfect English, "Shoot them and I will string your insides along the banks of the frozen river, you son of a bitch."

English, spoken by that savage, had shocked him momentarily. Long enough that the half-breed turned tail with those two and ran. He disappeared into the thicket of snow-covered lodges toward the bluffs where the rest of the tribe hid out and picked off half a dozen of the fine men from K Company. Even so, he would have shot them all, had his gun not suddenly jammed. Had the tables been turned and Gray Eyes had the bead on him, no doubt he wouldn't be here today, tracking the redskin.

But what was he doing here, all these years later, hauling white women off into the wilderness? If it were up to Laddner, he'd chase the bastard down alone. Screw the other idiot guards who wouldn't be able to find the ground with their hats if they threw them down. No, tracking this particular renegade was personal. Not because of the woman. He could care less about Essie Sparks or her virtue. She would get what was coming to her.

No, he had a score to settle with that half-blood savage on Lorenzo Ayers' behalf. And settle it he would.

He turned in his saddle to see the squat figure of Reverend Dooley approaching on horseback at a run. He was a little out of control, as usual, riding like a jack-stick toy. With arms and legs flailing, tugging the reins up by his chin, he looked precarious enough to fall at any minute from the animal who clearly knew he held the upper hand. Dooley was holding onto his flat-brimmed hat for fear of losing it as his horse raced to catch up with the ones parked near the banks of the creek, tugging grass.

Indeed, the horse skidded to a halt beside the creek and dropped its head down for a long drink, and the panting Dooley, who'd managed not to fly over the horse's neck, immediately parted company with the animal and put a safe distance between them.

He bent over with his hands on his knees to catch his breath. "Blasted animal!" he muttered.

"Reverend?" Laddner tilted a look at the man.

"He got a taste of freedom this morning and now he's a maniac."

There were few things more loathsome to Laddner than a man who couldn't control a dumb animal. "I'll send one of my men to ride back with you. You shouldn't have come out here on your own, sir."

Mollified by Laddner's apparent concern, the reverend waved a hand and straightened. "In truth, I despise the beasts and wish we weren't so confounded dependent on them. But they are a necessary evil, aren't they?"

Idiot. "Yes, sir."

"Any sign of them yet?" The Reverend Dooley shaded his pale blue eyes from the morning glare and peered up the creek at the men studying the banks on either side. The sun hovered high overhead in the blue August sky. They'd already lost the morning, gathering up the horses and hitting a dead end in the box canyon where they'd found the herd.

"In all these tracks here"—he pointed to the muddy bank—"there's only one set that's unshod. That belongs to the one carrying both the renegade and Mrs. Sparks. So far, we've found no sign of him crossing with the other horses here, so I believe he headed straight up this creek to throw us off. Sooner or later, we'll find where he got out."

The reverend whistled. "Impressive, Mr. Laddner. I didn't realize I'd hired a tracker."

You have no idea who you hired. No idea at all. "Yes, sir. Never had a redskin outsmart me yet. Not in the military and not now. I'll find him."

"And the boy?" he asked a little warily. "I need him back. Accounted for."

Laddner found the reverend tiresome, mostly because the man was a half-wit, but also because he was more politician than soul-saver. And nearly everything he did, where it concerned the school, was done with his own deep pockets in mind.

Not that Laddner gave a damn about the little bastard who'd run. He did, however, admire the little rounder his resourcefulness.

He'd had taken this job a year ago after spending the last decade and a half fighting Cheyenne, Crow and Sioux. Now that they were in their proper place, locked up on reservations and on agencies, the war was over. But he found this guard work beneath him. Until this morning, he'd intended to leave this employ shortly and look for a job better suited to his particular talents. But today, his reasons for having taken this job became clear. It seemed particularly appropriate that Essie Sparks was the one who'd been taken, since she'd been a thorn in his side since day one. Sometimes, justice prevailed in a world full of injustice.

"With our limited resources, the boy is the least of our worries at the moment, Reverend."

The reverend scowled. "Make no mistake. A scandal like this could ruin this school, affect subsidies I'm paid by the BIA, Laddner. Including your salary. I want this headed off before the Bureau of Indian Affairs learns what happened here. I want that boy back before everything we've done is undone by that renegade. And I want Mrs. Sparks out of the grasp of whoever took her."

"We'll find them." He turned an unsettling look on Dooley. "But when we do, you know what must be done with regards to Mrs. Sparks."

"Done? I don't follow."

Laddner glanced grimly up the creek, then at the mountain vistas beyond. "I've spent most of the morning thinking about it. What she must be going through. A fine girl like her. Raised right. That scar-faced savage..." He shook his head and fingered the grip on his pistol. "There's no doubt that he will...*defile* her, as is the wont of all savages like the Cheyenne. We both know the outcome. We've seen it. You must recall that Brassler woman they brought back to the mining camp, found after a few days with those heathens who'd stolen her. And she was not even high-bred. Still," he said, letting this point sink in, "she never was right again. Not fit for human company. Screaming if a man so much as looked at her...only thing she'd tolerate was a pup who wouldn't leave her side."

"We don't know—" Dooley began, but faltered as Laddner tilted a look at him one might aim at a poor animal stuck in the ice. Dooley's frown deepened. "In that case, we must pray for her salvation and sanity."

Laddner sniffed, staring down at the water ruffling down the creek. "I think it would be...un-Christian-like to leave a woman, thusly ruined, to suffer the degradation, the humiliation that would be her fate. Puttin' her down is a mercy only we can afford her. But it's your call, sir. Considering she's got no one in the world to look out for her in her condition...except maybe you. Sir. It might fall on you."

A pregnant pause stretched between them and Laddner watched the possibilities riffle across the reverend's expression.

Dooley reddened and reached for the reins of his horse. Awkwardly, and quite reluctantly, he pulled himself back up into the saddle. "You see that renegade, whoever he is, hangs for what he's done. That's all I want to hear about when you get back."

With a smile, Laddner touched the brim of his hat to the man. "Yes, sir. I will most certainly do that."

At the river, he set her down on a rock, bracing a hand there to steady himself. He led the horse to the edge, then stooped himself to gulp a few handfuls of water. The afternoon sun had nearly settled between the mountains, but it would still be light for hours yet.

"Soak your feet in the cold water," he instructed. "We will leave again when Náhkohe has rested."

With a petulant look, she did as he asked. The river this high up was icy cold and she gasped as her feet touched it. As she soaked, he filled his water skin and offered it to her. She drank deeply, ignoring her earlier reluctance about the receptacle.

She sighed aloud when she'd drunk her fill and handed it back to him. "What does that name mean, '*Náhkohe*'?"

"Bear," he said, lowering himself down on a rock beside her. "Because he's brave and has seen many battles." Gingerly, he lowered his pants again to loosen the blood-soaked strip of fabric from around his leg and allow some circulation to return. It began bleeding again in earnest. He covered himself again and rinsed the cotton in the stream. He squeezed the cold water over the wound with a hiss of pain.

He caught her watching him warily and he pressed the already wet cloth against the bullet hole in his leggings and leaned his head back against the rock behind him.

The wound needed a hot knife against it, which required fire, which they didn't—couldn't—afford to have. But he would lose either the leg or his life if he didn't take care of it soon. Perhaps once they crested the mountain and were out of sight on the other side...if his strength held...

"Please. You can unbind me now," she said, gesturing to her hands. "Where would I go now that you've got me in the middle of nowhere?"

"No."

With a frown, she pulled at the leather strip where it chafed her wrists. "What do you intend to do with me? Where are you taking me? At least I have the right to know."

"We've been following Little Wolf's trail since we started up the mountain."

Surprise replaced her frown. "What? Where? I saw nothing."

It mattered not to him if she knew how to follow a trail. It mattered little to him what this woman thought at all. "He is still hours ahead of us, moving faster alone."

"And the men from the school?"

He wrung out the cotton again and soaked it in the cold water. "They found the place where we left the creek over an hour ago."

The consequences of that information dawned in her expression. "Will they catch up to us?"

"Not if I can help it."

She stared at the swiftly moving water. "And what of me? Do you intend to kill me?"

He sliced a sideways look at her. She had reason to believe that, he supposed, considering how he'd put the knife to her throat. And dragged her off into the wilderness. In truth, he didn't know what he intended to do with her, but killing her had never entered his mind. "Do you always ask so many questions?"

"Do you always avoid answering them?"

"Most of the time," he admitted. His head ached and he felt like retching. But he took another sip of water to stave it off. Until today, the most English he'd spoken in the last year or so was with the whores at the Lucky Diamond Sporting House in Magic City, and with them, there was little talk. Still, Ollie made sure he was welcome there and he was grateful for that.

A pause that lasted only minutes stretched between them. Then Essie said, "I know your horse's name. Shouldn't I know yours? In case you die, I mean," she added, as if it mattered not to her either way. "That is, if I ever find my way out of this godforsaken place on my own, if you bleed to death." Glancing upward, her gaze followed what he first thought was a hawk, but was, in fact, a buzzard. "Won't someone be missing you? Your wife, perhaps?"

He nearly laughed. "*Wife*? No."

Leaning back against the rock behind her, she said, "You should do that more often."

Opening his eyes at that, he slid a look at her. "What?"

"Smile. It makes you look almost...civilized."

"Then I must remember not to do it." Without thinking, he moved his head so the curtain of hair fell across the scar on his left cheek.

The afternoon sun beat down on them and the river rushed by in a hurry to reach the waterfall that roared somewhere below.

"You needn't hide that on my account, you know. The scar, I mean."

"I wasn't," he lied, but knew it had become second nature to hide it.

She lifted her foot out of the water and touched the place on her heel that the rock had sliced open. "It does seem quite unfair that a scar on a man's face can only make him more intriguing, when on a woman, the same scar would be her utter downfall."

"Intriguing," he repeated incredulously. The woman was shamelessly naïve.

"Yes."

Now he turned to look at her. "And what would you know of scars? You, with your simple life, Essie Sparks?"

She jerked a look back up at him and her fingers darted to the locket that dangled at her throat. "I assure you, my life is nothing close to simple. And as for scars? Everyone has them. Some just carry them under their skin where they're not so easily perceived. To me, scars are a sign of survival. Perseverance. History, even."

He studied her from beneath his lashes. He couldn't see any scars on her. And, for all her talk, he doubted a woman like her would look twice at a man like him if they weren't the only two people on this mountaintop. But her life not simple? He would not lay money on that. She looked like all the other white women he'd met at school who'd had their lives handed to them without strings. Confident in their place. Self-contained.

Yes, everything about her seemed contained except for that hair.

That mop of red that had been tickling his nose for the

past few hours as she rode in front of him was something rare. That scent of lavender that lingered on her hair and—as he'd discovered when he'd thrown her over his shoulder—on the rest of her, too, had caused a tightening lower down that even the pain in his leg couldn't mask.

"A scar by any other name would still be a scar," he said at last, biting back the feeling that he was about to heave.

Her pink lips parted in shock. "Do *not* tell me you know Shakespeare!"

He tipped his head back against the rock. "Who?"

"You do! Don't deny it." She wound her hand in circles, trying to remember the words. "'A rose, by any other name, would smell as sweet. So Romeo would, were he not Romeo called, retain that dear perfection which he owes without that title.'" She got to her feet. "'Romeo doff thy name, and for that name, which is no part of thee, take all my—'"

Her foot slipped on the wet face of the rock and she lost her balance. She barely had time to cry out before she cartwheeled sideways into the river.

CHAPTER 5

He couldn't move fast enough to grab her. Into the frigid, fast-moving current she went, and almost as quickly she disappeared under the surface of the water and flew away.

Before he'd even lost sight of her he was ripping his rifle and shirt off over his head and limping along the bank of the river after her. Pain shot through his left leg like a hot arrow, but the fear pumping through him numbed it almost as fast.

She was flailing with her bound hands and gasping for air as she broke the surface ten feet downstream only to disappear again. He saw her surface two more times— clutching for a handhold on the slippery rocks—before he got ahead of her and threw himself across a flat rock, his arm extended.

"Take my hand!" he shouted over the tumbling water. Her green eyes stared up at him, wide with panic, as she reached for him, but her fingers merely brushed past his as the current swept her by.

Below them, maybe five hundred yards from the sound of it, was a waterfall. A big one. He shoved to his feet and ran downstream again. A cataract like that would kill her if he didn't get her out fast. He couldn't think about anything but finding a spot to save her. The sound of her gasping for air and panicked cries made his pulse rock against his insides.

His strides ate the soggy riverbank as he pushed to stay ahead of her, shoving aside branches and tangled shrubs. Finally, a deadfall appeared, lying half in the river. His best and possibly last chance.

He stumbled over a hedge of low bushes and sank down to crawl to the edge of the rotting log. Half lying in the water, clinging to the log, he reached out again for her as she spun toward him. "Essie! Take my hand!"

Her head bobbing half underwater, she looked up at him in real panic and reached her still-bound hands out as the river pulled her under, but this time as she slid by he grasped her wrist and managed to close his fingers around her slender bones and the rope ties. Using all of his strength, he stopped her momentum, pulled her out and dragged her up on top of him.

Falling back against the log, he held her atop him, unable to do more. "*Ómotómeotse!*" he told her. "Breathe. I have you." His fingers spread across her back, searching for the ties on her corset lacing across her back as she coughed and choked up river water. Quickly, he loosened the strings and she inhaled deeply.

Even then she didn't seem able to do more than lie sprawled across him, coughing and sucking in air. He held her, his hand slapping her back. Coughing, she pressed her cheek against his chest, her head tucked below his chin. They lay like that for half a minute before she seemed to come to herself. When she lifted her head from his chest, water still clung to her dark auburn lashes and her eyes seemed full of some emotion he could not name.

His own breath was still chugging in his chest, half from fear of losing her and the other half from the fact that he'd just used up what few reserves he had left. And yet in that moment, he had the impulse to kiss her. That must have shown in his eyes, because she got scared and rolled off him almost as soon as the thought entered his mind.

Her soaking wet chemise hid nothing from his view. He sat up and looked intentionally away from her, but couldn't get the image of her dusky nipples, so visible through the wet fabric, from his mind. "That was a fool thing to do," he muttered.

"A fool thing?" she cried, sitting up and pulling away from him. She sat between his legs on the log, crossing her arms across her small breasts with an accusing look. "I slipped. I almost drowned, thanks to you!" She held up her still-bound hands as proof.

They both could have drowned, because his next move would have been to jump in after her. Should it surprise him she was ungrateful? "You're lucky I caught you, or right now you would be heading over that waterfall below." He sat up, feeling dizzy.

"*Lucky*?" She shoved the hair off her face. "I suppose you expect me to thank you for that? After putting me in harm's way in the first place? Bringing me to the middle of nowhere and—"

"No need." Slowly, he pushed himself up to his feet, then extended a hand down to her. "Just don't do it again. Next time, I will let you drown."

She scowled at him. "Probably your plan all along."

He shook his head as the pain in his leg roared back to life now that the rush of danger had passed. He pressed a hand against it, feeling a wave of nausea swell over him. "You should watch your back with a man like me. You never know what I'll do."

She agreed with a silent glare, but wasn't fool enough to refuse the hand he offered to help her up. They navigated their way off the fallen log. But as soon as they were on dry land again, she shook him off. She was shivering with cold and probably fear.

In truth, fear had his insides tumbling around as well. Nor did he miss that every soaking wet bit of her was exposed, from the slender shape of her hips to the pink, puckered discs of her nipples and the outline of her small, upturned breasts.

The moment she caught his gaze on her, she brought her hands up under her chin to block his view. "Stop looking at me."

When he reached his discarded gun and shirt he tossed the shirt at her. "Put that on."

For a moment, she just stared down at it. She held up her bound hands. "I cannot. Just as I could not swim, bound this way."

He shrugged the gun across his back and untied her long enough to pull his shirt over her head, then he retied her. The woman might do any fool thing, like bolt into the woods like a scared deer, given half the chance. He was obligated not to let her die, since he'd been the one to take her, but this incident with the river only confirmed his determination to be shed of her as soon as possible. Somewhere safe. God knows where *that* would be.

Billings, perhaps. Or some other nearby town.

But that kind of future looked a long way off right now. And the distinct possibility existed that neither one of them would make it that far.

He tugged her along back to their spot on the riverbank where Náhkohe waited and tied her to a tree, away from the dangers of the water, then dropped to his knees, suddenly finding it impossible to stand. Feeling a wave of nausea roll over him, he retched into the river once, twice, before collapsing back against the boulder.

Only then did Essie notice that his bronze skin had gone pale and he looked terribly unwell. Pulling her from the river had spent the last of his strength. For which, she supposed, she should have been more grateful. But she was still too mad at him.

Leaning her forehead against the aspen sapling he'd tied her hands around, she said, "How long do you think you can go on this way? With that bullet in your leg? You need rest and a doctor."

"*They* won't rest," he said with a tip of his head in the direction of the men chasing them. "And I don't see a doctor anywhere, do you?" He surprised her by passing her the water skin to let her drink next. As she'd just drunk her fill of the river, she handed it back to him. He didn't drink.

Instead, he slammed his eyes shut and leaned back against the rocks.

Essie rubbed her damp mouth against the shoulder of his shirt. His scent lingered on it and it was, surprisingly, not unpleasant. So he had saved her life. And perhaps spent the last of his strength doing it. It was his fault she'd nearly drowned in the first place. What was she doing trekking across these mountains like a barefoot goat? She belonged in her world of sensible expectations and consequences she could anticipate.

She held her hand out. "Give me your knife. I'll take the bullet out." For the briefest of moments, those steely gray his flicked up to hers. He seemed to actually consider her offer, whether out of desperation or, more unlikely, hope, she couldn't tell. She could not read the man, which was probably just as well because she had no desire to understand him. Or, worse, to care about him.

He laughed. The sound was peculiarly without humor. "I give you my knife so you can finish what the bullet didn't?"

Essie snorted and looked away. Of course she wouldn't have *killed* him. She was not a murderer, no matter the circumstances. Unlike…possibly, *some* people she knew. But, heaven help her, the chance to make him pay, in some small measure—with the sharp tip of his knife—for all the torment he'd put her through since the day began wouldn't break her heart, either.

Ugh. That she'd even contemplated such vulgar anticipation shocked her almost as much as finding herself tied to a tree in the middle of the Montana wilderness. It was all *his* fault. He had brought her to such low imaginings.

"*Séaa…*" he murmured with a condescending grin."I came a little too close to the mark there, didn't I? What say you? Surprised you're only human, Essie Sparks?"

Ooh! How she hated him!

She leaned forward, leveling a look at him that made her feelings plain. "Do you know what I say? I say that you'll die here from stubbornness. From thinking you can somehow keep me as your hostage when I'm no good to you at all! They could care less about me. It's you they're after. Because they won't let some…some misguided—" She faltered, searching for the proper word.

"Half-breed?" he supplied, eyes closed.

She made a frustrated noise. "Some misguided *renegade* best them by taking what they think belongs to them. *And* I say that if you don't take that bullet out and stop bleeding, you won't have to worry about saving your leg." She leaned her head on the sapling between her arms. "*I say* with my hands tied here we will both die in this godforsaken place, sooner rather than later."

With surprising effort, he had rolled a look at her, mid-rant, and was studying her in the fading afternoon light. Against all common sense, she was struck again by his beauty, his rugged, effortless beauty—of which, she was quite sure, he was completely unaware. In fact, if anything, she supposed he considered himself without appeal, a conclusion with which she *should* heartily agree.

But nothing about this man was simple. Not the way his instinct to protect her seemed almost the equal of his instinct to ruin her today, nor the way he seemed able to crawl in her mind to know what she was thinking before she did. His complexity drew her and offended her at once. But when he looked at her, as he was doing now…despite the sudden sallow color of his skin, the awful scar bisecting his cheek or the bitterness in his eyes, she couldn't deny the effect he had on her. On both her heart and her female parts.

Then, as if he'd made some decision, he slid the knife from the sheath at his hip and, with an effort, crawled closer to the tree she was tied to. The blade glinted dangerously in the thin sunlight.

Instantly, she feared she'd gone too far, said too much. There was a darkness in his eyes that hadn't been there before—a warning.

She might have imagined the wounded look in his eyes when she flinched as the blade drew near. Yes, most certainly she had. Still, when he slid the blade between her hands and slit the rope that tied them, she couldn't quite believe he'd done it.

For a moment, she simply stared at her hands before scooting entirely out of his reach on her backside.

He gestured with his knife at the trail below. "Go."

"*What?*"

"Run back to them. Back to your pretty life."

"My pretty life? What would you know about my—Wait. You...you're letting me go?" Was this a trick? If not, he wouldn't have to tell her twice. She shoved to her feet and backed up a few steps, glancing over her shoulder down the mountain, at where she supposed the searchers were now, so far away. It had taken the whole day to get this far uphill. How long would it take her to go back down? What if the men gave up looking and disappeared? Could she find her way back on her own? On bare feet?

"Night comes quick up here," he said, his words beginning to slur. "Maybe you'll find your 'friends' before a cougar finds you. Or a grizzly bear."

She stopped in her tracks. *A bear? Or a cougar?* She glanced through the thick stand of trees surrounding them. *A million places for an animal to hide.*

"Then," she said, "I'll need a weapon."

"And I need a good leg," he said. "Seems we're both...out of luck."

She blinked. "You'll send me off with nothing to protect myself?"

Gesturing with his knife, he said, "Count yourself lucky I didn't take that pretty scalp of yours." He was still watching her, but through half-lidded eyes. "Savage that I am."

When she didn't move, he warned, "Sun's going down. What you waitin' for?"

She stepped closer to him, tearing the remains of the rope from her wrists. "Not that I care, but...what about you?"

A questioning look furled his brow, as if he couldn't imagine what she meant.

"You're...you're still bleeding."

He glanced down at the fresh blood seeping against his leggings. "So?" His gaze rose to meet hers. She opened her mouth then closed it again. He slammed his eyes and nodded. "I'll take care of the bullet myself. So I need the knife. Get out of here."

Essie frowned, uncertainly. "And you're not even going to tell me who you are to Daniel, or...or what this is all about?"

"Learn to live with disappointment, Essie Sparks. Like the rest of us do."

"Fine." Disgusted, she turned in an uncertain circle. "Fine. I'll go. Now that I've missed my train, and now that I'll...I'll have to buy myself a new ticket East." She glanced back at him, but he seemed not at all interested in her petty problems. "I hope you're happy. What was the point of all this? Did you always mean to release me in the middle of nowhere? As if it were all just a game to you? To leave me defenseless?"

"We are all defenseless without our courage, *vé'ho'á'e.*" Allowing his eyes to slide shut, he dismissed her with a flick of his hand. "I set you free. The choice to stay...or go...is yours."

Turning toward the vast mountains behind them, she felt suddenly overwhelmed. Find her way out alone? Her eyes stung, but she refused to cry. Heaven knew she'd managed not to cry this whole awful day. She wouldn't start now.

But of course she would go. Regardless what awaited her on the way down that mountain; leaving was a thousand times better than staying here, willingly, with him.

Turning back to tell him so, she was just in time to catch him pitching sideways onto the ground beside the river. Out cold.

Shocked, she stared down at him for a few long heartbeats, half expecting him to sit up, tell her his ploy was just a test. But he didn't. She couldn't even tell if he was breathing. Her stomach plunged. She'd never wished him *dead*, for heaven's sake. Dropping down beside him, she pushed her fingers against the side of his throat, paradoxically relieved to feel a quick, thready pulse.

An unladylike curse escaped her and she sat back on her heels.

Now what?

She tossed a look around at the darkening forest. It was not lost on her that she was officially on her own now, here, in the middle of nowhere. Or that leaving him here, in the forest…amidst the grizzly bears and cougars and other prowling predators she couldn't name, would mean certain death for him.

On the one hand, he'd gotten himself into this situation. This mess was not of her making.

On the other hand, he'd saved her from the river.

Something unreasonable twisted inside her. Concern? For a man like him?

She argued against such a possibility, but those arguments did nothing to diminish her feeling of responsibility. If she left him here, he would certainly die. If she stayed, the odds were just as good that she would.

She studied him for a long moment. The dark sweep of lashes that brushed his cheek. His face, savagely handsome, somehow looked less fearsome without his ever-present scowl.

Don't be a ninny! You just got lucky.

She tugged at the rifle, pinned behind him, but couldn't pry it free.

Take the knife for protection. Take it and get out of here. Now.

She reached for it, prying it from his lax hand. The feel of the thing, the heavy heft of it against her palm, troubled her somehow as she remembered how he'd held it against her throat. How he'd said he needed it for his leg. But the beginnings of panic scrambled inside her, shoving away any protests from her conscience. This was her chance to escape and she would take it. What fool wouldn't?

A few feet away, his horse lifted his head from cropping grass and snorted at her. And with that, her decision made itself. She would take the knife.

She would take the horse.

She would *survive.*

Catching the animal, she pulled herself up into the saddle, shushing the dissenting voices in her head. Any sane person would do what she was doing. Any woman with a lick of self-preservation would run as far and as fast as she could away from a renegade like him.

Anyone would.

Pulling her gaze deliberately from the unconscious man, she kicked the horse into a trot and headed back down the way they'd come.

CHAPTER 6

The buzzing high that had ridden for most of the day with Little Wolf shrank as the daylight faded. He had never been afraid of the dark until his nights alone in the Wages of Sin. But then he'd been confined and weak. Now, things were different. He was free. For the first time in two years, free and himself again. As much of himself, that is, as he could remember.

As he rode past trees and rivers and rocks, he unburied their names from his mind. *Hoohtsèstse*—the cottonwood tree—growing by the...*tóxeo'hé'e*—riverbank—and the...*sé...sée...séenēva*—boulder. It had been so long since he'd spoken those words aloud, he found himself doing just that as he and Lalo trotted through the darkening forest.

Still, with the sun sinking behind the mountains and the late summer moon rising in the east the prospect of his first night alone under the stars settled upon him uneasily. Perhaps he should keep moving through the night. He didn't feel tired yet, though he guessed Lalo did.

The paint pony beneath him had bravely carried him all day without complaint. But the horse needed rest and food. As he approached a wide field of summer grass, he pulled Lalo to a stop and dismounted.

He turned to look behind him. No one was following him. Perhaps they had decided to let him go. Perhaps they didn't care about Lalo or him enough to chase them down in the mountains. No one had noticed when the boy named Huckleberry ran away. No one even cared. And he was at least as unwanted as that white boy had been.

Perhaps the guards were still looking for their horses on a mountaintop far away. It gave him a secret pleasure to think of them scrambling up some mountain on foot to find those horses, cursing at the weeds and rocks in their way.

Then again, maybe he just could not see them following him. Maybe, even now, they were in the trees behind him, waiting until dark to take him. He looked back fearfully, but saw no one.

Hours ago, he and Lalo had crossed a river with a high waterfall at the crest of the last mountain. He had a full canteen—stolen from the stable guard, along with his skinning knife. But almost all of the food he'd pilfered for the trip had gotten wet in the fording of a river that had been deeper than it looked. A foolish mistake he was already paying for with a growling stomach. He took a still-dry cracker from his pocket and nibbled on it. Hunting with only a knife would not be easy. Berries might have to do.

Soon, he told himself, he would see his parents again. He feared they had forgotten him by now, for he had not seen them since the Big Hoop Moon, two cold winters ago.

He tried to imagine his mother's eyes when she saw how tall he'd grown. Would his father, a Dog Soldier, be proud of his escape? Would he give him a bow of his own? Would there be any more Sun Dances for boys like him?

He thought of his friends back at the school: John and Mark and Joshua, whose Cheyenne names he was never allowed to say and had forgotten. He already missed them, and wondered if he would ever see them again. Or if they would die before they could return to the lodges of the People.

Beside him, Lalo snorted, ears perked forward at something in the woods. Little Wolf stared past the lodgepole pines, deeper into the shadows where the silhouette of a young fox sat, dog-like, staring at him. Even in the deep shade of the forest, his red coat shone.

Reflexively, Little Wolf's hand went to the knife at his hip and he scanned the woods for the fox's brothers. But the fox seemed to be alone and made no move in his direction. It simply watched him curiously and yawned.

Little Wolf smiled and lifted a hand to the fox in acknowledgement. The fox's over-large ears twitched in reply, then he turned and disappeared into the forest.

From the gloaming dark, somewhere on a distant peak, came the sound of wolves howling. An answering pack yowled in the distance. He shivered. That was why the fox had vanished.

He mounted and nudged Lalo forward, his thoughts drifting back to a memory of his father settling a wolf cub in his arms when he'd been just a boy. One of the Dog Soldiers had found the cub alone in the woods and brought it back to camp. That cub had been raised up in the tribe, as tame as a dog, and Little Wolf had named him *Ésáa-hetseváhe*—He Is Not Afraid.

Ésáa-hetseváhe followed Little Wolf wherever he went. Others called them Big Wolf and Little Wolf, so inseparable were they. There was nowhere he went that the wolf would not follow. They'd had many adventures until the day the agency had taken all the children away and sent them to the Industrial School. It had been raining that day, so hard the mud puddles soaked their ankles and sucked at the axles of their wagons. Even then, the wolf had tried to chase after him, but his mother had tied the wolf to a stake so the white men wouldn't kill him. The rain hid the tears of all of the children that day and those of their parents. But it could not drown out the howls of *Ésáa-hetseváhe* as he strained frantically at the rope Little Wolf's mother had tied to him. He had howled and howled. If Little Wolf closed his eyes, he could still hear the confusion in his cry.

He wondered about that wolf now. Was he still alive? Had he gone off to find his own kind? Was he, even now, howling in the distance, calling for him?

Little Wolf tipped his head back to the rising moon.

"*Aaaahhh-rooooo*!" he howled into the still mountain air. "*Aaa-ahh-ahhrooo-rooo*!"

I am here, Ésáa-hetseváhe! I am Little Wolf and I am coming for you!

From somewhere far off, a lone wolf answered.

As Essie made her way downhill on Náhkohe, the lightness that had buoyed her at her escape leaked away fast, replaced by guilt.

Guilt she couldn't reconcile.

You took his horse and his knife.

I couldn't be expected to make it back barefoot, could I?

Why should she care? It served him right, taking her the way he had. And for what? To torment her for a day with his bullying and his accusing gray eyes?

He saved your life. Twice.

What if he did? He only did it so he could use me to his own ends.

She frowned. Was that right? How could she know? He'd barely communicated with her.

Still, scenes from the day flashed through her memory: him lying unconscious by the river; reaching his hand to her to save her; shoving her out of the way of bullets at the barn. His fingers, unlacing the strings of her corset.

She shook her head. *Do not make him something he is not. He wouldn't even tell you his name!*

"*Learn to live with disappointment, Essie Sparks. Like the rest of us do.*" He knew nothing about the disappointment she'd lived with. How could he? He thought her life was perfect.

But then...he knew as little about her life as she did about his. He was just a man. And she was just a woman. From two different worlds, true, but still...

She nudged Náhkohe and urged him into a reluctant trot. She had, after all, seen him, completely. Standing stripped bare in the creek as she bound his wound. She should have been appalled, and she *was*, but that wasn't all.

Her glimpse of him had fascinated her and terrified her, but worse was the undeniable rush of something foreign. A tightening. An indecent *wanting*. A shameful urge to—

To what? Touch him? Admire what lay nestled between his strong thighs? To wonder what it would be like to lie with a man like him? All sleek and muscled and—

Stop it!

It wasn't as if she'd never seen a man naked before. She'd glimpsed her late husband, once or twice when he'd forgotten to turn down the light. And certainly, she'd felt him touching her...down there. But she'd never been allowed to touch him back. Or look at him.

And he'd never stood before her, unashamed, like that moment in the river when her captor had.

All day, she'd been silently comparing the man himself to others she'd known: her husband, whose face she already struggled to remember. Or Thomas Peakin, the scrawny Pennsylvanian teacher who fancied himself her match back at the Industrial School and who had spent the last three days plotting ways to keep her there—as if she would ever stay for him. The married Reverend Dooley, who, at thirty-seven, was only nine years older than her but seemed more like twenty with his flaccid paunch and his sleep-starved eyes that made her feel vague guilt whenever her gaze met his. Even the awful Mitchell Laddner, the man probably chasing them now.

No, those men were nothing like the man she'd left lying by the river.

Nothing like those gray eyes that seemed to see inside her silences. Or remind her of how long it had been since she had a man beside her she could count on.

He could have left you tied to a tree while he slipped into unconsciousness. Maybe while he died. And then what would have become of you?

But he hadn't.

She passed a stand of ponderosa pines with their dark green summer needles glinting in the twilight and the horse dropped its head to tug at the rich grass slope, refusing to move.

Something rustled in the brush in the stand of brambles to her left and Náhkohe shied hard to the right. She nearly fell off, but clung on somehow. Her heart tumbled around inside her until a squirrel scurried out from under the brush and up a tree. The Appaloosa snorted and danced until he was pointed back up the mountain, then laid its ears back and arched its neck to look back at her, taking a few steps in the direction of the man they'd left behind.

She narrowed a look at him and reined him back. "Whoa!"

The horse tossed its head, obstinately.

"What?" she said. "We are going down, not up."

But the horse had other ideas and fought her, turning in circles as she tried to steer him the way she wanted.

Stubborn.

The horse wasn't having any of it. She supposed she'd be laughed at for thinking the horse had more compassion than she did. But possibly, that was true.

Ugh. What woman in her right mind would go back to a man who'd kidnapped her? What woman with any sort of conscience would leave him there?

She exhaled a sound of frustration and sighed. Finally, she gave the horse its head and without further encouragement, the animal, aptly named for a wild beast, took off at a run back up the hill.

He woke to an explosion of pain in his leg and someone—*that woman*—leaning over him. Firelight glinted off something—*the steel blade*—in her hands.

Before she could do more than gasp, he threw her onto her back, wrenched the knife from her and laid an arm against her throat.

"Trying to kill me?" he hissed, feeling the forest around him swim sideways.

Eyes wide, she shook her head, but did little more than croak at him. "I'm not—!"

"Knew I couldn't trust you, *vé'ho'á'e*—"

The woman choked, trying to catch her breath. But it occurred to him that he'd thrown his weight onto her and she could not get air. Even in the flickering firelight, he could see the blue cast to her lips as she struggled to breathe. He punished her for another few seconds before rolling off her and onto his back beside her.

He heard her suck air into her deprived lungs.

She coughed and choked, then rolled onto her knees away from him. "What is wrong with you!" she sputtered when she could finally talk. "That's what I"—she coughed again—"what I get for trying to help you!"

"*Help* me?" He proffered the knife as evidence. "With this?"

"Yes, for God's sake." She unfurled her other fist and thrust her open palm in his direction.

The pain in his leg flared again. For a moment, he couldn't quite grasp what he was seeing. Her hands were covered in blood. His blood. In the center of her palm, the thumbnail-sized chunk of lead that had come, apparently, from his leg. He looked down at the long slit she'd cut into the leather of his leggings. The wound was still bleeding.

He shook his head, feeling like a fool. "I thought—"

She threw the bullet at him and it bounced off his chest. "I know what you thought. You were wrong."

He rolled back against the ground and slammed his eyes shut. Nausea roiled in his gut again and he took a long, deep breath. "So I was."

"Apologize for trying to kill me."

He narrowed a look at her and thought about his options. He couldn't remember ever apologizing for anything in his life before and never to a woman. He didn't especially want to start now. But she had, no doubt, saved him a crushing agony, removing the bullet while he was out cold. Even now, the leg burned like an ember. "Sorry. I'm...grateful."

She picked up a fistful of dirt and scrubbed her bloody hands.

"Ha!" Her eyes flicked up to him with mock surprise. "That must have cost you. You're not welcome."

Squeezing his eyes shut, he asked. "How long was I out?"

It took her a few seconds to deign to answer. "An hour. Maybe more."

He groaned and rolled to a sit, remembering.

Darkness had truly fallen and stars were winking overhead. "The men. Where are they?"

"Coming," she said. "I think there were two of them on horseback, but still miles down the mountain. I saw their lantern light. But not for a while. Maybe they stopped for the night?"

"Or not." He rubbed his forehead where an ache had settled between his eyes. "The fire. You need to put it out."

She brushed the dirt from her hands. "Either I put that blade in the fire and cauterize that wound or you will leak blood until you die. Far be it from me to attack you again, so it's your choice."

She was right. He'd pushed himself as far as he could. "Do it," he told her, and handed her the knife.

Hesitantly, she took the blade and held the tip over the flickering orange flames.

"You started that by yourself?" He indicated the fire, feeling reluctantly impressed.

"Me? No. Your horse is really quite clever. All I had to do was ask and he gathered up the wood and everything."

She made a joke. He lifted one eyebrow in response. She'd obviously found the matches in his things. "Why didn't you run?"

She turned the blade in the fire until his dried blood sizzled on the edges and burned away. The metal began to glow orange. "Oh, I did," she answered, avoiding his eyes, turning the blade in the fire. "Your clever horse, again. He talked me out of it."

He narrowed a look at her. Another joke? He couldn't tell. Anything besides hostility was new. But he thanked whoever was watching over his broken life that the woman hadn't decided to go off on her own when he'd passed out. Anything that happened to her would be his fault. He'd dragged her out here into the middle of this nowhere place, where one wrong turn could be her last. Not to mention his.

Her red hair gleamed in the firelight, all wild and loose, so completely at odds with the smooth pale skin of her face. He didn't mean to stare, but he couldn't help himself.

Maybe it was her funny, bowed lips that turned down a bit at the corners, or her heart-shaped face, or her slender, well-bred nose that flared when she got angry, but not even the girl he'd once fancied himself in love with had incited such feelings of protectiveness as this woman did in him. Though, he saw now, she was no fragile flower like the girls he'd known back East who lived near the school his father sent him to. Pretty, stuck-up white girls who'd either thought of him as some kind of toy, or got secret thrills being seen in public with the half-breed son of a major university patron. *The oddity. The wild Indian.* Being seen on his arm made them feel somehow...generous. It had been fine with him. All of it. Until that last night. He blinked away the memory.

No, Essie Sparks was something else again. But he couldn't quite figure out what.

Turning to him, she held up the blade she'd removed from the flame. It was red hot and glowing. "This is going to hurt," she warned. "A lot."

He braced himself, picking up a stick from beside him and biting down on it. But nothing could have prepared him.

The sound came first, the awful sizzle and burn, followed instantly by the pain. He bit back a cry and flattened himself to the ground, scratching up handfuls of dirt in his clenched fists. Her cool hand tethered him as he felt himself sinking underwater. He took her hand in his and clutched it. And after a moment or two, she lifted the blade and he swam back to the surface, exhaling the breath he'd been holding with a low growl.

"It's over now." Her hands were shaking.

He gulped convulsively and nodded.

She pulled her hand away and set the knife down on a

rock to cool. "You did well not to scream."

So had she not to swoon, he thought, when rational thought returned. "I need…another piece of your petticoat."

After a moment, she complied, tearing another row of ruffle from the impractical thing. She turned back to him warily, eying his leggings. He took the cotton from her and gestured for her to turn around. "I'll do it myself this time."

A grateful relief softened her expression and she did as he asked.

He got to his knees—all he could manage for the moment—and lowered his leggings again, careful not to scrape against his wound. *Séaa!* The thing felt like he'd been attacked by ten swarms of wasps. He hissed out a breath as the cotton made contact with the wound.

"Frankly, I don't know how you rode as long as you did. You need rest now if you don't want infection to set in."

By the time he'd finished, the pain in his leg dulled to a throb. He tested it for strength. There was no time for weakness. Not if he wanted to live. Black spots swam in his vision, but he braced a hand against a tree for a moment before kicking dirt into the fire, extinguishing it.

That got her to her feet. "What are you doing? We *need* that fire. And you're in no condition to go anywhe—"

"I'm going now. Are you coming with me?" He limped to his horse and mounted slowly, pulling himself up awkwardly into the saddle without using his left leg. When he settled, he reached a hand down to her.

She glared up at him in the moonlight, torn. "Do I have a choice?"

"Between me and the grizzlies? Yes." And he meant it. He watched the possibility of running, on her own, flit across her expression.

Things that had seemed so straightforward this morning seemed less so tonight. Something had shifted between them now. Some balance of power. She'd saved his life. He'd probably ruined hers. But it was no use crying over what couldn't be changed now. There was nothing for him but to get as far away from here as he could. She couldn't stay here alone in the dark, without a weapon. She was impulsive, but not stupid.

Finally, seemingly against her better judgment, she reached a hand up. He closed his fingers around hers and tugged her up in front of him. And when she'd settled into the lee of his thighs, her back stiff and purposefully avoiding contact with his chest, he said, "Cade."

She turned fractionally, confused. "What?"

"My name. It's Cade Newcastle. The Cheyenne call me Black Thorn."

She jerked a surprised look at him, then turned back around with a "Huh."

A smile settled around his mouth and he nudged the horse into a walk, leaving the campsite and the men who hunted them behind.

Mitchell Laddner pulled his mount up beside the man Dooley had sent to accompany him on the hunt for the renegade. Jacob Moran was a man of few words and even fewer morals, and that suited Laddner just fine. He wanted complete control of this operation and Moran had made it clear from the get-go that he wanted nothing of the kind. He was a follower, Moran. Laddner planned to use that instinct to its fullest advantage in the pursuit of his goals.

Twilight spilled across the sky as stars appeared. Even with the moon up, the darkness up here in the mountains was nearly complete under the thick cover of evergreens. It made no sense to go on. The climb had worn his horse out and had likely done the same to the one he was pursuing. The trail of blood he'd followed halfway up the mountain meant one of their bullets had popped that damned renegade but good. And unless that Injun was a damned fool, he'd give himself a night to rest as well.

Unless he was already dead.

The mystery was the woman. Essie. He'd half expected to see her body lying in the trail partway up the mountain. What good was she to that Indian anyway? With two on that horse, she could only be slowing him down. It didn't make sense that he hadn't killed her yet. Unless he just hadn't used her yet. On account of the bullet. A matter of time, he supposed.

He signaled to Moran that they would stop beside the stream for the night and rest. They made camp and warmed a can of beans over a fire. Moran fried up a few pieces of bacon he'd packed, wrapped in paper, and the men sat back against a pair of rocks to eat.

"I reckon," Moran eventually said, filling the empty space between them with conversation, "we'll find 'em in the morning. They can't stay ahead of us on one horse alone. Can they?"

Laddner considered the fire. It occurred to him that spending the entire night here might be foolish. The man he'd met that day on the Powder River might not do the easy thing, or even the wise thing, but he would undoubtedly do the audacious thing. If they were going to catch him, they would have to outwit and outplay him.

"Done much tracking in your life, Moran?" Laddner asked.

He shrugged. "Gotta admit, I ain't. Exceptin' wild boar an' the like. Ain't never tracked no human being. No Injun, neither."

A grin curved Laddner's mouth as he shoveled in another bite of beans.

"You seem to know your way 'round a trail. You learn in the military?" Moran asked.

Laddner shook his head. "Raised up in the woods. My daddy was a tracker of runaways in his day. After that, deserters during the war and a galvanized Yankee out here. Taught me his trade. I joined up with the Western Army as a youngster to fight the Indians. I worked for Custer himself as a tracker for a time. He used to say I had the nose of a bloodhound."

"*Custer*? Whoo-ee! You're practically famous!" Moran frowned then. "But I heard all them soldiers under him died over at the Big Horn."

"If he hadn't sent me off to Major Reno with a message

that day, I'd be one of them. I managed to keep my hair."

Moran belched and contemplated his empty plate. "Poor woman. Mrs. Sparks, I mean. What do you reckon he'll do to her?"

"He'll kill her," Laddner said. "Bloodthirsty savage. What'd you expect?"

With a regretful shake of his head, Moran sighed. "If'n he don't kill her, she'll likely be a handful to tote down that mountain. Ain't seen a captive for a while in these parts, but them women's a god-awful mess, I hear, when they come back."

"She won't be coming back." Laddner popped the last of his bacon in his mouth, then stood to spill the dregs of his coffee into the soil near the fire.

"Well, if he ain't kilt her...?" Moran said, putting his plate aside.

"Then we must do our Christian duty." He walked to the stream and washed his plate with sand and water.

After Moran had chewed on that thought for a long minute, he joined him at the stream's edge. "I ain't much of a church-goer, but what would that be, exactly? Our Christian duty, I mean?"

Laddner sent the man a dark smile. "Well," he said, shaking the water from his metal plate, "we'll follow the Reverend Dooley's orders, of course, and put her out of her misery."

CHAPTER 7

———◆———

Essie woke to the sound of another waterfall when he stopped at dawn to rest the horse. They were at the top of a precipice where the river disappeared over an edge that collided with blue sky and tumbled for hundreds of feet, straight down. Fog still hugged the slopes of the mountains thickly, making visibility nil.

At some point in the night she must have fallen asleep because when she woke he had his arms around her, and her head had fallen back against his shoulder. For a moment, she didn't move. With his hands splayed across her ribs and the rest of her intimately pressed against his chest, he was holding her gently, protectively. The way, she had always imagined, a man should hold a woman in his arms.

But he instantly sensed her awake and loosened his grip.

"Náhkohe needs to rest," he told her.

She felt embarrassed for falling asleep. Horrified, really. And then she remembered she'd been dreaming about him. Some combustible, half-witted dream that made no sense, though she couldn't recall the thing now. But those female parts of her remembered. Throwing her leg over the horse's neck, she dismounted, holding Black Thorn's hand.

He followed her down, stiffly. His face was wan-looking and she wondered how he had managed to stay awake all night long. She knew he must be hurting and weak.

The simple feat of holding her up while she slept was remarkable, considering. But as she watched him, she knew there was no accounting for strength like his. He was a different sort of man from the ones she knew. Or had ever known.

The horse lumbered over to the stream and sucked noisily from it. Parched, Black Thorn—*should she call him that or Cade?*—bent and cupped his hand in the briskly moving water upstream from the animal and drank deeply, too, then splashed water on his face and the back of his neck. It took a moment for him to gather the wherewithal to stand again, but when he did, he caught her watching him as he swiped a damp hand down his face, looking dark and foreign and dangerous.

She meant to pull her gaze away immediately, but it caught on the water that clung to his dark lashes and trickled down his neck. It was, perhaps, fatigue that made such a small, intimate thing so fascinating. In fact, she was too tired to apologize for staring. She simply looked away to quell the unfamiliar curl of heat that had settled in her belly.

He gave her a "be my guest" gesture and she edged past him to take a drink herself. The water tasted good. Sweet and cold. She'd been thirsty. But even more, she told him, "I have to…I—I need some privacy."

He'd let her off the horse once last night to see to her needs, but it had been dark and he had no fear of her running off into a forest filled with bears and wild cats. Now, his gaze scanned the woods around them with a suspicious eye.

"Where would I *go*?" she asked pointedly. "We're in the middle of nowhere."

"I told you. You are free to go anytime you want. It is not you I worry about, but what lives in these mountains."

A chill ran up her as she allowed her gaze to follow his.

He pointed to a hedge of bushes not far away. "There," he told her. "Keep talking so I can hear you."

*So I can hear you...*She rolled her eyes and headed to the shrubbery. Horrifying. But what choice did she have? "What would you like to discuss while I suffer the humiliation of proximity?"

"Of...what?"

"What shall we talk about? The weather? Mr. Harrison's chances of beating Mr. Cleveland in the presidential elections this year?"

He didn't answer for a moment, then said, "Who?"

"Never mind."

From behind the shrubs, she watched him unbuckle his saddlebag and pull a piece of jerky from it. He took a bite but it seemed an effort for him to chew it.

"All right. How is your leg feeling this morning?"

"Fine."

His back was to her, so she couldn't read his expression, but he limped toward the tree as if it still pained him. "I suspect," she called through the hedges, "that you are exaggerating."

He glanced back with a reluctant smile in her direction, then quickly away.

"Can I assume," she asked, changing the subject, "that you are the one Little Wolf referred to as 'Black Thorn'?"

"The same," he answered, leaning his back against the tree to stare up at the morning sky. "It is what I am called by the *Tsitsistas*."

She peeked through the bushes to be sure he wasn't watching as she lifted her petticoats behind them. "*Tsitsistas*?"

"The People. The Cheyenne, to you."

She didn't know why it had never occurred to her that they called themselves something entirely different than their enemies did. "So if you are Black Thorn to Little Wolf, that makes you...his—?"

"Cousin," he finished. "He is my mother's sister's son."

"So your mother's Cheyenne and your father's...?"

"From Texas," he answered distractedly, staring down the path behind them for signs of their pursuers. "White," he added, as an afterthought.

It was the most information she'd managed to wrangle from him since she'd met him and she decided to press her luck. "Are they both still living? Your parents?"

"My mother died when I was fourteen."

So young to lose a mother. She finished and stood, shaking her petticoats into place.

"My father..." His voice trailed off.

"Your father?" she prompted when he stopped talking.

"I have not seen him in years."

"He doesn't live in Montana now?"

He shrugged, his expression stark when he turned to her as she emerged from the shrubbery. "He does."

"I'm sorry. I shouldn't have—that's none of my business. You should rest. Eat something more than...whatever that is you're eating." She shuddered again. Her stomach had been growling since yesterday, but she couldn't force herself to eat the malodorous—what had he called it? *Pemmican.*

But he didn't rest. Instead he limped to the pool near the waterfall, stretched out beside it and caught a fat trout—barehanded. He bowed his head and said a prayer over the fish before cleanly lopping off its head. Then he dug up some roots growing by the stream and washed them in the cold current.

"We'll risk a fire to cook it, before the fog clears," he said with a look at the spires of pines surrounding them. "You need to eat."

He needed food as much, if not more, than she did. How, in the space of twenty-four hours, had she gone from sheer terror to caring whether he lived or died from that bullet in his leg? But maddeningly, she did care. She supposed it was because he'd treated her mostly with kindness, the rope being the glaring exception, of course. But in that short space of time they'd saved each other. She imagined it was just *that* which made her feel some obligation to him. No, not obligation. Bond?

Perish the thought!

And while she was at it, banish the pang of desire that twisted in her belly when she rode beside him, felt his powerful arms around her, his chest and thighs against her. Or even now, when she allowed her gaze to roam over his long limbs, his strong, narrow hands and imagined them touching her in other places.

Her gaze flicked to the scar on his cheek. A nearly straight slash, faintly darker than the skin around it. Made by...what? A blade? An arrow? The furrow of a bullet? Curiosity only made her want to know him better, which was a foolish, foolish thing. Because getting to know him frightened her almost as much as it intrigued her.

He dug into his saddlebags and pulled out a tin of matches then dropped the fish and the wild onions in her hands. "You clean this. I will start the fire."

She bobbled the slippery thing in her hands with a horrified look. "Me, clean it? I have a better idea. Why don't I make the fire and you clean the fish?"

With a look that said it was women's work, he pulled his knife from his belt and handed it to her before limping off to look for wood.

That he trusted her with the knife shocked her. But, she supposed, he knew that if she'd wanted him dead, she would have accomplished that last night at the river. Staring down at the slippery thing in her hand, she reasoned, *It's just a fish. A fat, just-a-moment-ago-alive fish.* But she was hungry. Starving, actually. She had never cleaned a fish before, but now was as good a time as any to learn.

While she gingerly did as he asked, and tried not to gag, he gathered deadfall from nearby for a fire.

"How far behind us do you think they are?" she asked, trying to keep the optimism from her voice.

"I saw their fire late last night. I think they camped for the night."

Disappointment threaded through her. If he was right, they'd put miles between themselves and rescue. She glanced over at him, noting that he seemed almost relaxed as he built a small tepee of sticks with dry grass stuffed inside. Though somehow this morning, the prospect of finding herself at Mitchell Laddner's mercy instead of Cade Newcastle's felt...unsettling, to say the least. Not to mention that in order for her to be saved, it meant this man's certain demise. A possibility that held less and less appeal.

She turned to watch him gathering firewood. There was something primal about her feelings for him. Something she couldn't explain, considering her circumstance. Was it only that he'd done nothing to actually hurt her that had her thinking such things? But he had not only failed to meet that awful expectation, he'd actually risked his own life to save her as well.

"I owe you an apology," she said, watching him.

"For what?"

"I'm afraid I wasn't very grateful last night at the river. I surely would have drowned if you hadn't saved me. So, thank you."

A flicker of surprise crossed his expression before he lowered his head once more to his work. "And thank you for coming back. For cutting the bullet out."

"Then we're even, I suppose?"

Those gray eyes rose through a sweep of dark lashes. "We are."

A look passed between them that was not a simple evening of the sides. It was nothing like the looks he'd given her before. This was a look that said something had shifted between them. His gaze fell to her mouth then back to her eyes with some unasked question.

It seemed unthinkable that his look was enough to make her imagine kissing him. But she found herself wondering how it would feel to do just that. Would he be gentle? Would he ask her permission? Or would he be rough and brutal?

No, she couldn't imagine that. Forceful, perhaps. That thought stirred something warm, deep inside her. Did she actually *want* him to kiss her? But just then, two squirrels scampered up the tree beside them, chasing each other. The moment was broken.

"I've been thinking," she said, watching him bend down to blow on the small flame, "about Shakespeare."

From the corner of her eye, she saw him roll a look at the sky. Of course, a dimple appeared in his cheek when he smiled. Damn him for being so attractive and so hostile at once.

The fire caught and flared. He added smaller sticks. "What about him?"

"Then you admit it. You *do* know the Bard."

"The Bard?" he snorted then. "Yes. I was schooled when I was younger. Back East. A white boarding school." He picked up the fish she'd cleaned and rinsed it off with water from his canteen.

"But how did you manage to—"

"My father. He had the money and he preferred the white part of me. Wanted me to fit into his world." The bitterness in his voice twisted at her.

He could have fit in to the white world, she thought, if he cut his hair, donned white clothes. Though knowing him now, she guessed it would never be a comfortable fit for him. There was something exotic about him—the tanned color of his skin, those eyes, the strong shape of his nose. Those things all made him different in some indefinable way. Different and, God help her, attractive. But those things were merely external. In every other way, as well, he was distinct from any man she'd ever met in the world from which she came.

"What about your mother?" she asked.

Threading the fish onto two long sticks, he thought about his answer for a moment. "Gone by then from smallpox. My father didn't want me spending time with the People after that. As long as she was alive, he'd let her take me summers. But her death was the end of that."

At a great cost to him, she could see. "And now?"

"Now?" he asked, not understanding the question.

"Does he accept you as you are?"

He jerked a look at her. "You mean with this?" he asked, lifting the hair away from the scar on his cheek.

It was odd that in such a short time, she'd gone from being shocked by his scar to not even remembering it was there. "No. I meant as Cheyenne."

"Like I said, I haven't seen my father in years." Stirring the coals with a stick, he propped the fish over the fire and said, "As for the Cheyenne, they accept me. I live with them. I speak their tongue. But…" He stopped and looked through the smoke at the edge of the waterfall. "I am not one of them, either. Not really. I do not really belong in either world."

His admission, so deeply personal, surprised and touched her. "But perhaps it is only you who feels that."

Lifting a cynical gaze her way, he said, "I would expect that from a white girl, who grew up knowing exactly where she belonged."

Essie straightened. "If you're saying I can't imagine being an outsider, like you, you'd be wrong. I, too, am alone in the world. My parents, gone. My husband…" She fingered the locket and stopped short of admitting her biggest loss.

"You are married?" Suddenly he was interested in this conversation.

"No. Not anymore. He's dead." Had she said those words before? She could not remember. Nathan's death had been a private hell she'd simply survived.

"How did he die?"

"How? Well, one day he went to the shore and took off all of his clothes. He folded them neatly, then pinned a note to them. Then he simply walked into the Atlantic Ocean and started swimming. He never came back."

Cade lowered his head.

With a shrug, she fed more sticks into the fire. "So we have both suffered rejection, you see? We are not so different in that way."

"It was his own life he turned from, not you," he suggested, rotating the fish over the fire.

"Oh, it was me. It was definitely me."

"Is that what you keep in that locket of yours? A picture of him?"

Instantly, she dropped the locket as if it had burned her fingertips. "*No*. I don't keep pictures of him."

"Who then?"

"No one," she lied, looking away. "It's just…just a locket I found in some old shop in Baltimore. Touching it is just a…comforting habit, I guess." The locket and its precious contents were not for anyone else to know about. Certainly not the man who'd kidnapped her.

The fragrant smell of the smoky fish cooking drifted up as silence stretched between them. "So," she said, "shall I call you Cade or Black Thorn?"

"Cade is what my father's people call me."

She tipped her head in agreement. "Cade, then. So, you had schooling, and you lived in the white world, but you chose this, living with the Cheyenne." It wasn't a question.

"As a heathen, you mean?"

"I didn't say that."

He shrugged. "You thought it."

Casting a look backward, toward the direction in which they'd come, she said, "Perhaps I did think that at first. Before I knew you. You did threaten to kill me with that knife. But now…I don't know what to think of you. I have known men who are far more savage than you and their skin was white. Those men following us, even. One of them…well, it was because of him I was dismissed from the school. As brutal a man as any I've ever met. Did I tell you they dismissed me? I was to leave there yesterday on a train bound for…" She shrugged. "*Ah*, who knows where?"

He frowned at that. "Why?"

"Why was I dismissed?"

"Why, because of *him*?"

"I believe the reverend was afraid of Mitchell Laddner. I stood up to him. I said things…He went to the Reverend Dooley and the church called me subversive. Thought I was undermining their mission. Giving the children hope, God forbid."

"Hope? For what?"

"A future. Something more. In particular, Little Wolf, who is quite brilliant. Did you know that? He's miles ahead of the others. And he loves to read. He wants an education. He wants, perhaps, what *you* had."

He shoved a stick into the fire and stirred. "No, he doesn't."

"Why ever not? Why shouldn't he want it?"

"Because there's no place for a boy like him there."

"Then you would deny him? Just as Reverend Dooley would?"

"Nothing good will come of it for him." When he got that look on his face, she remembered, he became impossible. So she bit her tongue.

Cade got slowly to his feet and used his knife to peel two pieces of bark from a nearby aspen to use as plates. He didn't want to talk about what would become of Little Wolf as an orphan in this world if they found him. What chance did he have now that he'd landed himself on the other side of *vé'ho'á'e* law by stealing their horses? Essie could talk all she wanted about glittery-eyed hopes and dreams for boys like Little Wolf, but Cade knew what the boy was up against. What he'd now put them all up against.

He slid the fish off the sticks and divided it onto the makeshift plates, handing her one. She looked comfortable in his too-big shirt, which she'd tied with a piece of rope at her waist over her shift and the corset he'd loosened after she'd nearly drowned. Beneath her long, once-white petticoat, her toes curled into the pine straw at her feet.

"That smells heavenly," she said, settling down to scoop the fish into her mouth with her fingers. Rolling her eyes she moaned in delight with the first bite. "Oh. That is so…mmm-mm. I'm, *oh*…so hungry."

He kicked dirt on the fire and put it out before he focused on his own meal. His appetite was dampened by the pain in his leg, but he ate because if he didn't, he would not have the strength to go on.

He wouldn't have guessed she'd eat the fish with her

fingers without wrinkling her pretty little white nose. Complaining wasn't in her nature, it seemed, though she had plenty to complain about. But he shouldn't allow himself to be curious about her life anymore. Her reasons for trying to forget her husband were her own. What niggled at him, however, was the look that had stolen over her face at the mention of him and of that locket. It stood to reason her husband's loss grieved her. But she'd swallowed that grief and tried to forget it.

When Cheyenne women lost their husbands, they cut themselves, chopped off their hair, and often were stripped of all of their possessions. Even he, who had lived with and known the Cheyenne most of his life, found this harsh.

But in a way, Essie Sparks had done the same, keeping no reminders of her husband, no possessions that meant anything to her—even the locket which meant little to her. She had come here with nothing, to—

To what? Teach? Escape?

Steal the souls from the People's children?

Remember that. Remember how this all began. And where you must go. You have no time to ponder this woman's grief. Or imagine how to soothe it.

He finished his fish and tossed his bark plate into the river, watching it float downstream. A sound, like the retort of a pistol or the clatter of rocks colliding, came from the trail, somewhere behind them. His eyes met hers in alarm over the still smoldering campfire.

"What was that?" she asked.

With a curse, he shoved himself to his feet and peered down toward the granite cliffs they'd crossed yesterday less than two miles away. Two men, studying the granite face where Essie's foot had left a trail a blind man could follow. And, indeed, one of them was the man from the barn. The one whose face he would never forget.

"Hurry," he said. "We don't have much time." Limping toward his horse, he gathered up the reins and gestured for her to come.

She tossed the remains of her fish aside. "But you said

you saw their fire. You said they had camped for the night."

"I was wrong," he said, throwing himself up onto Náhkohe and reaching a hand out for her. "Come on."

Just out of reach, she stopped in her tracks to stare at him. He could see the indecision on her face. Wait for them or go with him? "What if I stay? What if that's enough for them? Maybe they'll stop chasing you."

"You'd be a fool to think so."

"What chance do we have to outrun them on one horse? They'll kill you if they catch you, no matter what I say."

"Do you see him back there? The one with his head down, watching the rocks?" he said, darkness creeping over his expression. She followed his gaze. "I know him. He is a killer of women. And he knows I know him."

Her face paled. "*What*?" She looked back toward their pursuers. He saw the recognition dawn on her face. "Mitchell Laddner? How could you possibly—"

"Years ago, on the Powder River, when he was a soldier. I'll never forget his face, nor will he ever forget mine, I suppose. Believe me or not. It is up to you now. Come with me or stay. But I would not put my life in his hands if I were you. Alone. Up here."

A shiver ran through her. He'd given her an impossible choice. He recognized that. But she was far better off with him now than with that man coming up behind them. He could only imagine what a man like that would do to a woman as beautiful as Essie, given half a chance.

She seemed to make up her mind then because something close to fear crossed her expression. Reaching for his hand, she let him pull her up onto the horse and settled herself in front of him. He gathered up the reins, but she delayed him with a hand on his wrist.

Half turning toward him, she said, "I have been at the mercy of men my whole life. First my father, then my husband, then the Reverend Dooley. I have been abandoned, dismissed, disregarded and kidnapped by men. But I am finished letting men decide my fate. And if I were to decide to trust a man, it would not be the man sniffing at our tracks. I choose to ride with you, Cade Newcastle. I choose it, because you're the first man to ever give me a choice." Her words settled in his chest like a fist. He slid his arms around her, brushing his hand against hers. She jerked a look at him. "Cade. You're burning up!"

"I'm all right." But he wasn't. Heat had settled in his leg and made him lightheaded. He needed to sleep, long and hard, and the medicine that White Owl knew of. Regretting all the times he had ignored the herbs and roots she picked in the forest for fevers, he nudged the horse into the rushing creek and followed it upstream for a few hundred feet before exiting. It was a small attempt at concealment, but it was all he had. It might slow his pursuers down for a short time, but they would catch up if he couldn't clear his brain enough to think of a way out.

On the other side of the creek, he kicked Náhkohe into a run.

CHAPTER 8

Little Wolf woke to the feel of a spider crawling across his nose. He batted the thing off him, sat up and whacked his head on the hollowed-out log he was sleeping in. With a grunt of pain, he rubbed the spot then peered outside. The sun had come up hours ago and Lalo was standing outside the log, stamping her hoof. Her whinny had woken him, he realized now.

Crawling outside, he took Lalo's velvety nose between his hands and stroked her. She was halter-tied to a branch, her saddle and bridle propped against the nearby log. The pony's ears were back. "You should have woken me sooner, Lalo."

"I reckon she should have, at that."

The man's voice behind him made Little Wolf jump and he turned to find not one but two men on horseback, staring down at him. They were strangers. Not from the school. The second looked even dirtier than the first.

"We was wonderin' what a pretty little paint like her was doin' out here on her lonesome," said the first man, who was chewing tobacco and paused to spit a stream of brown juice at Little Wolf's feet. "Good things come to them that wait. And look how we was rewarded, Payton. We got us a real, live Injun cub who speaks English."

Panic began drumming in his ears. The two men were dressed in oily, filthy clothes that were made of skins, with

Winchester rifles tucked in their rifle boots. Even from a few feet away, they smelled like they had rolled in a swamp bottom. Their appearance marked them as hunters of some kind. But the hunting was so bad in these mountains, Little Wolf decided he must be wrong. Perhaps they were hunters of something besides skins.

He gathered Lalo's reins in his hand and moved to her side. "I-I don't mean any trouble," he told the men. "I'll be on my way."

"Hear that? He don't mean no trouble, Nestor."

"I heard him. Imagine that? A boy of the Cheyenne persuasion thinkin' he ain't no trouble. What's your name, boy?" When Little Wolf refused to answer, he said, "I asked you a question, redskin."

Little Wolf lifted his chin and, thinking fast, said, "Huckleberry."

The man named Payton threw his grease-stained leg over his horse's neck and dismounted. "*Huckleberry*?" He laughed, walking slowly in Little Wolf's direction. "Well, we seen lots o' huckleberries on the way up here. Even et a few, but not another 'un like you."

Little Wolf backed up, gauging how fast he could throw himself up onto Lalo before they overtook him.

"Hey, Payton," said the other one. "I think this huckleberry's a runaway. All trussed up like a white boy, puttin' on airs. What d'ya think?"

"Well, he ain't no agency Cheyenne. Are you, boy? You's from that Bible-thumper's school down in the valley."

Little Wolf felt for the skinning knife tucked into the back waistband of his trousers. He would not let them take him back there. He would never go back.

"You reckon they got a ree-ward if we brought this here boy back?" Payton asked the other man.

"Doubtful. But value is in the eye of the beholder, ain't that what they say?"

"Beauty," Nestor corrected. Lalo shied as he spit more tobacco juice at Little Wolf's feet. "I believe they do say beauty."

"I guess that's about right. And this boy ain't no beauty, though."

"Nope." Nestor began to circle around to Little Wolf's right. Above them a hawk watched from a high-up branch in the pine and let out a plaintive sound.

"Unless you was Chen Lee or one o' his ilk. Then this boy might look real purty. And worth enough for a bath and a night with one of his girls. Maybe even two nights."

"None o' them girls for me. I'll take Ollie's girls any day o' the week."

While they argued, Little Wolf threw himself up on Lalo's back and kicked the pony. But he wasn't fast enough. The men grabbed the pony's reins and jerked her to a stop.

"Oh, no you don't, boy!" Nestor shouted, dragging him from the saddle and all too easily disarming him. Little Wolf kicked and punched at the man, but soon found himself face down in the dirt with the man's knee in his back. Behind him, he heard Lalo rearing in agitation.

"Tie him up good, brother," Payton said, holding Lalo firmly. "But try not to kill him. I got plans for this Injun cub that should make us a pretty penny."

Cade saw their lead steadily shrink as they raced over miles of rocky terrain, plowed through leaf-littered forests and watched their backs for hours until afternoon had settled the sun low in the sky. The men behind them each had a horse. Náhkohe was struggling beneath the weight of two of them.

The constant pounding against his leg had sunk him into a fog of pain hours ago. Still no trace of Little Wolf, despite watching the ground for sign. They had lost him.

Regret churned through him like a fever. Regret that he'd lost the boy, that he'd taken Essie, that he'd mangled the entire escapade from start to finish. And now, the men behind them were closing in and chances were good they would take Essie down, too, when they killed him. And that would be on him, too.

The blame was his for taking her in the first place. He

couldn't say what had compelled him. The sight of that long-ago bastard in the barn, the lost look she had in her eyes. Or something else. Something more primal.

Since the river, he'd fought the pain in his leg, trying to ignore it, but as the hours stretched by, his thoughts blurred and roamed out of his control, sparked by feverish swings between the urgency of their situation and the woman in his arms.

As they rushed across the terrain, he found himself distracted by her womanly softness. Once or twice his forearms had brushed the stiff corset around her breasts where it swelled to accommodate them. Imaginings filled his thoughts for minutes, sometimes hours afterward, picturing what shape they'd take if they were loosed from that corset. Imagining that his hands were cupping them.

Caressing them.

And her mouth…When his good sense failed him, he found himself picturing her mouth, wondering how she would taste. Were her lips as soft as they looked?

With her back pressed up against his chest, he could inhale her sweet scent—something between soap and violets—by simply adjusting his head closer. And despite everything, the pain he was in, the fever he could feel rising in his body, he found himself getting hard for her. Another ache atop an ache.

Foolish want. A woman like her could never want a man like you.

None of that mattered now. They were finished. The terrain here offered no shelter. No perch from which to hunker down, and ambush their pursuers. The men behind them had split up some time ago, intending to flank him. The mountains here had flattened out onto a broad grass-covered plateau whose edge seemed to meet the sky in the distance and plunge away.

The men chasing them were stronger of will than he'd imagined and better trackers. He'd done everything he could to lose them. Cut through rivers, up shale mountainsides and across limestone plateaus where no man could track another.

And yet, they had. And there was only so far he could push his horse. Náhkohe would run until his heart burst for him, but then what? What good would it do them only to be cornered by the one she'd called Laddner?

Not long ago, he'd begun seeing things: Little Wolf's mother, White Owl, thin and wasted by the coughing sickness, was standing near a rock, staring at the sweeping vista ahead. *Is she dead already? Or just an illusion? Am I already too late?*

His best friend from childhood—Wind On The Water—a boy who had never feared anything until the *vé'ho'e's* smallpox had taken him at fifteen—also appeared, beckoning him to follow. Cade had run a hand down his face to clear his vision, but Wind On The Water just stood near an overhanging rock, making the sign for something beyond his comprehension. And then it struck him.

Hotòame'ko. Buffalo.

Did Essie see Wind On The Water, too? Or was he losing his mind?

A chill chased through him. The sun was lowering again and he longed to stretch out by a warm fire wrapped in a buffalo hide and sleep. Náhkohe was coming to the end of his strength as well.

But the thought of Little Wolf and the woman in front of him kept him going. Where could the boy have gone? Was he lost up in these mountains? He was only thirteen. And whatever skills his father had taught him must have been ripped away by the damned school they'd kept him locked up in for the last two winters. Would he ever see him again? White Owl—wherever she was—no doubt wondered the same. Was that why she was haunting him now? *Because of your promise to let her see her son one last time. A promise you should never have made.*

He shivered again. Too many broken promises to count.

The sharp retort of horseshoe against rock somewhere behind them jerked him out of his reverie. He pulled the horse up short and turned to look. There, not a half mile back, were his pursuers. Relentless. Pushing their way past every obstacle.

She saw them at the same time. She glanced up at him, alarm in her expression.

He shook his head with silent warning and kicked the horse into a full gallop and shoved Essie down against the nape of the horse's neck. Náhkohe would not last long at this pace. He was as exhausted as they were. They were all clinging to the end of a very frayed rope.

As they raced toward the vanishing edge of the plateau, it suddenly struck him where they were. He hadn't been here for years. Not since his thirteenth summer on the hunt that would be his last with his mother's people. His mother had died that autumn. After that, there had been too few buffalo to hunt. And the People had left this place for hunting grounds north.

Buffalo.

This was Buffalo Jump. A huge, sheer, unsurvivable drop into nothingness. The bottom was a thousand feet nearly straight down. Whole herds of buffalo had met their ends here, driven off by the Cheyenne and Crow and other tribes who'd been lucky enough to use this gift of nature. And he and Essie and Náhkohe were heading right for it.

"Oh, no! Stop!" Essie gasped. "There's a cliff ahead! Slow down!"

But he didn't stop. He pushed the horse on. The chilly wind tore at them, cutting through their clothes and hair.

She gripped the saddle horn and the horse's mane. "Are you *mad?* You're going to kill us both!"

Cade clutched his mount hard with his legs despite the pain stabbing at him. He held his breath, his sight blurring, as he tried to remember where Wind had gone that day.

The whine of a bullet skidded past his ear in the thin air. *Damn!* He leaned forward and covered Essie with his body.

Then again, up ahead. Wind On The Water was there, beckoning him, as his horse raced toward the edge and he braced himself for what he was about to do.

* * *

Mitchell Laddner and Jacob Moran pulled their mounts up short a good ten feet from the edge of the cliff, staring incomprehensibly at the place where they'd seen the renegade and the woman vanish. They'd seen it with their own eyes from a half mile back. The lunatics had thrown themselves off the horse, sent the animal running and with barely a pause, had jumped off this damned cliff!

Jacob Moran looked white-faced and shaken at the prospect. He gave a low whistle as he cautiously peered over the edge. "That there's one hell of a drop, that is. See there?" He pointed down the steep cliff to the ground far, far below. "A thousand feet if it's an inch. No way we spot their bodies from here. Too far. Too foggy."

Laddner didn't care for heights and certainly not thousand-foot heights. He felt a cold sweat break out just above his lip seeing Moran standing as close to the edge as he was right now.

He cursed foully, wondering why, after two days of desperate running, the renegade had chosen suicide, thereby depriving him of the pleasure of killing the bastard properly. Laddner felt his stomach drop at the mere thought of making such a choice. He would take a rope over a fall like that any day of the week.

Dismounting, he began to remove his gloves. At a safe distance from the edge, he stared out at the big Montana sky with its pink edges curling toward sunset. The plains in the distance stretched on and on and on toward the Missouri River, many miles north of here. If one squinted past the fog hugging the mountains, one might just make out that green snake of water that would eventually roll all the way to the Dakota Territories before it hit the Mississippi. To the west, the mountains rose up like black crow wings against the pale blue sky. And to the east, the plateau they were standing on wrapped itself around the prairie below like a giant arm. It was, he supposed, as good a place to die as any other. Pretty as a painted postcard.

What a waste of a perfectly good day.

Disappointment and a certain sense of failure threaded

through him. He heard his old man's voice in his head, berating him for not riding faster, not hitting his mark at a half mile out. *You have a Henry rifle*, the old man would say. *Gun enough to hit your mark. Not man enough to make your mark.*

"We should go down there and find what's left," Moran was saying. "It'll take us the better part of tonight to get to the bottom and locate the remains. Guess they'll be wantin' some sort of proof."

"Look again," Laddner urged, though he made no attempt to get closer himself. "Try to spot them."

The other man glanced over the cliff's edge again. "Ain't no spottin' 'em from this height. Anything goes over, it's goin' all the way down."

"The girl jumped right over with him," Laddner muttered. "Guess he just saved me the trouble of what needed doing."

"What's that you say?" Moran asked with a frown.

"She'd clearly lost her mind. Would've been a mercy," Laddner said.

Moran stared at him, dumbfounded.

Laddner tugged the fingers of his second glove and pulled it off. He slapped the pair against his thigh, making Moran twitch and his horse shy sideways. "I suppose you'd have spared her, all broken like a sparrow mangled up by a dog? Even *she* knew there was no choice."

Moran shifted uncomfortably at the edge and scratched at his beard with his dirty fingernails. "She's broken, all right. Broken to bits. I don't reckon I'd have any say about savin' her or not, where she is now."

Laddner shook his head. He didn't expect a man like Moran to understand the intricacies of mercy. Still, it did disappoint him that he wouldn't get to see that Sparks girl get what was coming to her. He'd been looking a little forward to seeing what two days in the wilderness with a renegade savage would do to the snotty look she'd always worn when she spoke to him. Like she was too good for him. Like she had better choices.

Laddner mounted again and tugged his horse away from the cliff. "We'd best get started down and find what's left of them before the scavengers do. Then, all that remains is the boy. And when we find him, he'll wish he'd gone over with these other two."

Moran took another scan of the sheer drop below his feet and shrugged. "It'll sure enough be the Wages of Sin for him for a good long stay. Dumb little bastard. I never *will* understand why them redskin whelps don't—"

But Laddner had already kicked his horse into a gallop, leaving Moran behind in his dust, talking to himself.

With a sigh, he shook his head and mounted his horse. "And you can go fuck yourself, Mr. High and Mighty." He turned to look in the direction the Indian's horse had taken and cupped his hands around his mouth. To the endless valley below him, he shouted, "Run, damn you, horse! Run for your life!" And he added, under his breath, "If you know what's good for ya."

His words echoed over and over again until they faded away.

CHAPTER 9

Cade let go of Essie after they'd heard the second man ride off, unclamping his hand from her mouth and his iron-like arm from around her.

She flung herself as far away from him in the shallow cave as she could, furious with him for nearly throwing her off a mile-high cliff, only to stuff her into a shallow limestone cave just below the rim. Then he'd practically hogtied her with his arms to silence her. But that wasn't the worst. The worst was hearing what Mitchell Laddner had said about her, when he thought she was already dead.

She growled a sound of pure anger and frustration as she slid down against the far wall, glaring at Cade. Cold shivered through her. She'd never felt so alone in all her life.

"Don't say I didn't warn you about them," he said under his breath, eyeing her with what looked suspiciously like sympathy.

"Fine. You were right. Is that what you wanted to hear?"

He shrugged and tilted his head tiredly against the back wall of the shallow cave. Their escapade had clearly drained whatever remained of his reserves. He was still breathing hard from their jump.

She stared gloomily out across the valley, knowing that before sunrise, the men would be scouring the ground below for their bodies and coming up empty-handed. What then? Would they come back for them? Find them huddled here? Kill them both properly? She couldn't wrap her mind around it. "But why would he want to kill *me*? I've done nothing to deserve—"

"You're tainted now. Ruined. No doubt out of your mind."

"But you...you haven't—"

He sent her a serious look. "They wouldn't be wrong if you'd been taken by some Crow hunting party up here, or by the Flatheads, or even some renegade faction of the Northern Cheyenne. There's no love for whites now. Or ever, to be honest. It would have gone very badly for you."

She stared out over the lavender-colored sky at the valley. "I'd be past worrying about those two, is that what you're saying?"

"Or worse. The Northern Cheyenne have not taken a prisoner for many years now. Not since I've been with them. But I've heard stories."

"So have I. But you've been kind to me. Kinder than I expected."

That brought his head around to her. "It's my fault you are in this mess now."

Essie shrugged. "My life was a mess before you took me. A terrible mess." She turned to look at Cade. The sunset slanted across his finely carved face, painting him with a deceptively healthy color. In truth, he looked terrible.

The long days of riding, the loss of blood and the pain had taken their toll. She hated that she could despise him and care about him at the same time. That being clamped against him as intimately as any woman could be clamped against a stranger felt oddly safer than the alternative. And, yes, he'd ruined her life. But in some odd way, she realized that no one—not her late husband or her father, who had died years after her mother, who had died when Essie was young, or certainly, the men sent to rescue her—had ever protected her the way Cade had.

The cave smelled of the Montana wind that constantly

scoured it. It harbored dead grass and skeletal remains of small creatures who'd been trapped here. She shoved one away from her with a dry stick.

"This place," she said, staring at her surroundings. "How did you know it was here?"

"It's a buffalo jump. When the herds were plenty, the People drove them to their deaths over the jump for winter stores. For food and everything else. I came on a hunt when I was thirteen. My cousin, Wind On The Water, was chosen to play decoy, leading the buffalo to the edge covered in a buffalo hide." Cade stared out ahead, watching the clouds move in a flat line across the sky as the sun sank lower. "I remembered this cave. From above, it's nearly invisible. He jumped down here at the last moment…and…over the buffalo went."

She made a face. "How gruesome."

He shrugged. "Once, the buffalo jump meant life to the People. Now…this place just means death."

Now the buffalo are gone and so, for the most part, are the People.

"We can't stay here," she said. "They'll be back when they don't find us down there. They'll realize—" She stared at him, suddenly understanding. "But you knew that, didn't you? Before we even jumped. What was your plan?"

He lifted his hands, palms up. "I didn't have a plan. I was trying to save us."

But he hadn't. Not really. He'd merely postponed the inevitable. "We have to go. Now. While they're heading down there."

"Do you remember how we came?" he asked her.

"I—yes. Maybe."

"Good. Then you must find your way back."

"What do you mean I—" She gaped at him. "Oh, no. Y-you must be…joking."

"You're a clever girl. Try to stay just off the path in case they come back that way looking for you. Cover your trail as much as you can, the way I did."

He might as well ask her to juggle pigs! "It's…it's two

days back! Through the mountains. With…with bears and—"

He held out his rifle to her and slid his deerskin ammunition pouch off over his head. "Take these. I won't be needing them."

She didn't take them, but stared at him as if he'd somehow lost his mind. "What do you mean?"

The look he gave her was stark. "We both know I'll never be able to walk out on this leg. You'll have a chance without me."

Her eyes widened. "This is your plan? To wait here for them to kill you? No!"

He sighed. "I won't argue with you."

"And I—I won't leave you here for…*them*."

His eyes focused on her with effort. "You'll get away from me. It's what you wanted all along, isn't it? What do you care what happens to me?"

"I…I care," she blurted, before she could stop herself. "I mean…I have no wish to see you dead."

He tilted his head back against the stone and half grinned, something she'd almost never seen him do before. His grin dazzled her and made her want to cry at the same time.

"You care?"

She shook her head. "Yes. *Yes.* But don't make me say it again."

"All right." He stared down at the rifle in his hands, as if without it he would be lost.

"Come on, then," she told him.

He closed his eyes. "It was one thing to ride. I cannot run on this leg. Take the gun."

"No."

"Take it!"

"*No!*"

He shoved the rifle toward her again. "Go, *Mo'onahe*, while you still can. They will not be long."

"I am not going anywhere without y—"

"Go!" He shouted at her, then he sat up and forced the gun into her hands. He clapped his fingers over hers, around the barrel of his rifle. "I am sorry I took you. It was *ó'oht*. A mistake. Now go! Run. And don't look back."

Tears sprang to her eyes. She couldn't help it. He was sacrificing himself for her. How could she just leave him here to die? His skin was dry and hot against hers. His leg must be getting infected. He was right. He could never walk out. She wasn't altogether certain she could either.

She took the gun. "Fine. We have the advantage here. When they come back…*if* they come back…I'll shoot them before they can—"

"Don't be stupid. There are two of them. You could never kill them before they killed you. Both of us." He pulled his knife from its sheath and brandished it at her. "I won't ask again."

"You wouldn't—"

He bared his teeth and slapped the blade against his own throat. His eyes were fevered and bright and he wasn't thinking clearly. She felt tears leak from hers. *He might. He just might.*

"Don't!" she cried. "All right, all right! I'll go! But promise me you won't do anything. Promise me, unless they come, you won't do anything. I will find someone to come back and help you. I will not leave you here. I swear to you."

"Goodbye, Essie Sparks."

She stared at him for a long beat, until he lowered the knife and leaned his head back against the stone.

What she did next surprised even her. She leaned close to him and wrapped her arm around him. Pressing her face against his shoulder, she said, "Don't give up. Promise me."

She felt his hand spread against her back tentatively at first, then harder, as if he didn't want to let her go.

Lifting her head, she met his eyes. His silvery gray eyes that seemed too bright somehow. Full of need. They searched her eyes and then fell to her mouth. Impulsively, perhaps, and without asking her permission, he kissed her. A quick meeting of their lips that could hardly be misconstrued as anything but a goodbye. And truth be told, she could have resisted that kiss. She could have pulled out of his reach. But she didn't.

And when he broke the kiss, his fevered eyes searched hers for a long moment until she gave him a barely discernible shake of her head before he pulled her back to him and kissed her the way a man should kiss a woman.

His lips were warm, too warm, but unexpectedly soft. He threaded his fingers into the hair at her nape and pulled her closer still. Dipping his tongue into her mouth, he shocked her. Inflamed her. Nathan had never breached the seam of her lips—not once—or made *want* curl in her belly.

She filled her lungs with Cade's scent for perhaps the last time. She couldn't think straight now. Not when his mouth tasted as sweet as the fresh wind that buffeted them there in the cave, and his arms circled around her as if she belonged to him.

She didn't. She couldn't. But in this moment, she wanted to.

Somehow, she'd hoped to change his mind about staying behind, but she could tell this kiss was not acquiescence. It was farewell. And it broke her heart.

When she ended the kiss, she blinked and looked away, breathing hard, listening to the thud of her heart in her ears. "Promise me," she repeated, but her voice was small now.

He pushed her away from him with a shake of his head. "Go."

Slinging the rifle and ammunition across her back, she turned and climbed out of the cave and out onto the dark, windswept cliff.

The man with a braid of long gray hair and simple, sack-like, dark clothes leaned over Little Wolf, poking him with a stick and shouting something in a language he didn't understand. He blinked up at the bent old man through the smoky haze that circled the tent like a cloud, but his head felt muddled and thick from the sweet, awful smell. And in his mind, he could still hear the laughter of the two hunters who'd taken him as they counted the gold coins the old man had paid them for him. That had been hours ago, after they'd reached Magic City.

It was night outside. The raucous sound of the nearby saloons drifted to him. The moon shone through the flaps in the tent. His ankles were chained together by heavy manacles, and his hands, still bound, were tied above his head to a stout beam that supported the tent. Those men who'd stolen Lalo had left him here, sold him like a stockyard steer. He kicked at the chains on his ankles but only succeeded in rubbing his skin raw.

The old man brandished a knife in his direction with some sort of threat before slicing through the rope that bound him to the pole. Pain shot through the boy's shoulders as he lowered his arms.

He'd had seen men like this one they'd called Chen Lee before when he'd come here to Magic City with the supply wagon. These men mostly worked in nearby mines and on the railroad, or could sometimes be seen pulling carts full of laundry through the muddy streets, with their long braid trailing down their backs. They came from some faraway place, across the sea and far from the mountains of his people.

Chen Lee poked at him again, harder this time, and yelled again. He sat up, glared at the old man and captured the stick in his hand. For the briefest of moments, he played tug-of-war with him before the old man's slippered foot snapped around, catching him in the jaw and knocking him nearly senseless. Pain streaked across his face and he blocked the next blow with his still-tied hands. A stream of angry words spewed from Chen Lee's wrinkled old mouth, not a word of which he understood.

Sprawled there on the dirt floor of the tent, anger roiled up in his throat. Anger at his own foolishness for getting caught by those two men and at being sold for a handful of coin to this one. Anger at his powerlessness to stop any of it. All his foolish plans, gone to smoke.

The stick came down hard against his shoulders again and he cried out. He could feel the stinging welts rise on the skin of his back. Oh, if he had a knife, he would kill this old man, then steal that long gray braid of his. Then he would track those other two and kill them, too. But slower. Much slower.

In Wages, he'd spent long nights pondering the slow, painful murder of Sergeant Laddner. How the sharp edge of his knife would find the tender skin of his scalp; the look on the man's face as he stole his life from him. Thirteen summers had taught him to hate the white man, but now he understood that the People, who his grandfather had taught him were the center of the world, had enemies everywhere. No one could be trusted.

Risking a look up, he caught sight of a girl standing just behind the old man. She looked not much older than thirteen summers herself. Long, silky black hair, skin the golden, pearly color of a mussel shell he once plucked out of the river. Except for the dark bruise beneath her left eye, she was sort of beautiful. Her swanlike neck made her look proud beside the bent old man, and the look on her face, as she watched the man beating him, was half curiosity, half warning.

She shook her head slightly as Little Wolf raised his hands to defend himself against the stick, then her gaze darted back to the old man, who was speaking to her now and gesturing at him. She answered Chen Lee in a whisper, with her head bowed and eyes averted. Then she bowed to him and took a step closer, coming between the stick and Little Wolf.

She beckoned to him with her hand, then reached for him. "Lookee, boy. You come. Now."

Her hand was small and her fingers slender and long. Her nails were clean, but bitten to the quick. Anything seemed better than letting the old man hit him again, so he reached for her hand. With a quick crack, the stick came down on his knuckles and he snatched his hand back, biting back a cry. Again, the girl shook her head at him so that only he could see, then tipped her chin to get him to follow her.

Seeming satisfied at last when Little Wolf got to his feet,

the old man gestured, with a grunt of impatience, for him to follow. Little Wolf looked back at the girl, but she refused to meet his eyes. They moved through the smoky tent, past foreign men smoking pipes with half-dressed young girls lying beside them. Or on top of them. Or under them.

None of them looked much older than sixteen summers, and one looked younger than him. And the smoke coming from the pipes was not from tobacco or red willow bark, but something noxious that made him feel lightheaded just walking through it.

He'd heard of places like this. Here, in Magic City, there were many places men could go to lie with women, but only one with these dark-haired girls from across the sea. He'd caught sight of them once, each chained by an ankle to a stake in a tent, calling out to men passing by.

On the mountain, he'd heard Nestor and the other one talk of going to a brothel after they sold him, but Chen Lee had made it clear they weren't welcome at this one.

There were plenty of brothels that welcomed their kind in town. At least he would know where to look for them when he escaped this terrible place.

Attached to the smoking tents was a two-story building and they entered up a small flight of steps. Chen Lee shoved him toward a room down the hall where a disheveled young girl stood alone with her back against the wall, eyes downcast as they entered. There was one small, barred window in the room that opened to the street outside and the men passing by. The room was empty save a dirty cup on the floor and a pallet. In the corner, a covered wooden bucket stank in the close room. The man shoved him into the room and Little Wolf tripped and fell to his knees. More foreign words and the pretty girl leaned her head down to him and spoke.

Pointing to the bucket, she said, "You takee. Clean. *Kuai dian!* Quick, quick!" She let out a breath. "No go. Stay. Or else…" Slicing a hand across her throat, she laid her hand on her small breast and patted her chest.

Or what? "He will kill you?"

She bowed her head. "*Shi.* Yes."

He slid a disbelieving look at the old man who simply grinned back at him, rolling a pair of coins in his hand.

Was it possible that he'd actually found a place worse than the school? A place where these girls were no better than slaves? A look at the poor girl who was trying to blend in to the plain wooden walls answered that. No one would care about a Cheyenne boy any more than they would about these girls. They would not help him, or her. Even if someone did rescue him, he'd just be sent back to the school. Or worse. He was lost here unless he could find a way out.

Tears burned his eyes, but he bit them back. He would not cry or show that old man weakness. Instead, when Chen Lee yelled again, Little Wolf pushed the hatred from his expression and stood to face him.

"Where?"

"Come," the girl said, flicking a look in the direction of the old man. "I show."

Naturally, Essie did the exact opposite of what Cade had told her to do. She didn't run. Instead, she waited with the rifle propped on the ancient remains of a fallen tree, twenty yards from the edge of the cliff, above the entrance to the cave.

She was nearly completely exposed here herself, but that didn't matter. If they saw her, she would shoot them. She would not let them get as far as Cade.

A half laugh, half cry bubbled up inside her. Maybe she'd lost her mind a little out here in the wilderness. Imagine her, kissing him. Or plotting to murder two men. Even stranger, doing it to protect the man who'd kidnapped her. Though somehow, she'd begun to think of him differently. Not as a renegade. As a flesh-and-blood man, not an enemy.

About the staying, she had no choice, really.

Even if she ran, they'd chase her down. But first they'd kill him in some horrible way, if he didn't beat them to the punch himself.

She sniffed and wiped her nose with her sleeve. She'd lost her shawl somewhere en route, days ago, snagged on some branch somewhere and ripped away from her. The temperature was falling and she wished she had a fire. She pictured fire in her mind and let it warm her as she shivered. But soon, she imagined Cade's arms around her instead.

She squeezed her eyes shut to deny herself that fantasy. Because it wasn't just about his arms or the weight of him against her keeping her safe. It was him. Kissing her.

Gad!

Her feelings for him had changed, blindsiding her there in the dark, surprising her in their intensity.

But it wasn't possible. For either one of them. And that kiss notwithstanding, he'd made it clear he'd rather have died than let her stay to fight for him. He'd put a knife to his own throat! Right now, he was probably relieved not to have to worry about her anymore. She supposed—no, she was quite certain—he wished he'd never taken her at all.

Three hours had crawled by since they'd jumped, and the moon was hanging up high in the sky now. It was bright, though clouds were sweeping down from the north. Where the clouds weren't, stars smeared the blackness, twinkling with no concern for her and Cade's little lives. Their little disasters. For the first time since this whole misadventure had begun, she wished for darkness. Full, utter darkness.

Somewhere in the distance a wolf howled and another answered.

She huddled closer to the trunk and shivered, having almost forgotten about the wolves. There were more dangerous predators than wolves out there hunting her now. She clutched her locket, allowing the warmth of the metal to warm her fingers.

The men would reach the bottom soon and search for their bodies. Finding nothing, they would either retrace their steps or give up. The second option wasn't likely. But if they didn't return by morning, she would...

What? Try to find his horse? *Lost cause, probably.* Run

back to the school? Downhill, mostly, it might take her more than a day. And then what? No one would help him. The opposite, in fact.

There was no good answer. She was alone in the wilds of the Montana mountains with nothing but a rifle and her wit. Which felt about to fail her.

In her wildest dreams, she couldn't have pictured her adventure to the West ending like this. Maybe she would die tonight. Eaten by wolves or killed by animals of the human sort. Nor could she have pictured meeting a man like Cade Newcastle at all.

It wasn't as if he'd been nice to her. The opposite, really. *Except when he thought I wasn't looking. Or when he touched me. Or held me against him.* And she found herself imagining being held by him as if he actually cared about her. His strong arms around her in an embrace instead of…instead of whatever it was.

He had kidnapped her. But he'd been right all along. Laddner and his bunch had not worried at all about hitting her when they'd fired at them back at the school. They would have taken her death—if a bullet had hit her—as an inevitable, necessary evil. For once a white woman was taken, apparently, there was no coming back. No redemption.

But now look what she'd come to. Standing guard over the man who'd taken her. The man who'd treated her more gently than her husband ever had. Who made her feel like a woman for the first time in her life.

Remember who you are, Essie. Remember where you've come from. Was it only a few days ago she'd vowed not to allow herself to care again?

The farm of her dream came back to her then and she closed her eyes, thinking of Aaron. For a moment, she allowed herself to walk in that verdant green field with him, with the birds lifting off into the sky and the sound of cows in the distance. If she could only take back that day he'd died, when his sleep had taken him so deep that he'd never awoken. Her husband had blamed her, of course, for not being more careful. For not noticing that his little life was coming to an end. And though she wasn't the first to lose a child to a mysterious cause, Nathan had made certain she felt responsible. He couldn't forgive her. Or, more importantly, himself.

Which she understood, of course, because she couldn't forgive herself either. Fit for neither motherhood or marriage, she was destined to be alone. She'd made peace with that idea. Until Cade had barged into her life and turned it upside down.

It was starting to rain. Small drops at first, then fat, unrepentant splats against her skin. *Oh, God. What next?* She shivered and wiped her nose with the back of her hand. She should know better by now than to ask such a question.

A clip-clop of a shuffle sounded behind her above the drizzle of the rain. *A horse.* Essie froze. One step. Then another.

She whirled, pointing the rifle into the thick blackness. She could see nothing, but she tightened her finger against the trigger. The gun's tip wavered violently. Blood pounded against her eardrums. "Stop right there," she called out. "I have a gun."

Don't be stupid. There are two of them. You could never kill them before they killed you. Maybe he was right. But now, she would see. Because whoever it was wasn't stopping.

The hoofbeats came closer.

And then a horse emerged from the shadows like some kind of ghost. Slowly, head down, sniffing its way toward her. Dark, drenched with rain, splotches of white dappling its coat.

Náhkohe!

She let the tip of the gun collapse to the ground as all the strength left her arms. She threw the gun aside and got shakily to her feet, slipping twice before she managed it.

Walking slowly toward her, reins dragging on the ground, the horse dropped its head and exhaled an equine snort of a greeting. Essie threw her arms around Náhkohe's neck and kissed him. "You…you wonderful, handsome, brilliant horse!"

She was still shaking with cold and the horse's damp warmth bled into her. Giddiness flooded her and she began to shake with laughter. Who could have imagined the twists these last few days had brought to her life? And apparently fate was not finished with her. She would not die here. She would live. And so would Cade Newcastle.

Hurriedly, she tied Náhkohe's reins to the log she'd been hiding behind and slid down the rocky ledge to Cade, all the way praying he hadn't given up on her.

His eyes were closed as she slid the last bit down the rocky outcrop to him. She grabbed him by the front of his shirt and shook him. "Wake up. Wake up!"

With a flutter, his eyes opened and, after a moment, focused on her. The knife in his hand jerked up and he nearly stabbed her, but stopped himself an instant before it was too late. "*Séaa*! Essie?"

She stared down at the knife with a shaky breath, then back at him. "It's all right now. It's going to be all right."

"What?" He blinked up at her in the moonlight that spilled across the open ledge. "What are you doing here? I thought I told you to—"

"We're getting out of here. Can you stand?"

"I told you. I can't—"

"Náhkohe came back."

"What?"

"He came back. He's right up there. We're getting out of here. Both of us. C'mon. Let me help you. We don't have much time."

CHAPTER 10

———◆———

The rain got worse as they crossed the plateau, turning the dirt to mud. They rode back into the forest, wandering up into the rocky outcrops. Behind them, the rain dissolved their trail, hiding it as no amount of cunning could. They rode for hours through the dark, skirting the plateau to the east. Except for the body heat they shared where her back met his chest, they were freezing cold. Behind her, Cade shivered, but she couldn't be sure if it was the fever or the miserable cold that made him shake. It became clear that they would have to stop soon and get warm.

They looked for caves or any kind of shelter, but what they came upon, in the wee hours of the morning, defied all expectation. There, in the distance, sheltered in a canyon, surrounded by thick pines and nearly invisible, sat a handful of tepees with smoke rising in the rain. Cade pulled Náhkohe to a stop as an owl's cry cut through the sound of the rain. From the corner of her eye, she caught sight of an armed brave, perched on the high knoll, watching them. Down in the camp, the flap of a tepee opened and a gray-haired Indian emerged holding a gun. He pointed it directly at them. Cade raised his hand and shouted something to him in Cheyenne. The old man lowered his gun and shouted something back, motioning him in.

"Who are they?" she asked.

"Old friends." He nudged Náhkohe forward. "Part of Little Coyote's band. But since Little Coyote went into exile for killing one of his own, they've been at loose ends. This is a hunting party. Stay beside me. Say nothing."

Others emerged in the rain to help as he lowered her off the horse, then slid off himself, nearly falling on his bad leg. Two men moved to help Cade. A woman, not much older than Essie, took Náhkohe's reins and led him toward a makeshift paddock. Cade called after the woman, something about the horse, and she nodded, but not before sending a suspicious, downright hostile look in Essie's direction.

As the men helped Cade into the tepee the old man had emerged from, Cade turned to motion her to follow. "Come, Essie."

She was cold through and through and could not stop shivering, but this scenario was not one she'd been prepared for. The old man's woman held the flap and motioned her in, as well. She looked younger than the old man by a decade, but gray tinged her hair nonetheless. In her day, she'd been beautiful, Essie mused, but the years had taken their toll on her. If she felt the same hatred toward Essie the younger woman had, the older one thankfully checked it. Essie supposed Cade had vouched for her, but then again, this place was obviously a renegade camp. They could not be happy that a white woman had stumbled upon them.

Swallowing hard, she ducked under the tepee flap and into surprising warmth. Cade was already being lowered atop a buffalo-hide-covered pallet. The woman turned to pour something warm into two bowls as she grumbled to herself. She handed one to Cade and one to Essie.

"*Nomēne*," the woman told her.

"Drink," Cade translated as he peeled off the soaked deerskin shirt he wore with an effort. "It will warm you. And when you are done, take off those wet things."

Instantly, she backed up. "No!"

The woman looked at her askance and began grumbling in Cheyenne again, this time to Cade.

"I couldn't." Essie crossed her arms over herself. "Not here. Not in front of them." *Or you.* Water dripped from her hair onto her nose. She wiped it with one hand.

"Don't argue, Essie. You'll catch your death."

"If I don't die first of humiliation," she muttered under her breath, her hands still shaking so hard the broth spilled out of her bowl. She took a sip, then another of the rich soup and felt it instantly, deliciously warm her insides. She'd almost forgotten how hungry she was. If that was possible.

Purposefully, she kept her gaze from Cade, who was being helped off with his leggings by the old man who'd welcomed them before he covered Cade with a worn woolen blanket.

As she listened to them converse in Cheyenne, a beautiful language, full of sibilant sounds and gulped vowels, she glanced around the tepee. Around a center fire sat their few worldly belongings. They were poor-looking, but organized neatly. Buffalo fur beds were spread at the edges of the hide walls. A drying rack occupied a small space, hung with thin strips of some kind of meat. Ancient saddles and bridles sat propped beside the second pallet, along with several lidded, woven baskets and pots. Everything was in its place here.

Everything but her.

Seeing Cade slip so easily into this world reminded her that he was, indeed, one of them. Despite those things they shared in common, he seemed more at home here than he ever would in the white world. Hearing him speak Cheyenne made her feel all the worse for denying that language to the children at the school. It must have been like losing a limb to be forbidden to speak the language one was born to.

At least these people had no idea who she was or where she'd come from.

Even as she had that thought, Cade spoke her name in their conversation and they turned to look her way.

The old woman muttered near the fire, putting in her two

cents, while aiming a few of her comments clearly at Essie.

Cade must have seen her discomfort, because he said, "I asked them if they'd seen Little Wolf. They haven't. I told them you were his teacher and you were helping me find him."

"You told them who I am?" She shot a look at the woman near the fire. "Oh, Cade—"

"These two, Red Moon and Walks Along Woman, are cousins of my mother. They are family. You are welcome here as my woman."

Essie felt herself blush. As his woman? Her breath caught in her throat and her already thudding heart beat faster. Of course, he'd simply called her that to protect her. Hadn't he? Of course.

Their eyes met over the fire. His suddenly dark gaze lingered on her for a heated moment before sliding away.

That look made her remember his kiss again, as she'd been doing all night. The memory sent a wave of confusion through her. God help her, she wanted another kiss and perhaps another after that. She wanted to taste him again and feel him hold her, now that death was not at their doorstep. And, unaccountably, it didn't matter that those feelings made no sense. He had dragged her into another world up here in these mountains, a world that had little to do with the one she'd inhabited only a few days ago. She felt as if the moorings of her old life had been torn away and somehow, she'd been liberated.

But to think of such things here, now, when these people were sharing what little food they had, struck her as foolish. Even self-indulgent. It was nothing more than a fantasy to think anything good could come of this mess. His people— so beaten down yet so proud—hated her people and certainly hers felt the same. They belonged to opposite camps, firmly entrenched in their fear of one another.

And yet, these two had welcomed her into their home. She wondered, honestly, if her people—if she *had* people—would do the same for Cade.

Truth be told, the point was moot. He had done nothing

but regret taking her since the moment they'd ridden away from that school. Tomorrow, or maybe the next day, he would return her to her world and leave her there. She would be on her own again in a place where no one seemed to want anything from her and where she didn't really belong.

She finished the warm soup and set the bowl down beside the woman. The soup was the first thing she'd eaten in a day and her belly still felt empty. "*Hahóo*," she said softly, thanking the woman with one of the few words she knew in Cheyenne.

The old woman flicked a surprised look up at her, then at Cade, before shrugging with a nod. She lifted a worn blanket from beside the bed opposite the doorway and shook it out, then held it up like a curtain for Essie to undress behind.

"*Hahóo*," she repeated and proceeded to pull off her clothes. The soaked fabric sucked at her skin and made wet noises as she dropped them on the floor. When she'd finished, Walks Along Woman wrapped the blanket around her shoulders and Essie pulled it tight. She nodded her thanks to the woman who made some comment to Cade, who was lying under a similar blanket now.

"What did she say?" Essie whispered.

"She says you are skinny, like a buffalo calf. With no meat on your bones."

Self-conscious, she tightened the blanket around her.

"She wonders if *you've* been in the agency camps, too."

Starving. That's what she meant. Along with the rest of the Cheyenne.

Essie glanced at the woman, embarrassed now, and moved closer to Cade. "Did you tell them about the men following us?"

"Red Moon has already posted more guards."

She shook her head with regret. "We've brought trouble right to them."

"The rain has covered our tracks. At least I hope so. But we've evened up the odds. At least for a few hours." What little strength Cade had left was fading.

She hoped he was right. "What about your leg?"

He gave an involuntary shiver. "Walks Along is making a poultice. But mostly I need rest. We both do." He lifted up the buffalo robe beside him and gestured for her to climb in.

Naked!

Still shivering with cold, she thought nothing looked more inviting than that thick, warm buffalo robe, but she couldn't…she absolutely couldn't—

"And they're giving up their bed for us."

"Oh, but, no. I couldn't take their bed! That would be—"

"Rude to turn down such a gift." Cade met her eyes then with a warning.

Red Moon and Walks Along seemed half amused, half alarmed by their argument and spoke softly to each other in urgent whispers that she couldn't understand. Walks Along wrung out a warm cloth, soaked in some herbs she'd thrown into a pot of water over the fire. She headed toward Cade with the poultice. As she uncovered his bare leg to the thigh, Essie could see the redness around the wound beyond the burn she'd given him. It could be worse, she thought, but it looked painful. Walks Along carefully wrapped the cloth around his thigh. Cade squeezed his eyes shut and inhaled sharply.

"Be careful," Essie warned, but of course, Walks Along politely ignored her.

Getting to her feet, Walks Along mumbled something to Cade and shook her head as she joined her husband on the other pallet and settled into bed. Cautiously, Cade slid under the buffalo robe now, leaving the thin, wool blanket aside.

Still clutching the blanket, Essie felt for the locket at her neck. The metal felt as cold as she did. Though she was grateful they'd found shelter, she felt as out of place here as a thistle in a field of moss.

"Will you get under the covers?" Cade said. "There are still a few hours until dawn."

What difference did it make now if she slept beside him naked? She'd seen all of him before and was already a fallen woman, according to Laddner. How much further could she fall? And if they blamed her for surviving, then let them cast aspersions. No one seemed to give a fig about her survival except Cade Blackthorn.

"Fine." Still wrapped in the blanket, she shimmied under the buffalo robe beside him and pulled it up to her chin. "But I'm keeping my blanket."

"Suit yourself. There are better ways to get warm."

"Don't even try…" she warned under her breath and rolled so her back was to him.

Beside her, he sighed. Exhaustion and frustration colored that sound, and for a few minutes they lay still beside one another, listening to the crickets—or maybe they were frogs—chirping in the rain. Soon, Red Moon's gentle snores joined the mix. Still, Essie couldn't stop shivering. She'd probably never been as exhausted as she was right now, on the verge of a complete breakdown as the night's events played back in her mind. But she couldn't relax. How close they'd come to dying!

And, more ironically, to *living* for the first time. She felt tears sting the backs of her eyes and she snuffled into the blanket wrapped around her hands.

Cade rolled toward her then and pulled her against him, into the crook of his big, warm body, wrapping his arm around her and tucking his hand against hers. She froze for a moment there in his arms, but it was no use fighting. And soon, she found herself leaning into his warmth.

"S-so cold," she whispered.

"Shhh," he said against her ear, his warm breath in her hair. "You will be all right, *Mo'onahe*."

The frogs chirped and whirred into the still night. Her shivering slowed and she felt her tension soften like warm tallow against him.

"What does that mean? *Mo'onahe*?" She whispered it awkwardly; wrongly, she supposed. "You called me that before."

"It means"—he rubbed her fingers with his own—"beauty. Now close your eyes. Rest."

But that word, *Mo'onahe*, sang in her ears for a long time after, snuggled there against him in the dark. She found the locket at her throat and tucked it between her fingers. And just before she dropped into a dreamless sleep, she thought, *I am a fool.*

They slept that night and part of the next day. And after Essie awoke, she let Cade sleep more. Twice, Walks Along Woman dressed the wound on his leg as he slept, wrapping it with herbs in a poultice, but even that didn't wake him. The last few days had taken a toll on him that had left him exhausted and weak.

As for Essie, with her clothes finally dry, she dressed that morning under a blanket. She watched him sleep, accepted food and companionable silence from Walks Along. She heard Red Moon and several of the other men ride out of camp late that morning. They were gone for hours and returned with nothing but small game, which his wife cleaned near the fire. Out of sympathy for Essie's uselessness, she gave her the job of hanging the sliced-up meat on the drying rack near the fire. She did so gratefully and without complaint.

They ate a rabbit stew for dinner with flavors Essie had never tasted before. When night fell again, she curled up beside him under the buffalo robe, leaning against his warmth. He stirred long enough to slip his arm around her and pull her close to him. She fell asleep that way again, tucked into the curve of him.

Sometime later, instinct jerked Cade awake. It took him more than a moment to drag himself out of the nightmare he'd been having and realize where he was.

His arm tightened around the woman whose back rested against his chest. She was still sleeping, tucked against him like she'd been designed to fit there. Her chest rose and fell beneath his arm in a steady, even way that calmed the sudden plunge of his heartbeat.

His dream came back to him in fragments, but the bristling tug of a rope around his neck lingered there in the dark. He believed in dreams, as most Cheyenne did. But if it was a warning of things to come, then so be it. At least for the moment they were safe.

How long had he been sleeping? It felt like days. He had a memory of rain lashing the tepee, but now the night was silent except for the crickets chirping outside and the soft crackle of the fire beside them.

His skin was cool and dry. Bless Walks Along Woman and her medicine. He felt almost human again. Weak and sore, but better.

Looking up toward the smoke hole in the tepee, he caught glimpses of stars.

A hard rain would have washed away their trail if they were lucky.

Lucky. A strange word to use, considering not much had gone their way since this whole thing had begun. Yet here they were, both still alive. An ending even he could not have predicted a few days ago.

How had they come to this? One minute she'd been fighting him, and the next, she was sleeping willingly in his arms. She was exhausted, as he was. But he was not fool enough to think it was motivated by anything more than necessity.

He turned back to her, pressing his nose against her hair. It was something he'd unwittingly done many times over the last few days. Though the lingering scent of soap had worn off sometime during their plunges through trees, rivers and death-defying escapes, that essence of her that had drawn him that first morning was undiminished. He felt himself tighten with want.

Which was all wrong. Even he recognized this. Take away the circumstances they found themselves in and she was like every other white woman he'd ever known. If they'd met on the street, she would have snubbed him. Walked past him. Even now, he supposed.

But she would have lingered in his mind on any day. For more than a day, though he had no right to imagine even friendship with her after what he'd put her through.

He hadn't planned to take her. Reckless decisions were his trademark, according to his father. But this one was, perhaps, the most reckless of his life, second only to the decision he'd made to liberate his nephew in the first place.

He slid his hand up and rested it on her ribs. She felt small beneath his palm. There was no changing who and what he was. And he would never be enough for a woman like her. But it didn't change the fact that he wanted her. Wanted her like he'd never wanted another woman.

Probably since the first moment he saw her. Despite everything he knew and didn't know about her, she was a light that drew him. A light that reached into his darkness. And despite the hot bolt of desire that poured through him whenever she was close, and even now, pressed against him, the imaginings of something more itched the back of his mind. More of what, even he couldn't articulate yet.

Maybe that bullet had knocked something loose inside him. He had no business with this woman. But the past few days had nothing to do with good sense. He should hate her and she should hate him. But he admired her when she fought him and argued and stood her ground. When she'd stayed with him, back in the woods, when she could have abandoned him.

Firelight flickered nearby, glimmering in her red hair. He breathed in her scent again. Smoke and rain and…Essie.

If he had any sense, he would take her back and make sure he never came within a mile of her again. God knew what would happen if he did.

CHAPTER 11

In the morning, Cade was up and gone when she woke. The others were nowhere to be seen either. Suddenly frightened that he'd left her, she dressed quickly and stepped outside the tepee. A soupy fog still lingered along the backs of the horses standing tied beneath the trees. A hunting party was readying to leave. Beside them, she was relieved to find Cade, sitting on a log near the creek with his leg outstretched, in conversation with several men of the band.

She felt barely decent, in a vagabond sort of way, in his long shirt and her trail-muddied petticoats—bare feet and all. So she wrapped herself in the blanket again.

Fragrant wood smoke rose from every tepee and several large dogs wandered camp, looking for scraps. On a much smaller scale, this camp might have been any camp twenty years ago, before her kind had routed the Cheyenne from their territory. The place seemed orderly and peaceful, even, despite the armed guards perched on lookouts on rocks high above them. But the impoverished band had left the reservation and come into the mountains to hunt. Their people were still half-starving down below with the game wrung out of the Yellowstone Valley like water from a wet rag. The buffalo, antelope and deer were nearly all gone. The wolves decimated whatever was left and the Cheyenne were forced to settle with the remainder. A bitter pill to swallow after so many bitter pills.

Some, she'd heard, had begun farming, homesteading reservation land to feed themselves. She supposed this small hunting party was not the only one up in these mountains, but if they were caught off the reservation, there would be consequences she hardly wanted to imagine.

In the light of day, she counted four tepees, eight men and a handful of women. A working camp; there were no children here. Essie headed toward Cade. The memory of him holding her last night wound around her like a warm breath of air. She'd woken once or twice in the night, her backside nestled against the curve of his belly, his arms around her. She'd felt safe. Impossibly safe, in the arms of the man who'd stolen her. A man as at home in an Indian camp as the buffalo robe they slept on. She couldn't quite wrap her mind around the change that had happened between them, but seeing him now across camp, talking to the others—looking handsome and dangerous and completely...completely   himself—stirred   something thrilling inside her. Something she was quite sure she'd never felt before.

She made it only halfway across the camp before she felt a hand on her arm. It was Walks Along Woman, who spoke to her in Cheyenne, then held out a pair of worn, soft-looking moccasins.

Essie stared down at them in surprise. "For me?"

The older woman shoved them into her hands.

"I don't know what to...Thank you. *Hahóo*," Essie said, accepting them from her. "Very much."

The woman nodded curtly and, in spite of herself, allowed her mouth to twitch with a smile. As she walked away, Essie admired the soft moccasins. They were not new. They were worn, well used, cut from deerskin, and plainly decorated with beading of blue and green across the top. Hours of work had gone into them once upon a time and it wasn't as if this band had anything to spare. That included shoes. But Walks Along had simply given them to her because she had none.

Hugging them to her chest, she glanced around the camp to find the younger girl from two nights ago, who'd taken Cade's horse, staring at her now. After getting caught looking, the girl glanced Cade's way, then stalked off in the other direction. Essie sighed. She wanted to tell the girl there was nothing to be jealous of between her and Cade, but it would do no good. She was here as Cade's woman, a pretense she needed to keep up.

There was a creek running through the canyon, not far from the camp, and Essie walked there to wash her feet before putting on the shoes. Her feet were a mess, with cuts and bruises all over them. She looked like she'd run a footrace through a briar patch.

"Morning," Cade said, appearing in the clearing nearby, startling her. He looked better. Still favoring his leg as he walked, but better.

"I woke and wasn't sure where you'd gone," she said. "How are you feeling?"

"Human again. I lost a day, I hear. I'm sorry."

"Don't be. You needed to rest. I'm glad you're still with us."

He tipped his head with a smile. "Did Walks Along Woman give you those?"

She nodded. "I don't know why she would do that for me."

"Because you needed them. That's how it works here."

"Their generosity shames me."

He sat down beside her, easing his leg gingerly in front of him. "You would do the same for them."

"Would I?" She lowered her feet into the chilly water and rubbed the tender bruises with her fingers. A cloud of dirt muddied the crystalline water. "I'm not sure I would have before"—she lifted her gaze to meet his—"before we met. I would have been afraid. Like I was afraid of you."

"I gave you reason." Beside them, the creek ruffled by over buried stones and fallen branches, glimmering in the early morning light. "What about now?"

"Now?" She gave a quiet laugh. "I think I will never be that girl again. The one you stole in the middle of the night."

He studied her hands for a long moment before turning to stare into the creek. "I must take you back."

An inexplicable sort of disappointment knifed through her. Disappointment which made no logical sense. Of course she should be relieved he was taking her back. Of course she was. She blinked up at him. "I know. I suppose it will relieve you to be rid of me at last."

He didn't reply, but merely stared out over the water, as if his thoughts were already elsewhere.

"At least you could lie," she muttered before turning her attention to her feet in the cold, clear water.

"I could," he said, "but I won't. I won't be relieved. But it's what must be."

She exhaled a sharp breath. "Do you find it odd that we know each other so little after all we've been through?"

He frowned, but didn't answer.

"Tell me something about yourself," she said softly.

"What?"

"Something you've told no one else."

"Why?"

"It isn't too much to ask, is it? Considering."

"And if I do?"

She shrugged. "Then I will, in turn, tell you something. If you want."

"I am not that interesting."

She laughed.

"That's funny?" he asked in all seriousness.

She straightened her expression. "I was just imagining what my old friends back in Baltimore would say if they heard you say that. You would, by far, qualify as the most interesting man any of them would ever meet. Yet they would be shocked to their very cores if they could see me in your company."

A frown pulled at his brow and a muscle worked in his jaw. "I am sure they would."

"No, I don't mean that," she said, touching his arm. "I only mean that my life in Baltimore was exceedingly safe. Or so I thought. Even the man I married, I thought was safe. It turned out to be quite the opposite. So, being out here in the wilds of Montana Territory wearing nothing but my…well, *unmentionables* and your shirt, with you…well, no one could have conceived it for me. Which is why, sometimes, our expectation for our own life is the very thing that keeps us from who we might become, because we cannot see the open doors for the walls we erect around ourselves. Much less walk through them."

"There are no open doors here, Essie. Not with me. And you would do well to keep those walls intact."

She wouldn't argue this with him. Not now. "Whatever the outcome of this," she said softly, turning away from him, "I've decided I won't regret it. Not a minute of it."

"Not the kidnapping? Or the blisters on your feet? Not the pain in your backside or the days spent running with the likes of me?" When she shook her head, a disbelieving smile tipped one corner of his mouth. "You are a puzzle, Essie Sparks."

"No more than you. So will you? Tell me one thing?"

He lifted a small, flat stone from the riverbank and skipped it across the water. "What do you want to know?"

She rubbed her foot thoughtfully, her fingers numb in the cold water. "Anything." But her eyes drifted to the scar on his cheek before she checked the impulse to ask about it.

He turned his face self-consciously. "This? This is no secret. It is common knowledge hereabouts, in fact. It happened a long time ago."

She waited for him to go on.

His jaw worked as she watched him wrestle with whether to tell her the truth. "All right. I was seventeen. My mother was dead by then. My father had shipped me off to a white boarding school back East."

"A boarding school?" Nothing like the boarding school she'd just left. "You?"

He laughed. "Imagine it."

With a shake of her head, she disagreed. "I can imagine that quite clearly, as a matter of fact."

Did he wince at that? Possibly. But that, too, was erased from his expression quickly.

"Anyway, there I was, a half-breed amongst Boston's best."

"Don't call yourself that."

His eyes were hooded as he turned to her. "Why? Everyone else does."

"I don't. And you shouldn't. Now, go on."

"*Seáa*. Are you always this bossy?"

She smiled. "Sorry. Please, do go on."

He took a deep breath, then draped his wrists across his bent knees. "After I'd been there a few months, my...heritage came out at the school. Behind my back, they called me a breed. To my face, they were much too polite for that. Still, I was a curiosity. I intrigued them. Especially the girls at the sister school down the road. They were spoiled, rich girls who liked their boys wild and a little dangerous. Being a *wild Indian*, I fit right in."

"You must have been quite the thing, then. Handsome as you are." Essie glanced up at him through her lashes with a smile.

His cheeks actually took on color at that. "Believe me when I tell you, I was little more than a"—he searched for the word—"*mascot* to any of them. A sideshow animal to be seen with. And there were more than a few who wanted to be 'seen' with me. I was young. Foolish. At first, I didn't care if I fit in. But there was this girl..."

He paused, staring down into the water as if he might find the memory of her face there.

"Her name was Delilah. And like the fool boy I was, I actually thought I was in love with her. Even knowing better. I would have done anything for her. She was wilder than most. Richer than most. She could ride a horse as well as any Cheyenne brave and we would ride together at breakneck speed across the grounds. There was nothing she feared. Nothing. Except her father.

"And all that wildness pulled me to her. She made me feel like I was...somebody. Like I mattered. And for a while, I allowed myself to believe I did.

"But her father got wind of rumors. About the half-breed boy she was secretly seeing. And he burst into her room one night, catching us...together. Before I could even react, Delilah had grabbed a knife from somewhere she'd kept hidden from me and slashed me across the cheek, crying *rape*. I can still hear her screaming. Rushing to her father's arms..."

"Oh, Cade—no."

He shrugged. "Naturally, I was arrested, expelled. My father fixed things somehow and wired me train fare home without a single word to me. And when I got home, he refused to hear my side of it. He barely spoke to me except to warn me not to leave the ranch or show my ruined face in town. I had shamed him. So I did the only thing that made any sense to me. I left. And I never went back."

All that explained so much, and yet left a hundred unanswered questions. Questions to which she wanted answers. But what she said instead was, "I'm sorry, Cade. About all of it."

"It is in the past now. I hardly think of it anymore."

"Or her?" she asked.

"Her, least of all." He lifted his gaze to her again, allowing it to travel along the lines of her shoulders, her neck, her face.

"What?" Self-consciously, she smoothed down the wild mess of her hair.

"I was thinking of...you just reminded me of a deer I once saw."

Her fingers paused in her hair. "A deer? I remind you of a deer?"

He laughed. "Oh, she was a beautiful doe. All sleek and pretty, standing under the New Planting Moon, ready for summer. But it was her eyes I was remembering."

She began to separate her hair into three strands for braiding. "Her eyes? They were blue?" She sent him an ironic half smile.

"Brown. A deep, dark brown."

"Ah." She frowned at him. "That clears things up."

"I was just a boy that day I was hunting her. She didn't know I was there. I had her in my sights and had the bow primed at her heart. But then she looked up at me. Straight at me. With those eyes."

"What about them?"

He shook his head. "I don't know. She lifted her head and stared right at me, sure that I wouldn't hurt her."

"And…did you?"

"No."

Her fingers faltered in her hair and she turned to face him. "And what about that deer reminds you of me?"

"*É-hetseváhe.* She was brave. Fearless."

"She was just a deer. Perhaps she didn't know what you intended. Or, if she did, perhaps she was hoping you would find the good in her. To save her."

Cade glanced up through dark lashes at her. "Like you, she didn't need saving. She took her freedom with that look. And then…she was gone."

"It's strange you think I'm either brave or fearless. I'm neither of those things. On the contrary. And there are many who would argue that I *do* need saving, if from nothing else, from myself."

"Says who?"

She stared down at her hands. "Well, in his infinite wisdom, the good Reverend Dooley. And, of course, there was Nathan."

"Your husband?"

She bit her lip. "Yes. My late husband."

"The one who deserted you."

His words hit her like a gust of wind. Why she'd never thought of it exactly that way, she couldn't say. But yes. He *had* deserted her when she'd needed him the most. But by then he'd had nothing to give her.

"Your turn."

She'd almost forgotten they were trading memories. "All

right." It took her a moment to work up the courage to speak of it. She had told no one about Aaron since she'd come West. She supposed it was time. "We...we had a child, Nathan and I."

Surprise etched a line between his eyes.

"Our son, Aaron, was the sweetest boy. Perfect, if small, with eyes like mine and his father's blond hair. He was very young when he died. He'd hardly lived, really. One hot summer afternoon, he simply didn't wake up from his nap. There was no fever, or sickness. No bedclothes over his little face. No obvious reason for him to be dead. He just— one minute, it seemed, he was learning to smile at me and the next, he was just...gone."

"I am sorry."

She stared at the water, watching it tumble over the rocks. A breeze ruffled the water and swirled a leaf inside a little eddy there. "Nathan blamed me, of course. Because who else was there to blame? God? Far be it from Nathan to blame Him. So I was at fault, for not watching closely enough, for doing the laundry that afternoon instead of sitting over my son's cradle to be sure"—tears suddenly clogged her words—"to be sure he didn't stop breathing. And Nathan was probably right. It *was* my fault. What mother doesn't notice her child is dying?"

Cade swallowed thickly beside her.

"And Nathan couldn't forgive me. Maybe he couldn't forgive himself, either, for trusting me with our son. Maybe that was why he walked into the sea. Those who didn't outright blame me tried, in some backhanded way, to comfort me. They told me it was simply Aaron's time. At two months. God's will. That my little boy was in some better place than right here in my arms. That I would become stronger for this loss or that losing him was some trial sent by God to see if I had faith enough. If I was brave enough. And I wasn't. I'm not. And I don't."

She stared at the moccasins in her hands and rubbed her thumb over the beadwork on them.

"So I ran away. Came here. To that school. And now, I'm

here in a camp full of strangers, with you." She lowered her eyes.

He shook his head. "Perhaps you didn't run away. Perhaps you ran toward something."

"It would be nice to think so."

"He did not see you, your husband. Or he could not have blamed you."

She blinked up at him. "Ah, but how could you know? You hardly know me."

One side of his mouth lifted in a gentle smile. "I see you, Essie Sparks."

And in his own quiet way, he absolved her. Gratitude welled up in her and the emotion filled her eyes. For the first time, she wondered what it would be like to be with a man who wanted to see her. Really know her.

"I have to take you back," he said before she could fantasize more about the impossible. "We must go soon, before those men follow us here."

"Yes," she answered.

He pulled a small beaded pouch from the back waistband of his leggings. Daniel's medicine bag.

Her eyes widened. "Where did you find that?"

"They did." He gestured to two braves who were walking toward the horses. "Two days ago, before the rain. They were hunting just southeast of here. When they heard I was looking for White Owl's son, they feared it might be his."

"You know it's his. You gave it to him."

Cade nodded. "There are only two ways he would part with it. If someone took it from him, or if he left it behind him intentionally for someone to find."

"By someone…you mean, *us*? But he doesn't even know we're looking for him."

"He dropped the bag at a fork in a hunting trail this band has used for years. There were hoofprints of two other horses beside his pony's. I do not think it was the men tracking us. They were too far west then. Whoever was with him, they were heading down the mountain, toward Magic City."

Oh, no. She pulled her feet out of the water and brushed them dry. "If we know that much, we have to go after him. God knows who's got him or why. But at least we have an idea now of where to look."

"Where *I* will look," he corrected. "You can't come."

What? "Of course I'm coming. I will not just...He was my—"

His eyes darkened to a steely gray. "Being with me isn't safe for you. They can't see us together."

"Not safe? Do you think being back with them will be safer for me? They want to put me down like some...some rabid dog!"

He got unsteadily to his feet, favoring his injury. "I will get you on the train. I will find the money somehow. I owe you that much."

She blinked up at him. His words pricked her heart. What an idiot she was, imagining...Of course he'd simply been keeping her warm last night, keeping her safe out of some sense of duty the last few days. He wanted her gone, too. Fine. She knew perfectly well how to be alone, how to stand on her own two feet without any help from a man. Especially a man like him.

She turned away and stared downstream where one of the men from the camp stood, fishing in the shallow pools. "You can do what you want, but once we get back, you can't make me go anywhere."

"Essie—"

She got up and started to walk away.

"Essie!"

She turned to him. "What? I told you I am through letting men choose for me. If I decide to look for Little Wolf when we get to town, then that risk is mine. Not yours. If you don't want to go with me, then that's your choice."

He grabbed her arm and tugged her closer, holding her by the shoulders. He stared off over her head at something. "If I had chosen well, I would never have brought you into this. You would not be barefoot up here in a poor Cheyenne hunting camp, wondering if you will die tomorrow." He lowered his gaze to her, his gray eyes searching hers. "If I had chosen well, I would have met you on another road. One that did not lead to disaster. But we are here, on this broken road now. And we can only make the best of it."

"Oh. Is that what we're doing?" She tried to pull her arms free but he held her firmly.

"If things had been different—"

"What? You wouldn't treat me like a child?"

He dropped his hands, irritation burning in his eyes. "Maybe if you didn't act like one."

Her mouth fell open in indignation. "Oh, really? A child?" She glanced around to see if anyone had heard her and she lowered her voice. "Says the man whose life I saved twice!"

They were beginning to draw stares and, with a flash of annoyance, he dragged her fifteen feet away, putting a thick pine tree between them and the others.

"Let go of me!" She twisted in his arms.

"Yes, you saved me. Twice. And I saved you. That is not what I'm talking about and you know it."

"Then what exactly are you talking about?"

"You know what I mean." He braced one hand above her on the tree, frustration tightening his expression. "We should not even be having this conversation."

"You mean the one where we discuss all the things we can't possibly have in common? With you cast as the villain and me as the poor damsel in distress? Where you explain that whatever we've come to mean to each other is strictly based on circumstance? And for that reason and a thousand others, like your bloodline, like the scar on your face, that we're as alike as fire and kerosene?"

"Yes," he said. "That one."

"Well." She exhaled sharply, looking away so he wouldn't see what was in her eyes. "Don't flatter yourself. Because the only thing we actually have in common is the fact that we both care about that boy and want to keep him safe. Believe me, the sooner you and I can part ways, the better."

He was silent so long that she actually looked back at him. Some fierceness had crept into his expression as his gaze slid down her features, filled with emotions he couldn't seem to formulate into words.

"So, if we're finished here—" she began, pulling away from him, but he caught her by the shoulders and pressed her back up against the pine tree.

"We're not."

Her eyes widened because, land sakes, he was scaring her a little now. She glanced to either side of her to see if help was on its way. Of course, none was. So she pinned him with a look that dared him to challenge her.

Instead, he shook his head, and dropped his mouth on hers and showed her exactly what kind of challenge he could mount.

CHAPTER 12

———◆———

His mouth crushed against hers without gentleness, as if trying to prove something about his own brutality. But what she felt, instead, was his wildness. His loneliness. Some aching need for connection. His tongue pillaged her mouth without invitation, but she had no desire to deny him. She wanted to feel his mouth against hers, inhale his breath and taste his kiss again. He could deny all he wanted that something good had sparked between them, but this kiss was all the proof she required that the opposite was true.

Dragging her hard against him until they fitted one another like blades of grass, he sank his fingers into the hair at the nape of her neck. A sound of need echoed against her mouth that only stirred the embers heating inside her.

The coil at the center of her tightened and every nerve ending came alive. His kisses were nothing like Nathan's had been—chaste, Presbyterian efforts of duty. And while this kiss had more passion than Nathan could ever have mustered, it was, she could tell, meant to end things between them. But if ending things was his intention, his plan backfired miserably. Dampness blossomed, unbidden, at the juncture of her legs and her nipples ached against the fabric of her shift. She felt herself melting against him as he punished her mouth with his kiss and the evidence of his own hunger pushed up hard against her belly.

Then, as if he'd only just realized how far out of bounds that kiss had gone, he tugged her head backward, breaking the kiss, his control wrecked and his expression more than a little lost. He took a step away from her, rubbing his palms on his thighs. "That..." he said, his breath coming hard, "is why we cannot be together. That can never happen again."

Outrage darkened her expression. "You kissed *me*!"

"And you kissed me back."

Clutching the tree behind her, she stiffened. Feeling dizzy and bruised by his kiss, his words cut her deeply. She was in no mood for rejection, especially when it came from the man who'd *kidnapped* her. Against her will, her eyes filled with tears. "What did you expect, then? A paper cut-out in your arms? A woman who couldn't, or wouldn't, kiss you back? Did you think to scare me off if I should dare try to? How very male of you!"

He loosed an oath and spun away from her. "You have no idea what you're playing with, Essie."

"If anyone is playing games here, it's you."

He turned back to her. "Do you think that kiss meant nothing to me? That you mean nothing to me?"

"I don't know. Do I?"

A sound of frustration vibrated in his throat and he took her by the shoulders and dragged her close to him. "You do not seem to grasp your situation."

"My situation?" She let out a bark of laughter. "You mean, mine alone? Yes, I'm quite sure the past few days of running for our lives across the dangerous mountains of Montana, nearly drowning, almost falling off a thousand-foot plateau and now, taking refuge in an encampment of enemy Cheyenne who should, by rights, despise me—if all that wasn't enough to convince me that at any moment the sky could fall, the earth could drop out from under me and/or I could die"—she shrugged off his hands—"perhaps the whole thing is, indeed, beyond my grasp. After all, if losing a child and a husband in the same year didn't send me into a darkened room for the rest of my days, or the very idea of walking away from everything I'd known to risk a whole new life in the wilds of Montana Territory couldn't kill me, or wake me up to the dangers of moving forward in my life, God knows what will."

"You may think you know," he said, looming over her, "what the future holds for a white woman returned from captivity in this country, but I assure you, you don't. If you think you were alone before, you've never known aloneness. The few who manage to survive are locked away for the rest of their lives, or at the very least, shunned. No respectable white man will have you. You're spoiled. Ruined. Probably crazy. Certainly violated."

She glared at him. "Oh, how disappointed they'd be to know no such thing had happened." He pressed her back against the tree and she could feel the sharp edges of the bark through his shirt.

"But I've wanted it to. It was all I could do last night not to rip that blanket away from you and pull you under me. Touch you"—his fingers slid down the side of her face, then drifted down her chest to the tip of her right nipple, underneath the shirt he'd given her—"everywhere. Taste your skin on my tongue. Slide myself inside you and feel your slick warmth around me until you moaned with pleasure."

She lifted her chin, her breath coming quick and shallow. "And why didn't you?"

He blinked back the rest of what he'd been about to say and stared at her.

"I thought so." She turned and walked away from him, but he caught her with his hand.

"What's that supposed to mean?"

"Never mind."

"Tell me." His voice sounded breathless now, the way she felt.

"You talk about fear, as if I'm the only one who has something to lose here. But I think it's you who's afraid, Cade."

"That's a dangerous thing to say to the man who's kidnapped you."

"Perhaps. If I were afraid of him. If he hadn't protected me since that first moment, with his own life. But I'm not afraid of you, Cade. And I'm no girl. I'm a woman fully grown. So don't pretend that thinking of me as your hostage to push me away is for my sake. At least admit it's for yours."

"You don't know what you're talking about."

"Then I guess there's nothing else to say, is there?" This time, she tugged her arm from his grip and headed back across camp, leaving him behind her.

Cade didn't follow her. Instead, he limped downstream, following the water as it made its way downhill. Each step a burning reminder that he deserved to be alone.

Séaa!

What a fool he'd been to kiss her again. In all the years since Delilah had cut him, never once had he allowed himself to touch a proper white girl, much less the days he'd spent with his arms wrapped around this one. Except that when he was near her, all he wanted to do was what he had just done. And more. Maybe he had used that kiss to push her away. Maybe he thought he'd scare her, or anger her. Which he had. But he'd never intended the kiss to backfire on him the way it had, nor send want crushing through him like a herd of buffalo. Had he not already damaged her enough? Had he not taken away every shred of dignity she owned?

"Don't pretend that thinking of me as your hostage to push me away is for my sake. At least admit it's for yours."

At least about that, she'd been right. He *was* afraid of what might happen with a woman like her. Risking all the things she made him crave was not on the table for him. She could go on about his reluctance to move forward in his life, but she didn't know him. Didn't know what he'd been through or what had made him who he was. If she did…

Walks Along Woman appeared a few feet ahead, scrubbing some laundry by the creek. She looked up when she heard him coming. He pivoted and began walking back the way he'd come.

She spoke to him in Cheyenne. "Have you learned the manners of the *vé'ho'e* since you left us, Black Thorn? Do you not stop to say hello to your oldest cousin?"

He turned back to her with a regretful shake of his head. "Forgive me, cousin. Good morning."

She nodded, wishing him the same before turning back to her work.

He stared downstream, feeling awkward, like the boy he'd been when last they'd been together. "I am in your debt once again. Thank you for taking us in."

"You would do no less for us." She studied him. "How is your leg today? Has the heat left it?"

He rubbed his thigh without thinking. "It's better. Much better."

"Rest is a healer."

He couldn't argue that. "Your poultice is what helped most."

Pleased, she said, "The old ways still work, in spite of the whites' attempts to rub them out of us." She let her gaze slide up his considerable size. "I still see my sister's son in your eyes, but you have changed, Black Thorn. Grown dark. A thunderhead cloud carries less trouble than you," she said, turning back to the rock she was washing upon. "Is it that white woman of yours?"

"Her name is Essie. And she is not—" He stopped short of what he'd been about to say as Walks Along Woman glanced up at him in expectation. "She is not like them."

Walks Along nodded with a small smile. "She is not a sheep like most of the white women I've seen. That much is plain."

His face heated, realizing she must have heard them fighting.

She smiled knowingly. "Red Moon and I have shared blankets for so long, he knows all my crooked paths and how to pick his way around them." She smiled up at him. "But that is because we are both old now and have put many disagreements behind us."

He lowered himself onto a rock beside her and stared out over the water. Across the way, the branches of a low-hanging shrub floated on the ruffled water. The music of the creek sang along the surface of the rocks hidden just underneath.

"She belongs to herself, not me," he admitted. "We are not meant for each other."

"Why not?"

"Because..." He faltered, unable to articulate the exact problem.

"Because she is not a Human Being?" Walks Along shrugged. "Your heart also pumps with white blood, cousin. And yet, our world is also yours."

"It is not the same. Her world cannot be mine. Not anymore."

She turned to him fully now. "You were born to straddle both worlds. Both the Human Beings' world and the white one. This will always be so. To deny that part of you is like asking a fish to deny his scales because they only run smooth in one direction. Without them, what would protect him from the sharp rocks in the river? Or the fox that wants to eat him?"

"It is my father, and not me, who denies that part of me."

She patted his hand, then squeezed out the shirt she was washing. "I think you are wrong. I knew your father. He was good to your mother and she loved him. It is true, she missed her life with us. But your father let her come with you every summer. And every autumn, even after her death—until we were moved to the Territories—your father would cut twenty cows from his herds to be delivered to us. Their meat kept us alive after the buffalo disappeared. And when we returned from the long walk from the hard place, nearly starved, those twenty cows appeared again one morning. A gift from him."

Shock filtered through him. "*What*? How did I not know

this? I always thought those cattle were from the agency."

She snorted. "The agency? We were lucky to get scraps, what the agents didn't steal for themselves or sell. They have done their best to starve us with their lies. Without your father, many of us would have died. His only request was that you should not learn of his generosity."

He scrubbed a hand through his hair. "But why?"

"He is as stubborn as you, cousin. You know why, I think."

Because he didn't want Cade's bad opinion of him swayed by a good deed. He wanted Cade to forgive him on his own. The memory of their falling out still pained him, when he allowed himself to think of it. His father's leap to judgment still burned him like a hot coal. Yet it somehow surprised him to imagine that his father must feel the same sort of pain as well.

"Perhaps it is time to put this bad blood behind you," she said. "This is why I have told you the truth. Because men can be as stubborn as buffalo following the grass. Sometimes they forget to look to see what is around them."

He shook his head. "I have to find Little Wolf and take him back to his mother. I promised her I would bring him to her before—"

"Cousin…" Walks Along touched his hand again. "My heart aches to tell you, but…you are too late. Her spirit walks with the ancestors. The wasting sickness took her soon after you left."

The news caught him off guard and his hands curled into fists at his sides. His aunt, gone? So fast?

"Even if you had taken the boy and gone straight back," Walks Along said, "you would have been too late."

He stared off at the ridge of the mountain where the morning sun was beginning to spill light like honey over the ridge top.

"Little Wolf is alone in the world now," she continued. "He will not find his way back here to us. Like the others, he is too changed."

"I will bring him back," he promised.

"He will not be happy here." She sighed. "He can no longer talk the talk of the Cheyenne. The way of the Human Beings is almost disappeared." She gestured at the poor camp behind them. "They have murdered us, stolen our homes, our buffalo, our hunting grounds and our children. They have ripped away all things from our children that make them Human Beings. When they come back to us, they are like lost buffalo calves standing alone on the prairie. They are buffalos, disguised as birds. But they are broken and do not know how to fly. But you…" she said, pointing at the glistening stepping stones jutting from the water. "You are like those rocks in the creek, going from here to there." She glanced back at her tepee, where Essie had gone. "And maybe she is what is standing on the other side."

"Do not! It only cuts deeper," Shyen Zu warned Little Wolf, who sat in the sweltering heat of a keeping room, tugging ineffectively at the filthy metal manacle on his ankle. "Many die of…of sickness here."

Releasing the metal with disgust, Little Wolf folded his arms across his knees, ignoring the bite of the metal against his skin where it had already cut him. He looked at the girl who'd been the only one here to befriend him and speak to him in a language he could understand. Her English was broken and simple, as his had been once, but she had saved him a dozen beatings already with her knowledge of Chen Lee's peculiar tastes. On the other hand, he'd taken a dozen beatings already for infractions of rules he still didn't understand. And frankly, hoped he never would.

There was a window in the keeping room that let fresh air in. Outside that window, he could hear the sounds of the street, where the world of Magic City moved along without him. Wagons, horses, the sound of trains pulling in and out of the depot. The lowing of cows in the stockyard, trapped as he was here in this prison, awaiting what?

He had no way of knowing how or if he would ever escape this place. Those men had sold him to Chen Lee, as if they had the right. He had seen money change hands. Now, he was no better off than Chen Lee's slave girls, sold into this life of misery. It was, he guessed, only a matter of time before he was used as the girls were by some customer with a taste for boys. But he would kill any man who tried. That vow he had made to himself the first night, shackled in the room next to Shyen Zu's, listening to her bed bang against the wall and the grunts of the man rutting inside her.

At fifteen, this life had not yet stolen her beauty, as it had many of the other girls'. She was much in demand because of that. Three or four men a night chose her from the window. Most of them were Chinese. Some were white, though even he knew that brothels were segregated by race. Chinese men could not use the women in white brothels, though the rules were slipperier the other way around. So the men, banned from the white brothels here in town, for violence against the girls or for other reasons, found their way here, to the bottom of the brothel barrel. No one knew or cared what happened to these girls. They were invisible. Like him.

This world, with its sickly sweet smell of opium, made no sense to him. No Cheyenne woman would ever be abused the way these women were. And no Cheyenne boy would find himself enslaved like he was. He would die bravely in battle first.

Beside him, Shyen Zu curled up with her head beside his knee. "You thinkee run? Escape?"

"Yes."

She shook her head. "No use. Better be good at what he want."

"Emptying piss pots and cleaning laundry?"

"*Shi.*"

He pressed a hand across her back, meaning to comfort her, but she flinched at his touch before allowing it like a cat leaning into a palm. He could feel each of the bones in her back. She was like a fragile bird. "There are more of us than him. We could overpower him," Little Wolf said quietly. "Escape."

Shyen Zu stiffened at his suggestion. "I have thought this, too. But the others…they too scared."

"Are you? Too scared?" he asked.

She curled her hands into fists. "I am only one."

"Now we are two. Maybe there are more."

"He will catch—then kill us."

He did not doubt this. Yesterday, a worn-out-looking old woman named Gi Lan, whose hair was going gray, was locked in a cell without windows inside the house. A lit candle was all she took into the room with her, except for a small vial Little Wolf watched Chen Lee tuck into the torn bosom of her gown.

Before Gi Lan had turned from the door, she'd met his eyes. He'd expected to see something there…Fear, anger…even hostility. But what he'd seen as the door was closing on her was resignation. Nothing really, at all.

"Why is she in that room?" he'd asked Shyen Zu later.

Shyen Zu ran her hand, matter-of-factly, across her throat, in the universal sign for death.

"What? Why? Is she sick?"

The girl shook her head with a shrug because he didn't seem to know anything. "Once she a beauty from my province. *Jiansu*," she'd told him. She counted out twelve on her fingers for him. "This many when she come to San Fran-Cisco. Now, here. She too old." She counted again on her fingers to twenty-four.

Shock poured through him. Twenty and four? She looked closer to fifty.

"Men not choose her. Today she die. She must drink—" She searched her mind for the word, then made a face like she was choking.

"Poison?" Little Wolf supplied, appalled.

"*Shi*. Yes. Chen Lee gives her to drink. Or he"—she demonstrated the wringing of her neck—"when the candle die. But she choose drink. Quick-quick."

"He's…forcing her to kill herself? But…why? Why not just let her go?"

Again, she stared at him in all his ignorance. "Go? Where? She no one. No use now. Finished. No good here. No—" She gestured lewdly with her index finger into the circle she made with her other hand.

Anger had curled through him anew. Was that to be Shyen Zu's fate as well? Or his? If he hadn't realized the danger they were all in before, he did now. And hours later, he'd seen two girls carry the thin, limp body of Gi Lan out of that room and toss her onto the back of Chen Lee's wagon. She would be buried somewhere out of town, without a word or a marker, like many of the children at his former school. She would be forgotten as easily as she'd died.

In the two days he'd been here already, he'd begun to understand that Shyen Zu was on the same road the other girls had already chosen—resignation. They had been sold into slavery young and knew nothing else.

Now she had dismissed the idea of escape with the shrug of her thin shoulders. But he was not ready to give up. He had escaped the school and he would escape this place. But if he did, he would find a way to take this frail bird of a girl with him. There had to be more for them in this world.

Somewhere.

Chen Lee burst into the room holding the stick with which Little Wolf had become so familiar, and roughly unlocked the manacle from Little Wolf's leg. He spat out a few unintelligible orders at Little Wolf, which he took to mean it was time to empty the piss pots again. Without warning, the cane cracked along Little Wolf's spine as he got to his feet and he cried out, grabbing the stick to wrestle it out of the old man's hands. Instantly, he knew that had been a mistake. One of Chen Lee's bodyguards stepped up and tossed Little Wolf against the wall.

Pain rocketed through his shoulder and it was all he could do to keep from crying out. But he kept silent, refusing to make eye contact with the man. Slowly, he got to his feet as the old man loosed a stream of Chinese oaths and what, he supposed, were warnings.

Yes, he would escape this place before they killed him. But first, he would count coup on Chen Lee, and maybe even take his scalp.

Red Moon loaned them one of his ponies for the trip and now Essie followed Cade and Náhkohe down the steep trail, her pony nose to tail with his Appaloosa. Essie was grateful to put some distance between her and Cade. They'd already ridden for hours and they'd spoken no more than a few words.

The trail that led down the mountain toward Billings wound past creeks and waterfalls, outcrops of granite and summer-browned meadows. They passed a series of small, mirrored lakes, littered with fallen trees where beavers had been at work. Overhead, a hawk circled lazily, following them out of curiosity as if they were just regular people passing by and not two lost souls with no idea what tomorrow would bring.

As her pony picked its way down a rocky slope behind his horse, she tried not to watch Cade, but her eyes strayed to him over and over.

She couldn't deny what had blossomed between them, but she wanted to. She wanted *not* to want him. Not to feel anything for him at all. As he, apparently, did for her.

Except for that kiss. That kiss hadn't felt like nothing.

As they moved through the forest, she tried to imagine her life after him. After this. How she would go back to her life as it had once been. Alone, perhaps for the rest of her life. If he was right, and she was truly marked as a ruined woman, then quite possibly that kiss they'd shared was the last one she'd ever have.

The thought sent an empty, sharp pain through her.

And lovemaking? Well, that would be finished, too. A fate that, until now, hadn't seemed so bleak. But now…just the thought of his kiss, the sweet slide of his tongue against her own, the press of his arms around her and the jut of his desire against her belly, made her understand that loss in a whole new way. Was it so wrong of her to want him? Just once?

She could be satisfied with once, couldn't she? Store that one time in her memory to pull out now and then, when she would recall each and every detail? It would be enough, wouldn't it, to have that memory?

Ahead, he bent over the horse's neck to study the ground, then slowed Náhkohe to a stop. Beside the trail, trampled paintbrush lay browning in the cool air.

"What is it?" she asked.

"We've picked up their trail again. Three sets of hoofprints. They weren't too worried about leaving a trail. Or at least, one of them wasn't. I wouldn't put it past Little Wolf to have deliberately moved off the path."

She looked off down the mountain. In the distance, she could see Magic City, otherwise known as Billings, perched on the prairie floor. From here, it looked like a collection of toy blocks some child had forgotten. But smoke from an approaching train drew her gaze farther north. A train that would, one day soon, take her away from all of this. From him.

She worried her bottom lip with her teeth. "How much longer 'til we get there?"

"Dark, most likely," he said, turning in time to see her shiver. "Cold?"

She nodded. She'd been cold for days. Even the afternoon sun couldn't chase away the chill that had settled inside her.

He pulled Náhkohe beside her, untied Walks Along Woman's blanket from behind his saddle and draped it around her shoulders. "You should have said something."

Not if my life depended on it. Tugging the blanket close, she said, "What happens when we get there?"

He looked away at that. "You'll ride into Billings alone. I have a friend there. Ollie Warren. She runs the Lucky Diamond Sporting House. She'll help you."

"A...sporting house?"

"A house of sin," he clarified with a small grin. "They don't come any better than Ollie Warren. She'll see you get set up at a decent hotel and will get you on the next train out of town. She'll do that for me."

Really. "A hotel? How do you expect me to go to any decent hotel in Billings, looking like this? I might as well wear a sign, declaring 'I survived! Just barely!'"

He chuckled at that. "Ollie will see that you have new things, get cleaned up. C'mon." He nudged his horse forward and she followed him down the slope.

"You make it sound so easy," she called after him. "But this…Ollie Warren doesn't know me from a woodchuck. What makes you think she'll help me?"

"Because," Cade answered, "she owes me."

Curious. "And what about you?"

"What about me?" he asked.

"Where will you be as I'm collecting your favors from Ollie Warren?"

He sent a quick look back at her, flashing those silvery eyes in her direction. "I'll wait back in Coulson for her to bring me a change of clothes. Something that will help me…blend in."

Cade 'Black Thorn' Newcastle would never blend in anywhere, no matter how hard he tried.

"And then?" she prodded.

"I told you. I'm going to look for Little Wolf. We've settled all that."

"In your mind," she muttered.

"What was that?"

"Nothing. But I suppose you think Mitchell Laddner will just call a truce. Let the matter slide? Has it not occurred to you that he and his cohort are probably in Magic City by now, as well? Possibly waiting for us to show up?"

"The last thing he'll expect is for me to head to town with you. They're probably doubling back to the school by now."

That sounded like wishful thinking, but it was useless to argue with him. After all, he would do what he would do, and she would do what she had to do.

Cade's horse tossed its head suddenly and stuttered to a stop. Her horse whinnied, too, and backed up with a jerky motion. Cade threw his arm out in a gesture meant to protect her, but from what, she could not see. And then she heard it.

The bloodcurdling roar of a bear.

Not twenty feet away, crossing the path, stood a huge golden-colored bear that stood as tall as Cade on his horse, with two cubs beside her. Her gaze was locked on Cade and Náhkohe as she lumbered forward on two legs.

"Run—" Cade whispered, pulling his rifle from the boot of his saddle. "Go back up the trail!" As he spoke, he backed his horse up. But the bear opened its mouth in a fearful yawp that could certainly engulf a man's entire head.

"Cade!" Essie gasped as her horse reared and she flew off its back.

CHAPTER 13

━━━◆━━━

She landed with a hard thwack on the trail, sprawled on her back. Pain shot through her head. Stars swam in front of her eyes and her lungs didn't seem to be working. Distantly, she could hear the fading sound of her horse's hoofbeats as it ran away, and she lifted her head to see the bear lowering to its four legs to make a run at them. *Oh, no. No, no, no!* Cade roared at the bear and waved his arms like a madman. For a moment, the bear seemed confused. Or angry. No time to decide which.

"Give me your hand!" Cade shouted, without taking his eyes off the beast. Náhkohe's eyes rolled white and he tossed his head in fear, dancing in place and fighting Cade's direction.

Get up! Get up! But catching her breath enough to stand seemed ridiculously hard. She rolled onto her side and pushed herself onto her elbows.

"Essie! Now!" He shouldered his rifle and put a bullet in the ground at the bear's feet. That seemed to startle her and the bear jumped back. Her two cubs hustled away into the forest behind her. But furious, the mother bear did not back down. She roared again, a sound so deafening it made Essie's ears ring.

Lumbering forward, the animal pawed at the air in Cade's direction with deadly threat. This close, Essie could smell the rank, musty odor of the animal's breath and every meal that had left its golden-colored coat brown with blood.

Gasping, she pushed herself to her feet as Cade fired another warning shot at the bear. Closer, this time, so a piece of bark flew up at the animal's face. Cade backed a terrified Náhkohe up beside Essie, then reached down and yanked her up behind him. She clapped her arms around him as the mother bear lowered to all fours and stomped the ground with her two front paws.

With his gun still aimed at her, he shouted something at the bear in Cheyenne. The animal roared fiercely one last time, then—impossibly—she turned and ran after her cubs into the woods, disappearing from sight.

For minutes, still shouldering his gun, Cade watched the woods, waiting for the bears to circle back. But it seemed they had gone. The whole thing couldn't have lasted more than thirty seconds, but it had felt like an eternity.

It wasn't until he reined Náhkohe back down the trail that she felt her lungs unlock enough to actually take in a deep breath. She couldn't stop shaking. "I thought...I thought we were dead."

"And well we could have been." Without much encouragement needed, the horse broke into a nervous lope downhill.

"What about my horse?" she asked over Cade's shoulder. "The little traitor..."

Cade rested a hand on the one she had wrapped around him to calm her. Oh, and she was so grateful for that touch.

"He'll find his way back to the camp, I hope. We'll just have to manage with one."

The rush of fear that had poured through her for the last few minutes now left her feeling weak and shaken. "If Náhkohe had balked, too, we'd both be dead now."

"They're gone now. They won't be back."

The horse's flanks were wet with sweat and quivering every bit as much as she was. She smoothed one hand on Náhkohe's muscled backside. "Good horse. Good boy."

"You all right?" Cade asked. "You took a good fall."

"I think so. My pride is wounded, but the rest of me will be all right." But her head still ached and her back felt like that bear had stepped on her.

He didn't reply, but he squeezed her hand and they rode in silence for a few minutes at an easy lope. The trail widened through stands of pine and aspen that crowded the slope on either side of the deer track. Below them, a meadow appeared and sprawled beneath a cerulean blue sky. When they reached the meadow, Cade slowed Náhkohe to a walk so he could snatch some tall grass as they walked by.

Now that the whole thing was over, it hardly seemed real now. But they had just come as close to death as at any other time on this crazy journey so far.

"Most would have shot her where she stood. But you didn't. Why?"

"She and her cubs belong here. We are the intruders."

True. Until the bear eats you.

"When you spoke to her…in Cheyenne…what did you say?"

"I told her I did not want to kill her, or leave her cubs orphans. I asked her to go and leave us alone. That today was not a good day to die."

"But she could have killed you. *Us,* actually."

"But she did not."

A nervous sound escaped her. "Well, the children at the school told me that long ago, their people could talk to animals."

"Some of the old medicine men still can," he said, pulling the water skin from his saddle to offer it to her. "I am not one of them. My words to that mother bear were more of a…prayer than a request."

"A prayer?"

He shrugged. "Not the same kind as yours."

"*Mine?*" She reached for the locket at her throat. "I haven't said a prayer since my son died. I don't much see the point."

He half turned to look at her. "I didn't mean to—" he

began, but she shook her head as she took the skin from him and pulled out the stopper.

"It's all right," she said. "It doesn't matter. But I am quite glad you guessed right about that bear. It could have gone badly."

"There is no place more dangerous to be than between a mother grizzly and her cubs. She was torn between protecting them by attacking us or running. She chose to run."

That, she understood. She would have done anything to save her son. Anything. But there was nothing she could do. And run, she had. All the way to Montana, to meet Cade Newcastle in a most unlikely way.

She drank from the skin and handed it back to him, watching as he did the same. Her eyes fell to his throat, how it moved as he swallowed. How the water spilled over his lips and trickled down his jaw. Some dark impulse had her wishing she could follow the track of that water with her tongue and—

She turned sharply away, horrified at the direction of her thoughts. Imagine, her, wanting to do something like that. It was unseemly. Indecent, even. Perhaps it was their brush with death that made her think such things.

He pulled one sleeve across his mouth and looked back at her. And when she met his gaze she was surprised to find him watching her with a look so stark he couldn't disguise the heat behind it.

"We'd best hurry," she said softly. "If we're to make it by dark."

His jaw tightened. With a nod and without another word, he nudged Náhkohe on down the mountain.

By late afternoon, the rain had started again and as they rode they shivered under the blanket Walks Along had given them. There was a chill of late summer in the air. Cade could feel her tremble behind him, though she did not complain. He was anxious to make town by nightfall, but he could tell she was at the very end of her tether for strength and he knew he had to do something to get her warm before going on.

Up ahead, he saw what looked like smoke rising through the trees. But it wasn't smoke. He knew this place. It was sacred for the Cheyenne. He remembered it from when he was a boy. He veered off the trail and headed toward it. If she noticed, she said nothing. She had her face buried against his back and the blanket covering her face.

Some small voice warned him that he was simply avoiding the inevitable. That once they reached the bottom of the mountain, things would be at an end between them and he would never see her again. And he knew that was right. But he dreaded it. How strange that he should come to care about this woman in so short a time.

No, *care* was the wrong word. He'd cared for women before—women like White Deer, back at Red Moon's camp, who had never made any secret about her feelings for him. But White Deer wasn't for him and he'd never felt for her what he did for Essie Sparks. Not even—especially not—Delilah had come close, though at the time, he'd thought he loved her. That had been some twisted lust on his part. And the bad judgment of youth.

No, what he felt for Essie couldn't be put into words exactly. Wouldn't be defined by anything as simple as lust. Though he did lust after her. He'd lost count of the times he'd turned away from her so she wouldn't see the evidence of that hunger that cut through him when she was near.

No, it wasn't simple lust, but some emotion he had never felt before. When he'd kissed her back in camp, he'd nearly lost control. When he'd felt her return his kiss, slide her tongue against his with a hunger that shocked him, he'd longed for nothing more than to carry her back to the tepee and make her his for once and for all. Brand her with his seed and forbid her to ever take another lover.

But for both their sakes, he hadn't. He wouldn't. He'd vowed that to himself. Not only because choosing a white woman—much less *this* white woman—was impossible. But allowing her to choose him was even worse. Yet, every step they took closer to town meant a step closer to losing her for good.

It took only a few minutes to reach the hot spring tucked into a nest of rocks overlooking the valley. One of the few that had a reliable temperature, this hot spring was a favorite amongst the Cheyenne and was often used, in the old days, for those with winter in their bones. It had always seemed to him that nature itself had carved this hot spring there to be used on a day exactly like this one. The water here smelled faintly of sulfur and was crystal clear, with curls of steam rolling across the surface.

"What is that?" Essie asked when she lifted her head to see why they'd stopped.

"That is your salvation." He slid off the horse and helped her down. In the rain, they walked to the edge of the spring, with Essie staring like a child at the steaming water. "It's a hot spring. And it will warm you to your bones. Take off your clothes."

She jerked a look at him, shocked.

"I will wait for you over there," he assured her, gesturing to the rocks behind them. He started to turn but she grabbed his arm.

"You would have me go in alone?"

"Are you afraid?"

"What if I were?"

"I think you're not afraid of much, Essie Sparks."

She blinked at the water, listening to the rain patter the glassy surface. The pool was barely twenty feet across and ten feet wide and not deep enough to drown in. Below the surface, benches of rock sat haphazardly along the edges beneath the clear water. "I'm afraid I'll never see you again after tonight."

He said nothing, but he supposed the set of his jaw encompassed all the conflict he was feeling about that very same thing.

For a long moment, she just stared at him, her look changing from stark to something much more complicated. A look that warned him not to take anything for granted

with this woman. He started to turn, but she lifted her chin
and arched a brow, wordlessly daring him not to as she let
the blanket fall away from her shoulders and drop to the
ground.

"I will go in, if you will come with me."

As he watched, she loosed the rope she'd tied like a belt
around her waist and tugged the shirt he'd given her over
her head, leaving her in her damp underthings. His gaze
fell, against his will, to the thin cotton fabric of her corset
cover that clung to her breasts, where the dusky peaks of
her nipples showed through the dampness.

A hunger, sharp and uncontrollable, knifed through him.
He clenched his fists.

"I am not a girl, Cade, I'm a woman. Fully grown," she
said, pulling the corset cover off over her head. Her auburn
curls tumbled damply about her shoulders and that gold
locket she loved so much dangled at her throat between her
breasts. "If you think you can ruin me, then you're too late. I
was ruined when you met me. And you can take me back
tonight, as I am, and leave me and never see me again. But
if, as you say, I'm to be shunned for the rest of my life"—she
slid a petticoat off her hips—"never to know a man's warmth
against me, or inside me, well, then I'm asking you. Give me
something to remember. Some memory I can pull out when
I'm old and can hardly recall what it was like to feel this. At
least then I'd know what it's like to be held by a man who
really wants me."

He wished he could look away, but she refused to allow it.

"And if I'm wrong about that," she went on, "couldn't
you…just pretend?"

Pretend? Do you have no idea what you do to me?

The last of her petticoats slipped to the ground. "Pretend
that you care about me and that we'll see each other again
when this is all over? That you and I will not be saying
goodbye tonight?" She reached behind her and unfastened
the button on her last petticoat and let it slide down her
slender hips. All the while, she refused to release him from
her steady gaze. So he watched and got achingly hard as she

let her underthings drift to the damp ground, one at a time.

The rain continued to fall. Water clung to her cheeks and lashes and she glanced up at him through that dark, wet fringe. He felt his mouth go dry. "I do not have to pretend to want you, Essie. I have wanted you since the moment I saw you in that room. Since the moment you flashed those eyes at me and warned me not to cut you again."

She released some breath she'd been holding and her eyes, already damp, glistened with tears. "That seems like forever ago."

He nodded. "This can only end badly."

"It's already bad. What can it matter now?"

"You tempt the darkness to ask such a question."

"Then let us tempt it." With a flick of her fingers, she undid the first hook on the corset with a pop. Then the next and the next, until it, too, fell away and her small breasts bobbed free of the contraption. "We should do everything in our power to fight back against what they expect of us."

He'd learned long ago that the fates were nothing to be toyed with. But if tomorrow was, indeed, his last day on earth, would he not regret pushing her away? Would he always wonder what it would feel like to cup her breasts in his hands? Dip his fingers into her and taste her everywhere? Yet could he imagine himself walking away from her after?

Seáa! He would think of that later.

His fingers found the hem of his deerskin shirt and he pulled it up and over his head, tossing it aside. Then he dragged her up against him and kissed her deeply. Shifting her mouth against his, she made a sound of need, there in the rain, and flattened herself against him, curling her hands around the back of his neck and threading her fingers in his long hair, pulling him closer. And after he'd ravaged her mouth, he slid the gathered top of her shift down over her shoulders and undressed the last of her.

Naked, her body was everything he'd imagined. Slender and pale, with the womanly flare of her hips where he rested his hands. His gaze drifted from her perfectly shaped breasts—whose nipples were puckered from the cold or the kiss—to the nest of auburn curls at the apex of her long legs.

"Get in the water," he told her, turning her by the shoulders toward the pool. Without further argument, she did as he asked. He tied Náhkohe to a tree and, with a quick tug, undid the leather drawstring on his own leggings and dropped them to the ground. He followed her in.

She didn't even pretend not to watch or that she didn't notice his erection. There was nothing shy in her gaze as it followed him until he'd sunk to the neck in the steaming pool and swam to her.

He pulled her close, anxious to feel the press of her breasts against his chest again. "You are so beautiful," he murmured against her ear.

"You don't have to say that."

"I only speak the truth."

She slid her hands over his shoulders under the water then pressed the flats of her palms against his chest. Her mouth found his neck and he exhaled as she tortured him with her tongue. Beneath the water, she wrapped herself around him and he cupped her bottom in his two hands, drawing her up against his hard length.

Floating with her, he closed his eyes, his heartbeat stuttering at the feel of her there. She moved her hips up and down him, sliding over him. He pulled her harder against him. He could take her right now, for the longing of the past few days peaked in him like an avalanche, crashing over him in wave after wave of hot desire.

Steam rose between them and eddied between their bodies where it could find a space. Her mouth moved up his jaw and then to his lips again for a quick peck before drifting to the scar on his cheek to linger over it with soft kisses. He nearly pulled away from her, but she held him there and met his gaze intentionally. "This," she said, kissing the scar again, "is your history. And that makes it part of you." She arched a teasing brow at him. "It makes you dangerous and a little roguish and I like it."

After years of despising his scar, he was hard pressed to believe it could be anything but ugly. But as he studied her eyes, he realized he believed her. He sent her a devilish look. "Is it a rogue you crave?"

"Yes," she said simply. "But only if that rogue is you." She gave a shy laugh then, as if her comment had startled even her.

This woman! He swam with her to a ledge of rocks, lifting her onto them, just enough so that he could access her breasts. One at a time, he lingered over her dusky nipples, warm now from the steamy heat of the water. She let her head fall back as he sucked them, one at a time, just hard enough to make her moan in pleasure. Her breasts, he marveled, were small and perfect and fit perfectly in his hand with a weighty heft that sent a new kind of ache to his loins.

The rain continued to fall, and she slid down into the water and kicked away from the ledge, beckoning him toward the chest-deep middle. They ducked in and half out of the pool as they rolled through the water, kissing and half sinking below the surface, laughing when they ran out of air before starting again.

He forgot about everything but her. And he especially forgot all the promises he'd made to himself. Because who could not, in this woman's arms?

"I feel wicked," she murmured against his ear as they sank to their necks in the steamy water. "It must be the wildness of where we are."

His mouth explored her throat and the small hollow at the base of it. Her necklace with its gold locket floated at her breasts. "You feel wicked because you're naked with me. In a hot spring. Here, wrap your legs around me." He lifted her onto his chest underwater and she wound her arms around his neck and her legs around his waist. The tip of his hard erection brushed the entrance to her. As he watched, she closed her eyes and shuddered.

"*Mo'onahe*," he murmured in her ear. "You are so beautiful." Pulling his hand from her back, he slipped it between her legs and touched her slick, sweet center. Her response only made him harder. She curled against him, squirming against his touch.

"Oh! Cade!"

"Do you like that?" he whispered. "What of this?" He lifted her in his arms until he could reach her breast with his mouth again and licked her pink nipple as he swirled his finger inside her.

"Yes," she breathed. "Oh, yes, Cade."

She pressed her mouth to the top of his head and brushed kisses down the side of his face until she reached his ear. Tracing the outline of it with her tongue, she tortured him there until he couldn't take it anymore and he caught her mouth again with his. He kissed her deeply. Her tongue swirled against his and slid against his teeth. She tasted of rain. He kissed the drops on her lashes then took her mouth again. He couldn't seem to help himself. She was like a thirst he couldn't quench. He couldn't get enough of her.

He lifted her, set her back up on the rock ledge again to taste the place he couldn't taste underwater. She watched, wide-eyed, as he nudged her knees apart and dipped his mouth to the soft curls between her legs to taste her there. Her shock was soon replaced by soft moans of pleasure and he felt her hands draw his head closer yet as he laved her with his tongue.

"Is this…oh! Is this even *legal*?" she murmured, head thrown back, welcoming the cool rain on her face.

"Do you care?" he said, lifting his mouth from her with a smile.

"Oh! Only if you stop!"

Essie had never imagined such a thing. Not in her whole married life had her husband touched her the way Cade did. So gently. So tenderly. Wanting her to feel pleasure as if that was his only goal.

But she wanted to touch him, too. She'd longed to run her hands along the strong muscles of his arms and now, with his arms stretched up and his hands around her waist, she did just that, exploring all the dips and hollows where the muscles of his upper arms contracted and relaxed. Drawing her closer to his mouth, he sucked at that sensitive nub, lifting her hips practically off the stone where she sat. Until she thought she might explode. But instead, he released her and climbed up to her there on the rock, his hard length meeting with the place he'd just abandoned.

Working up her nerve, she slid her hand downward until her fingers closed around the slick, velvet warmth of him. He shuddered into her hand, nearly losing control. He was big, bigger than her husband had been, and she suddenly longed to have him inside her. To feel what that would be like. But she moved her fingers along his shaft, teasing him with her touch until he could take it no longer.

He dragged her close to the edge and poised himself at her opening. The pressure of her need had her hips nearly bucking at his touch. "You are sure?" he asked.

"Oh, Cade, how can you ask? Please. Please."

And he obliged, sinking himself into her slowly at first, then with long thrusts that drove him deeply inside her. He filled her completely. She forgot to think. She forgot where she was. Neither of them had much control or even wanted it. Because the primal rhythm of his thrusts got faster and faster, his hips slapping against hers with a sound that only curled her want more tightly. She felt herself slipping off some metaphorical edge—as if to lose herself this way was to spin completely out of control. But she didn't care. She *wanted* to lose control. She *wanted* to disappear into him. She pressed her face to his shoulder and felt the clutch, deep in her belly, of some otherworldly pleasure she'd never felt before. Harder and harder he pounded against her until she spun over that edge and she cried out loud, feeling him spend himself inside her, hot and explosive.

After they came together, they collapsed against the ledge for a few breathless moments before he drew her back into the water to hold her tightly against him. He kissed her again and again and murmured things in her ear in Cheyenne that she didn't understand. But she didn't care if he was saying goodbye. She only wanted to hold on to this moment, this memory, and keep it with her forever.

CHAPTER 14

It took them until nearly sunset to reach the beginnings of civilization, riding through what was left of the on-again, off-again rain. But shivering and damp, wrapped in borrowed blankets, they stopped at the outskirts of what remained of Coulson, an abandoned hamlet less than a mile from Billings, or what many called Magic City. The new railroad town up ahead was alive with activity even at this hour and the streets were lined with kerosene lamps that were burning already.

Cade surveyed the thriving railhead town a half mile down the road. From here, they could just make out the sprawl of new cattle pens that lined the south side of the new Union Pacific tracks. With the north bank of the Yellowstone River at their feet and the towering, red rim rock of the Sacrifice Cliffs behind them, the mountains had given way to a sprawling valley that had become the hub of every bit of commerce in Montana Territory. Billings had earned the nickname Magic City because it had grown almost overnight once the railroad laid claim to that section of land, bypassing Coulson.

In a matter of two years, Billings had blossomed from a meager gathering of thrown-together tents he'd had the personal misfortune to occupy, into a genuine town, complete with two-story wooden buildings and nearly four thousand souls.

His mixed blood and his father's name had effectively saved him from reservation life, and he'd worked for the past few years in nearly every growing concern his father didn't own in these parts, including laying track for the Union Pacific and cutting timber in the mountains west of here. There was a fair to even chance he'd be recognized by someone from the Newcastle spread here, and the possibility settled over his skin like itchweed. He had no desire to see his father and the feeling was clearly mutual.

The lonesome whistle sounded from a train arriving from the East—probably St. Paul—frightening Cade's horse.

"Whoa," he soothed, keeping the exhausted animal from bucking.

Essie clung to him and managed not to fall. She was worn out and beyond anxious to be finished with riding, now that they were within sight of the town, and he couldn't blame her. He was near the end of his resources as well. They'd reached this place the long way around, not all that far now from where they'd begun.

The warm effects of their lovemaking and the hot water of the spring had dissipated hours ago on the ride down and both of them were shivering and wet through.

The cold dampness was like a knife in his bones after so many days of it and he longed for a warm fire to sit beside. And he wanted to share that fire with her. He wasn't ready to let her go. To say goodbye. He needed to say something and he hadn't yet found the words. But it was too late for such things now. They had both known it was coming to this.

He would not meet her in Billings as he'd told her he would and she seemed to know it. It would be far easier to make a clean break, knowing that Ollie would have her on a train by tomorrow morning, before anyone was the wiser. A new life. A new beginning. That's what she needed.

He threw his leg over Náhkohe's neck and slid off. With only one horse between them, she would take his into town and leave him with Ollie.

There were a dozen abandoned buildings here and most were showing signs of two years of neglect, with falling-down siding and holes in the roofs. To their right stood the empty Bender Bros. Livery, which had recently pulled up stakes and relocated to Magic City. If he was lucky, there might be somewhere to warm himself while he waited for Ollie to come with a change of clothes for him.

He held the horse's reins and watched Essie stare at the city's outskirts—with longing? Not that a woman like her belonged in a backwoods place like Billings, but at least she'd be among her own kind. Not attached to a man like him for her very survival.

"Remember what I said," he told her. "Keep to the side streets. Do not meet anyone's eyes. Ollie's place is near the stockyards halfway—"

"Down Missouri Avenue," she finished. "I know. I know the plan."

"You have the money I gave you?"

She nodded, patting a pocket in his shirt.

"I am not so sure this is a good idea," Essie said, breaking into his thoughts. "Leaving you here. How is your leg?"

"Fine. Nothing a good bed and some food won't fix." Hunger gnawed at his belly, as he was sure it did hers as well. They'd gone through the little bit Red Moon and his band could spare them.

"Besides, we agreed—" he began.

"I know. I know." She turned to regard the distant town, biting her lower lip. Her face, no longer smudged with trail dirt, gleamed in the moonlight. Her curls tangled in the cool evening wind blowing down off the mountains.

"See that my horse is well fed and has a place to rest. Ollie will see to that, too. The Headquarters is the best hotel in town. After Ollie's, if it's safe, get a room there for the night. Sleep. It's too late for Ollie to get me clothes tonight. Morning is soon enough. Have her bring Náhkohe back to me."

"But what about—"

"No more," he said, holding up one hand. "It is decided."

She sighed heavily. "*You've* decided."

"It's best for you."

"Or you," she contradicted.

He tightened his hand around the reins. Not him. Definitely not him. The idea of watching her ride off without him was like a knife in his gut. "Essie. It's already late."

She nodded again, staring off at the town up ahead. "What happened between us, back there…"

He reached up to take her fingers in his. "If anything…if I got you with child…"

She lifted her finger to her mouth to silence the question. "It was my choice. Remember that."

He would only remember that he wanted her as much as she wanted him. And that he might have planted his child inside her. "But if you are—"

"I will be long gone from here. I wouldn't have you feel obligated to me because of a child. So think no more about it. Tomorrow, I'll take a train to somewhere far from here and we will never see each other again."

She leaned toward him and kissed him, lingering on his mouth for a moment longer than necessary. Then she said, "Goodbye, Cade. I'll never forget you." And with those words, she nudged his horse and started off.

"Essie Sparks!" he called before she'd gone far.

She pulled Náhkohe up and turned back to him, her expression hopeful and wary, the cool, chinook wind blowing her hair across her face.

"You are *vé'otsé'e*!" he called to her. "A warrior woman! Know that."

A wavering smile lifted one corner of her mouth. She nodded and kicked her horse and took off at a lope toward town.

He stood watching her for a long time, until she disappeared from sight, before turning back to the livery.

You're a fool. A damned fool for letting her go.

A woman like that comes along once in a lifetime. If a man's lucky. Which, God knew, he was not. Nor did he deserve her. He'd done enough wrong in his life to know he'd never be the kind of man she should be with. But he couldn't stop imagining that she might, somehow, overlook all that was wrong with him, to see what his heart held.

"I wouldn't have you feel obligated to me because of a child...Tomorrow, I'll take a train to somewhere far from here and we will never see each other again."

Yes, tomorrow she'd be gone and his choices along with her. She'd said nothing about her destination. Just something vague about somewhere warm.

Still, if somehow he survived this mess, maybe he'd find her. Maybe he'd never stop looking for her until he found her. And if he was wrong about their chances, maybe she'd even let him love her.

You are *a fool, to even hope.*

He turned and walked back toward the livery. Almost to the double doors, he caught a movement in the dark to his right, but before he could even react, the butt of a rifle slammed into his face with the force of a brick.

Pain exploded there in his cheek and he found himself suddenly sprawled on the ground, clutching at dirt.

Ohhh, hell.

Two dark shadows leaned over him, blocking the stars.

"You look surprised to see us, half-breed. You didn't think we'd give up that easy, did you?"

Stunned, Cade grabbed ineffectually at the ground, trying to roll to his knees.

A foot caught him dead center in his belly, lifting him off the ground and knocking the wind from him. He clutched his midsection and wheezed in a breath.

"That's for all the trouble you put us through, trying to catch you," Mitchell Laddner told him. "And this is for her."

The rifle butt came at him again and smashed into his head.

And the stars above him winked into utter darkness.

CHAPTER 15

The back door of the Lucky Diamond Sporting House opened at Essie's tentative knock and a modestly pretty young woman with dark hair and far too few clothes answered the door. In the background came the sound of a tinny piano playing "Buffalo Gal," and the hum of conversation and clinking whiskey glasses in the busy enterprise. The fragrance of perfume wafted out the door. Perfume and the smell of food. Real, warm food.

"Come back around eight if'n you want a biscuit," the girl said. "After the girls eat. Right, Pink?"

From behind her somewhere, a man grumbled, "That's it. Come back at eight. How many times I got t' tell you folks not to bother me 'til then?"

A biscuit? Essie's mouth watered and her stomach growled, but she shook her head. "I-I didn't come for a biscuit."

"Well then?" the girl inquired, giving Essie's damp, disheveled appearance a once-over.

Essie cleared her throat. "I'm looking for Miss Warren. Ollie Warren?"

The woman tilted a patronizing look at her, scrunching her painted lips, like she'd heard that question a hundred times before. Maybe even before noon. "Sorry. If you're lookin' for work, Ollie ain't hirin'. An' for certain she ain't hirin' you."

"I'm not," she began, brushing the hair from her face, "looking for work. A friend of hers sent me."

The whore slapped a hand on her barely clad hip. "And just who would that be?"

"Look, could I please just speak to Miss Warren? It's very important."

"First off, nobody calls Ollie Miss Warren. 'Cause she'll slap you upside the head if you do. Second of all, unless I know your business, you can forget about seein' Ollie altogether."

Essie's expression flattened with stubbornness and not a little embarrassment that this…woman was looking at her as if she were no better than a rag-picker. Granted, her filthy petticoat was almost a decent brown color with mud and dirt and her hair was—

"Hey, Lucy!" some man shouted from another room behind the girl. "My lap is still waitin' for your sweet little ass!"

Lucy shouted back, "Hold your horses, Landon! I'm comin'!" She shook her head at Essie and began to close the door, but turned back to add, "Just a piece of advice, sweetie. We've all seen hard times. But there's a bathhouse just down the street. Two bits'll buy you a hot soak and a mostly clean towel to dry yourself off with. If I was you, that's where I'd begin."

"Wait!" Essie wedged her muddy moccasin in the door and pushed back. "Wait. I'm perfectly aware of how I look, and it's none of your business how I got that way. But I would appreciate it if you would tell *Ollie* that Mr. Newcastle sent me. With a *personal* message."

Some of the snide slid off her expression. "Newcastle junior or senior?"

"Junior," Essie answered, fairly certain she was right.

Lucy's brown eyes went wide and she studied her anew. "*You* know *Cade*?"

"Yes," she said, biting back the sting of knowing that Cade was on a first-name basis with this sporting girl. She glanced behind her, anxious to get in off the street before she was seen. There were wagons and pedestrians all over the place, even in the alley, but no one was paying her any mind. Yet.

"Well, in that case," Lucy said, "wait right there."

"Can I wait inside, please?"

Lucy glanced at the alley behind Essie, then reluctantly stepped aside to let her in. "Don't you move. I'll be right back. And I ain't makin' no promises."

Lucy disappeared into the next room and Essie rubbed her arms, peering around the kitchen. The man who'd spoken earlier, Pink, turned and eyed her suspiciously. Pink, a middle-aged man—as wiry and dark as a mahogany twig, but strong-looking—was standing over a pot of something on the stove. The delicious smell nearly made Essie faint from hunger on the spot.

There was definitely chicken involved, she divined, and herbs—sage and rosemary—*ohhh!*—and probably potatoes with onions, maybe some sweet carrots—

"You keep them eyes o' yours in your own head," Pink warned grumpily and, too late, Essie realized she was licking her lips. "This here stew is for them workin' girls out there, not for the likes of every Mary, Sue and Harry that comes knockin' at the back door for handouts. You get biscuits. That's it. Don't know how many times I gotta say it."

Essie shrugged. "Anyone who gives handouts to the hungry at the back door can't be nearly as grumpy as you pretend to be."

Pink huffed and sent her a narrow-eyed look before turning back to his stew, but she caught the hint of a grin there. "Mighty uppity for a gal who looks like she ain't et a solid meal in more'n a few days." He tossed her a small, fluffy biscuit from a pan cooling on a board.

"Oh! Thank you." Backing up against the door, she cradled the biscuit and wolfed it down like a hungry dog. Pink shrugged and went back to his work. She supposed there were plenty of folks in these parts who went hungry instead of striking it rich here as they'd hoped. How fortunate she'd been in her life to have always had food on her table. And how spoiled.

As she chewed, she purposefully turned her attention to the rest of the room to get her mind off the food. A long, oak-planked table occupied one side of the room, flanked by bench seats under a white-curtained window. The kitchen felt welcoming. Well, except for Pink's suspicious stare. But she'd wager it was the man's cooking that made this place feel more like a home than the brothel it was.

The door Lucy had walked through led to a finer room with carpets and crystal-hung lamps. She could see several settees and caught glimpses of men with half-naked women settled on their laps. Less than a week ago, she wouldn't have been caught dead in a place like this. But now she felt grateful for the sanctuary, temporary as it might be.

This was yet another first in a long line of firsts that had happened to her since she'd arrived in Montana. Standing inside a brothel.

Behind her, a female cleared her throat.

Essie spun to find a handsome, auburn-haired woman standing in the doorway of the kitchen, with the petulant Lucy at her side. The woman's indigo satin skirt gave an imperious swish as she entered the room but as she took in Essie's disheveled appearance, she slowed to a stop.

"Well," she said, "you wouldn't be the first girl who's fallen on hard times to knock at my door. Or even the first Cade has sent my way. Though Lucy tells me you're not looking for employment."

"I'm sorry to trouble you"—she glanced at Lucy—"Miss Warren."

"It's Ollie. And ain't no trouble. Any friend of Cade's is a friend of mine. What can I help you with, Miss—?"

"Sparks. Essie Sparks." She swallowed past the dry lump in her throat. She flicked a look out the window at where she'd left Náhkohe tied to the rail. Ollie followed her look.

The woman's lips parted in alarm. "That's his horse."

"Yes."

"Where is he?"

"Back in Coulson. He sent me to you for help."

"He…all right?"

She answered with an equivocal nod. "Can we talk privately?"

Without taking her eyes off her, Ollie said, "Pink? Would you take that Appaloosa outside back to the stable and get him out of sight? Rub him down? See he's fed an extra ration of oats. Looks like he's been through somethin'. Looks like you both have."

Pink disappeared outside to tend to the horse. As she watched him go, days of shoving aside the toll of their struggle seemed to pool in her legs. The shaking that began there seemed to move through her in a wave of fatigue.

Ollie took her arm and guided her to a bench at the table. "And you'd best sit down before you fall."

"May we speak privately?"

The madam tipped her chin at Lucy and the girl dutifully left the room.

"I would offer you something more comfortable—you look as if you might appreciate something more comfortable—but my comfortable seating is…occupied just now. Sit right there. I'll get you some stew."

The biscuit had only whetted Essie's appetite and against her will, she glanced at the pot on the stove.

Ollie moved with the grace of a woman at ease with herself, without apology or uncertainty. She was tall. Taller than most women, and big-boned in a handsome way. She was not what Essie would call beautiful, but something about the way she held herself reminded her of a girl she'd once known in school, who might have been a wallflower but for the men who always seemed to buzz around her.

Ollie set a bowl of stew down in front of Essie. The deliciousness of the fragrance nearly made her forget to use a spoon.

"Eat first. Then we'll talk."

The woman watched her as she wolfed down the stew.

"I'm afraid it's been a while since I had a good meal," she said when she finished, feeling almost human again.

"Thank you so much."

Ollie folded her hands on the table. "Now, tell me."

Essie nodded. "This will probably sound far-fetched, but perhaps not if you know him."

"Go on."

She proceeded to tell her the story of their adventure, from the first day to the last. Ollie listened without a hint of judgment on her face until Essie finished at the part about leaving him behind in Coulson.

"First off," Ollie said, "I figured out who you were after one look. Your name's on pretty near everyone's tongue hereabouts, being taken by a Cheyenne renegade."

Essie felt herself color at the thought that she was already infamous here.

"Second, I am both relieved and dismayed to hear it was Cade did the taking."

"It's not…it wasn't as black and white as it sounds."

Ollie shrugged, as if she already knew that. "Let's pray it stays a mystery to everyone but you. And you say the boy ran away before Cade could get him? You're sure he wasn't hiding? I haven't heard one thing about a missing boy in all the gossip. Only that you were taken."

That surprised her. "I'm sure. He took his medicine bag with him. It was his only possession. He wouldn't part with it willingly. And if he took it, he meant to run. And then, days later we found it—well, we didn't find it, exactly. Cade's friends did. But Little Wolf had dropped it on the trail. And there were two others with him. Not Indian ponies. White men's horses. We fear someone took him. Cade thought he might have left the medicine bag behind like a…a clue. So we'd know it was him."

Ollie shook her head. "Two men, huh?" She glanced out the darkened window at the street traffic still passing by. "Well, regardless, I'd say Cade should've thought twice about going to take that boy in the first place, but it would do little good. He abides by different codes, that one." Ollie smiled. "And to tell the truth, I'm quite fond of him."

"Yes," Essie said, staring at her hands.

"And so are you," Ollie surmised. "Unless I'm mistaken. Quite a twist in a story that began with a kidnapping, no?"

"Please don't call it that. It'll do no good to call it that."

"All right. What do you need?"

Essie felt relief pour through her. "He needs new clothes. He might be recognized. He needs clothes that are not…Cheyenne. And mine…well, clearly…"

Ollie eyed her ruined things. "Uh-huh. I won't ask where the rest of your duds went."

"Cade gave me some money. But since, apparently, everyone is talking about me, I have to think about how to handle it." She pulled the money from her pocket and laid it on the table. "He didn't want to risk being seen with me. Not for his sake, but for mine. Especially with him looking—"

"Like a Cheyenne?" Ollie finished. There was no meanness in her eyes, when she said it. Only unexpected compassion.

"Yes."

"They think you're probably dead, you know. Most everyone. Or, at the very least, ruined and crazy by now."

She met the woman's gaze head-on. "If I am ruined, it's of my own doing. The crazy part? Maybe."

Ollie patted her hand. "Take it easy, sweetie. I can see that it would take a lot more than what you've been through to ruin you. Or make you crazy. Underneath that layer of trail, there's a formidable woman. Pretty, too. I'd hire you myself, if I thought you were meant for a place like this, but you're not. I can see that, too."

Her kindness surprised Essie. "I will take that as a compliment."

"As it's meant. I'm afraid your…ordeal…has been all the talk in Magic City for days now. If anyone knows it was Cade involved with the fiasco at the school, I haven't heard it."

"And I want to keep it that way." For reasons she couldn't fathom, her eyes watered as she said it.

Ollie studied her for a long beat. "Which presents

something of a problem for you and him, no?"

With her hands locked together on the table, she said, "There is no me and him. There's only two people caught in a very…precarious situation."

Ollie sent her a knowing smile. "Precarious. That's one way to slice it."

Essie jerked a look up at Ollie. "It's the boy I'm worried about. I need to find him as much as Cade does. It's my fault he ran away. My fault he's probably fallen into the hands of…God knows who? There are bad men out there."

Ollie sat back in her chair. "But you don't see Cade Newcastle as one of 'em?"

"No." She dropped her face into her hands. "He never hurt me. Not once. And he could have."

"Yes," Ollie said. "Yes, he could have. But that's not the sort of man he is."

"I have to fix this, Ollie. For the boy and for Cade. No one can know he was the one who took me. And after we find Little Wolf…well, I'm sure that will be the end of things. Between us, I mean."

"I see."

"You can't." She got to her shaky feet and moved to the window, staring out into the darkened alley "And I'm not sure I understand either. I feel…as if whoever I was before has been flung about and scattered by the wind up in those mountains. Nothing is as it was. Nothing. Especially not me."

"That's how it is with men, Essie."

"Not men. *That* man."

Ollie put her hand over Essie's. "What can I do to help?"

"He needs food. Clothes. White clothes. You must—" She stopped. "I mean, if you would, could you go tonight? He told me morning is soon enough, but I'm afraid for him."

"And what about you?"

"He wants me to go to The Headquarters for the night, then board a train out of town in the morning. But I…I'm not going."

"Oh?"

She shook her head. "I intend to look for Little Wolf, with or without him."

The older woman looked at her long and hard. "Montana Territory is a rough place. I expect you know that already. It ain't for the faint of heart, or mostly, for women on their own. I speak from personal experience. The girls who work for me, they know. And I don't recommend lookin' until you find your last resort like they have. It's not up to me to tell you what to do. But I will warn you that a woman on her own ain't safe in a place like this. The best you could do would be to hop on that train and head back home. Leave what's happened here behind you. I can keep you here for the night, if you like, put you on a train in the morning and that'll be the end of it. I reckon it's what Cade is hoping for from me."

Essie stared at her hands for a long moment, then shook her head. "I know you're right. Of course you are. Logically. If I could go and live with myself, I would. If not for Cade, I would have been on that train days ago and turned my back on the boy because I didn't see I had a choice. But that was before. Now, everything is different. How I saw things. What part I played. As for Cade, all I could think about for the first two days was how I would get away from him. But now…"

Ollie tilted a sympathetic look at her.

Essie patted the pile of cash on the table. "There's enough here to get us new things. Ready-made things. If we could impose on you to buy them for us, I'll be gone straightaway. We don't want to bring any trouble down on you. I know this is asking a lot—"

Ollie stopped her with a hand. "See this place? It belongs to me. I say what happens here and what don't. And if we're honest, I owe Cade a debt I wasn't sure I could ever repay, so you've done me a favor, really. Now. What about the folks lookin' for you? You got family you want to tell you're alive and well?"

Her gaze drifted to the white-curtained windows. "I have

no one. So you needn't worry. I'm on my own. But I'll be careful."

"Figured that's what you'd say." She got to her feet. "First things first. When Pink gets back, I'll have him draw you a hot bath. Then I'll see what I can come up with in your size." Ollie scanned her figure. "There should be something decent around here. Meanwhile, I'll get Cade some food and scrounge up some duds for him. You say he's at the Benson Bros. Livery in Colson?"

"That's right."

"And I'll bring Cade a fresh horse to ride."

What she offered was more than what Essie had expected. "Thank you seems insufficient after everything we've been through, Ollie. But…thank you very much."

Ollie shrugged. "You can thank me after this mess is all straightened around. 'Til then, none of us will be at ease. C'mon. Let's get you lookin' presentable."

Jedediah Sampson, sheriff of the burgeoning town of Billings, sat with his mud-caked boots propped up on the two-planked bench that served as his desk, playing solitaire. One of the two cells to his left was occupied by a snoring cowboy, and Sampson beaned the man on the head with a carefully aimed walnut through the bars of his cell.

"Bingo!" he cackled as the snorer jolted awake and sat up.

"Aw, hell's bells, Jedediah, will ya quit it? I'm trying to sleep here," the prisoner complained.

"This ain't no hotel, Lackaway. Me usin' *you* for target practice is small price to pay for shootin' up the lobby of the International."

"I had my reasons," Lackaway grumbled.

"A whole bottle of 'em, to be exact. When you gonna give up that drinkin'?" Sampson asked with a laugh.

"When you do, I reckon." Lackaway rolled with his back to the sheriff, putting an end to the conversation.

Since that would never happen, Sampson figured he'd have regular company in his jail for a good long time to come. If he didn't have to shoot the idiot first.

"I'm lockin' up for the night, you old bastard. Sleep it off. I'll be back in the morning."

But before he could do more than reach for his gun on the peg behind his desk, the front door burst open and two men, holding up a third man by the arms, blew into his office along with a gust of cool wind.

Sampson unfolded himself from the chair and stood—all six-foot-eight of him—understanding immediately that the unconscious man was not just another drunk. He was an Indian. And as the men holding him tugged off their hats, he recognized them as well.

"Well, look what the rain washed down from the mountains. You fellas look a little worse for the wear. And so does this Injun. What is he, drunk?"

They dumped him on the floor at Sampson's feet, out cold. He was bleeding from the head and ears and his face had a dark, swelling bruise running alongside the old scar on his cheek. From that scar, he recognized him immediately.

"What *is* this, Laddner? This is Tom Newcastle's half-breed boy, Cade."

Laddner wiped the back of his hand across his face, leaving a streak of Cade Newcastle's blood there. "I don't give a flying damn whose son he is, but this here is the renegade who stole that woman from the school. We've been chasing him for days and finally caught up with him over in Coulson tonight. I expect there's a reward for the likes of him. We've come to collect it." Laddner propped the stock end of his rifle on the sheriff's table and spit into a brass spittoon poised just at his feet.

"Where's the girl?"

"Probably kilt her," Moran said, sliding a look at Laddner. "Ain't that right, Mitch?"

"He was alone when we found him. If she's anything like the others, she's lying gutted and scalped up in the high country somewhere. We must've missed her."

Sampson frowned, then squinted at the pair. "He alive?"

"Alive enough to hang. I would've saved you the trouble on my own, but I thought the reward might say 'alive,' so here he is."

Sampson rubbed his chin with the back of his beefy hand. "Folks hereabouts are stirred up by this trouble. Most folks thought those days of Cheyenne stealing women were over. I heard there was a boy missing from the Industrial School, too. There was some speculation he might be involved in all this. Any sign of him?"

"A boy?" Laddner slid a troubled look at Moran. "Didn't see no boy. But then, I suppose we could've missed him, too, up there in all the trees."

Sampson bent down to feel for a pulse in Cade's neck. Satisfied he was alive, he straightened, wanting to be rid of these two men as soon as possible. He'd never liked Mitchell Laddner and he'd heard stories about his tactics at the school. Stories that made his skin crawl. Cade Newcastle's condition here spoke for itself. This rough country drew men like Laddner like flies to honey, but they didn't live by any code he could point to except their own self-will. Still, if Tom's son did this thing, there'd be no helping him. He knew Tom Newcastle personally and he dreaded telling him that the culprit responsible for kidnapping a white girl was his son.

"The town took up a collection," he told Laddner, "considering there was not just kidnapping, but assault and horse thievery. There's a two-hundred dollar reward on the head of whoever is responsible. You say it's him. I say, how do you know?"

"We've been trackin' him for days. Plus, there's the scar on his cheek. I saw it that morning he took her from the barn. Clear as day. It's him. Just ask the Reverend Dooley. He saw him, too."

"What you say is true, then you two earned yourself some money tonight. For now, help me get him into that cell. I reckon the doc should have a look at his head. You boys got him good."

Newcastle moaned as they moved him, but didn't wake

up. Sampson noticed the bloody slit and bullet hole in the man's leggings then. "You shoot him, too?"

"I expect that was my bullet that hit him that first day when we were tryin' to save the woman. He left a fine trail of blood for us to follow part ways."

"After they went off that buffalo jump, we thought they was both dead for a while—" Moran began, with a disbelieving laugh, but Laddner elbowed him silent.

"Buffalo jump? And he's still breathing?" Sampson shook his head. "Nobody survives that jump. That place is haunted. See any ghosts up there?"

"These two, we thought, for a while," Moran said. "Still can't figure how they survived."

"Like I said," Laddner interrupted, "she's likely dead and gone. When can we expect our money?"

They backed out of the cell and Sampson locked it shut. "I'll be checkin' in with Reverend Dooley, as you said, and then there'll be a trial. Circuit judge is comin' back to town in a week. We'll get him on his feet by then."

"He's a damned *Indian*," Laddner complained, as if that was enough to convict him.

"He's the son of a prominent rancher hereabouts. That gives him rights. I'll see the doc takes a look at him tonight. Wouldn't do to have him die without a fair trial, would it?"

Laddner spit into the container near his feet again. "You just be worryin' about getting us that money, sheriff. Meanwhile, I don't much care how that half-breed son of a bitch dies."

CHAPTER 16

Ollie stepped back out of the shadows of the building she'd been passing as she'd caught sight of the two men entering Sheriff Sampson's office, with what looked like Cade slung unconscious between them.

Her heart had dropped at the sight. *This is bad. Very bad.*

The two had lingered in Sampson's office for all of ten minutes before exiting. Now, as the men disappeared down the street, she headed toward the small building whose lamplight spilled through the windows and out onto the street.

By now, Sampson was usually locked up and home for the night. She knew Jedediah Sampson as well as she knew any man in this town. A former trapper, he was a solitary type who'd gotten this job not only for his formidable size, but because he seemed to have a moral center that was lacking in other men. He lived alone in a small house up the street and frequented her place at the end of every month. He was one of her few personal customers and there was never any money exchanged in the bargain. First, she thought it good business to keep pleasant relations with the local law. And second, she liked him quite a bit. At her age, she only made room in her bed for men she gave a damn about.

She left the tapestry bag full of clothes she'd been

carrying to Cade outside Sampson's door before entering the office. Above the entrance, a little bell rung.

Sampson was strapping his gun belt to his hips and looked up at her with a smile.

"Ollie."

"Jedediah?"

"What a nice surprise. What brings you out so late? These being business hours for you."

She shrugged. "Surely I don't need a reason to stop by and say hello to a friend."

"Well, I'd be plum flattered if I didn't think you had something else on your mind." He sounded wholly unconvinced and glanced over at the man lying in his cell. "Couldn't have anything to do with my guest, could it?"

She lifted her brows in feigned ignorance. But at her first good look at the man on the cot, she couldn't manage to gulp back her gasp of dismay.

She whispered a curse under her breath.

"Yup. He's stepped in a deep pile of it," Jedediah agreed. "I was about to go fetch Doc Watley. Unless you're of a mind to do it for me."

Unable to drag her gaze away from the wreckage, she said, "Yes. Of course. I-I—"

"He's a friend of yours, isn't he?"

She nodded, unsure of how much to say about his situation to Jedediah without making everything worse. "I don't know what you think he's done, but—"

"Murder, maybe. Kidnapping, at the least. Horse thievery. All of them hanging offenses."

"Murder?"

"That girl he stole is missing."

Ollie bit her tongue. She hadn't gotten to where she was in life by being an impulsive fool and she wasn't about to open her mouth, even to Jed, about Essie Sparks until she knew what was what. "I'll get the doc," she said. "But I'm asking you to keep an open mind, Jed. Cade's no murderer, whether he's living the life you or I would choose for him or not. And he's no horse thief, either. I know him."

"Not every man lives up to your expectations, Ollie. You must know that by now, too."

"What I know," she said, "is I trust my own gut instinct about men. And that's rarely steered me wrong."

"Maybe this is one of those times. You do know that he was accused of raping a white girl many years ago at that fancy school his father sent him to. It ain't common knowledge around here, but Tom confided it to me once. Boy's got the scar to prove it."

The scar! That mark had always been a mystery to her, one of those things he'd kept private. But she had no doubt that if there was a story to be told about what happened, it was his side she'd believe. "A man who rapes a woman doesn't do it for the sex, Jedediah. He does it out of pure meanness. Out of a hatred for women. To show her who's boss and to beat her down. And that doesn't change in a man. That's who and what he is. Cade has never, *ever* hurt one of my girls, or me, nor done anything even close to that since I've known him. And I've known him for a good long while. That sounds like a one-sided tale to me. So I don't believe it. And you shouldn't either."

He folded his arms over his massive chest. "I ain't the judge. Just the law. It won't be up to me to untangle the mess he's in once he gets in front of a judge."

"I'll remember you said that." Ollie gave the low-cut basque bodice on her blue silk gown a tug. "I'll be right back with Doc Watley. Don't you let anything happen to him. Or you'll answer to me."

Essie could not sit still. She paced the small room Ollie had given her, long after she'd finished with the delicious hot water bath the woman had arranged. After the briefest of naps, she'd changed into clean clothes lent to her, begrudgingly, by Lucy. The silk bodice of the bright green gown puckered for lack of volume, but the rest fit as if they'd been born twins. The dress had a narrower skirt and smaller bustle, which was all the fashion now, and looked like it might have come directly from a "Godey's Lady's

Book." It made all of her old things back at the school seem woefully out of date.

"You could use a bit more up there, if you know what I mean," Lucy had advised, cupping her own ample bosom in two hands for effect. "But then we can't all be perfect."

Essie laughed. "They'll have to do, since they're all I have," she agreed, though the possibility of stuffing her camisole with rolled-up socks did, embarrassingly, occur to her.

"Bend over," Lucy said and tapped Essie not so gently between the shoulders. "Now, give the girls a shake. That's it. Let the corset be your friend."

That'll be the day. But when she straightened, miraculously, her breasts looked fuller and, well, perkier. And the bodice lay smooth across her bosom.

Pleased, Lucy stepped back with her hands on her hips. "There's hope for you yet, town girl. You clean up real good."

"Thank you, I think."

"Anyway, not to worry. Cade Newcastle's an *ass* man...I mean..." She gulped back her faux pas. "Well...so I hear." She actually blushed. "What I meant to say was—"

"I suppose Ollie told you everything." Essie glared at the girl from beneath her lashes.

"Only on a need to know basis. And since she left me in charge while she's gone, I needed to know."

By now, Essie was already imagining him in bed with Lucy or probably all of the other girls here. Kissing them. Touching them as he had her. He was a man, after all. On his own. Of course he would.

"You needn't worry. He's not mine, Lucy. We're...I'm not sure what we are. Strangers, I suppose." Except for the time he'd made love to her in that spring. Held her through the night. Saved her.

Lucy made a *tsking* sound. "And you two together all that time? Alone? Seems like a wasted opportunity, if you ask me."

Essie stayed silent, her thoughts traveling over the last

few days together and all the moments that hadn't been about her being a hostage.

"'Course, maybe him bein' a half-breed and all, maybe that's just not your cup of tea. You wouldn't be the first town girl to hold such an opinion."

"First of all, I'm not a town girl, so stop calling me that. I'm a—I *was* a teacher. And second, whatever is or is not between Cade and me, it's our own private business. So I'll thank you not to call me a bigot to my face."

"Well," Lucy said, "I see that bath washed some of the timid right off'a you, eh? And just so you know, 'town girl' is the name we give every woman hereabouts who ain't one of us. Which makes you a town girl. And as far as Cade goes, ain't a female hereabouts who hasn't given him the old up and down. But even though he's Tom Newcastle's son, most of the town girls wouldn't be caught dead with a breed. Which is a shame, 'cause as lovers go—and we don't get too many of those in here—he's an ace. A five-carat stone. And that ain't sayin' nothing about what I think of him as a man. Well, I imagine you've gotten a taste of the kind of man he is by now. I can't think of another one I'd want at my back if the cards all went wrong. You ask Ollie. She'll tell you what's what."

Essie stared at her, speechless.

The girl put her hand on the door handle but said, "You school-learned girls? Sometimes you're the thickest ones when it comes to men."

And with that, she'd gone.

Now, Essie paused at the window to stare out onto the darkened street where oil lamps dotted the muddy strip called Minnesota Avenue in little splotches of light. *Even though he's Tom Newcastle's son*...Lucy had said. All she knew about Cade's father, aside from the fact that he'd rejected his own son out of hand, was that Cade didn't like talking about him. He didn't like talking about himself at all, from what she could tell.

It was the girl's certainty that Essie was a bigot that made her want to scream that she wasn't. She wasn't a bigot. She had no feelings either way about his Cheyenne blood. But she supposed, if she were honest, that wasn't exactly true. She'd never ignored the fact that he was half-Cheyenne. Naturally, it had been quite apparent from the moment they'd met. In fact, he'd used it against her. But as the days passed between them, she'd simply stopped noticing.

Was simply *seeing* the difference between them bigotry? But how could she not see their differences? They existed. They had ceased to matter to her, but they still existed. He was who he was, and she was who she was, and there was no changing that. But in truth, she couldn't think of anything about him she would want to change, except, perhaps his stubbornness. Certainly not the kindness he'd shown her. Or how he protected her at every turn. And not the way he looked—as beautiful as any man she'd ever met. Or how it felt when he touched her. Kissed her. Wrapped his warm weight around her and held her.

No, there was nothing she'd change about him, except the fact that he wasn't here, beside her. So if she was guilty of anything, perhaps it was that she wanted him more than he did her and she would just have to live with that.

She had the gut feeling that getting her to supply him with new clothing had merely been a ruse to get her to ride away from him. And now that Ollie had taken him fresh clothes, he might be miles from here already, looking for the boy, which she couldn't very well hold against him. Finding Little Wolf was all that mattered right now.

She sat on the chair beside the washstand and turned her face toward the window. If those men brought the boy into town, where could he be? Where would she even begin to look?

Think logically. Step by step. Where first?

She closed her eyes. *Think.*

The two men with him were surely up to no good, else Little Wolf wouldn't have been forced to drop his medicine bag or leave a sign on the trail down the mountain. He was certainly hoping someone would follow him, or at least understand he was in trouble.

She imagined the three of them riding into town.

Three. Three horses.

Lalo.

Essie's eyes popped open. Of course, Lalo. The pony he'd stolen from the school. That pony had to be here somewhere. Or at least, someone might have seen it, passing through, if not the boy. If, indeed, Billings was their destination, Lalo would be here, too. Not likely on the street, but stabled somewhere. At a livery?

She shot to her feet.

How many of those could there be in this small town? Perhaps they'd even sold the horse, in which case someone could identify them.

Essie began to pace the small room. Ollie had advised her against going out on her own. And it was dark. She shivered, knowing that Ollie was right. But waiting until morning seemed unthinkable. What might happen to Little Wolf between now and then?

Quickly, she hurried out of the upstairs room and down to the first floor by the back stairs that led to the kitchen. Pink was at the sink, cleaning up the last of the dishes from the evening meal. She hurried to his side.

"Pink, I have a favor to ask."

"No more biscuits. They's all gone for t'night." Then he turned to look at her and his eyes went wide. His gaze swept down her in the gown Ollie had given her. She knew she must look considerably better than she had a few hours ago. But Pink smiled at her for the first time and gave her a nod of approval.

In the next room, the piano plinked away with another song she didn't recognize, along with the raucous sound of laughter and conversation.

"Those biscuits were incredibly delicious, but that's not what I wanted to ask."

"Don't you go tryin' t' butter me all up, Mrs. Sparks. It won't do you no good. I only make biscuits in the afternoon."

"Pink, it's something else entirely."

He stacked the last plate onto the sideboard. "Well, what is it?"

"I need...I need an escort."

He jerked his chin backward in surprise. "You need a *what*?"

"I need a man. To accompany me. Just for a little while. It's dark and it's late and I can't go alone."

He raised an eyebrow in agreement. "Go where?"

"I'm looking for a horse."

"A horse?" Pink looked relieved. "Well, I can get you one of those. We got half a dozen in our—"

"Not any horse. A particular horse. A horse that was stolen and is, possibly, stabled here in town somewhere."

"What for you need *that* horse?"

"That horse will, hopefully, lead me to the men who took him from the boy I'm trying to find. A boy who's missing and desperately needs my help. I cannot impress upon you enough how urgent this is."

Giving his smooth brown head a scratch, Pink frowned at her. "I ain't supposed to leave this place at night. Girls, they might need me."

"I know. But it won't take long. I have money. I'll pay you."

Insulted, he turned back to his dishes. "Ain't about the money."

Essie glanced out the glass window in the door at the darkened alley. "I only thought...for your trouble. But forgive me if I insinuated that you needed money to help me. I know that's not why you said no. But I think Ollie would make an exception for this. It's about Cade's nephew. He's the one that's missing and we both fear something bad might have befallen him. That horse, his pony, is my only clue as to where he might have gone."

Pink threw the dishrag into the water and left her standing there, disappearing into the salon where customers and girls mingled.

Well, that went badly. Naturally, she'd mangled it all. Which left her on her own.

Hanging on a peg by the door she saw a red, crocheted shawl which she pulled down to wrap around her shoulders. At least Ollie couldn't claim she hadn't tried.

But before she could turn the knob on the door, Pink reappeared, wearing a patched brown jacket and looking like a dark raincloud.

"Well, if we's gonna go, let's get it done."

A smile broke out on her face. "Oh, Pink. You're an angel."

"I ain't no angel. And I ain't fond of barns at night—bats and owls 'n such—but let's us get it over with in a right hurry, 'fore Ollie come back."

With a quick nod, she tightened the shawl around her shoulders and headed out the door.

Cade swam up from the darkness, fighting the heaviness that held him down. Voices drifted toward him in waves and he tried to pick them out.

"No broken skull, is my guess." *A man's voice, low and steady.*

"His cheek? It looks bad…"

And…Ollie?

Where was he? In a bed. Hard. In a place with echoes.

He felt the weight shift beside him as someone stood.

"Not sure I can say the same for that cheekbone of his." *A doctor?*

"How can you be sure?" Ollie's voice now, coming from nearby. "About his head?"

"Tuning fork makes a certain sound on healthy bone and less so on fractured bone. I can hear it with my stethoscope and to me, sounds like he got lucky."

Lucky?

A wave of pain crashed through him. He kept his eyes closed. Feigned sleep. Afraid he knew exactly where he was.

"…put in a few stitches back there and in a couple of days, head'll feel good as new. Not much I can do for the cheek, though. Looks like maybe someone kicked him."

Even now, he could recall the sight of that rifle butt coming at him.

"...needs rest...been through a lot the last week," the doctor continued. "I'll check back in the morning if you want."

"I ain't sure that's necess—" the other man began.

"I *want*," Ollie insisted. "I'll pay for your time." He heard the sound of a few coins exchanging hands.

"You heard her, Doc. See you in the mornin'?"

"You will."

The sound of footsteps across a hard floor. A door opening with a little jingle bell. Ollie's fingers brushing his hair off his face.

He forced his eyes open and attempted to sit up. Pain knocked him back.

"Settle down, honey," Ollie told him, pressing him back to the cot. "You're hurt pretty bad."

He groaned and slammed his eyes shut again. "Ollie. Where...where am I?"

"In jail. Billings. But I expect that's no real surprise. Considering..."

A curse fell from his cut-up mouth. "Laddner."

"That's the one."

"Essie?"

"Safe at my place," she told him. "Don't you worry about her."

Gingerly, he touched his broken lip with his tongue, then fingered his tender cheek. "Get her on a train in the morning."

"You better be thinkin' about your own self, Cade. Because they aim to hang you. And not just for stealin' that horse the boy took." That didn't seem to surprise him either. "They think your girl's dead. Up there in those mountains. They think you killed her."

He half grinned. "Good. Better that than what they'd do to her if they knew she wasn't."

"Don't be a fool, Cade. You tell them she's alive. If you don't, I will."

He grabbed her arm. "No. You won't. And don't you tell her where I am either."

"I'll do no such thing, you stubborn, mule-headed—"

"Yes. You will. I'm a lost cause anyway, Ollie. They'll hang me and then destroy a good woman. She doesn't deserve that. So you won't." He squeezed his eyes shut, waiting for a wave of pain to pass. "But I need you to find the boy, Ollie. He's…he's in trouble and I need you to find him."

Relenting, she patted his hand. "Don't you worry about him now. I'll find him, if he's to be found. You try to get some rest. I'm not giving up on you, Cade, so don't think you'll get off that easy. What were you thinkin', takin' that town girl anyway?"

"Instinct."

"Huh. Well, that Cheyenne instinct of yours could use some polishing up, I'd say."

Cade watched her through half-opened eyes with a rare fondness. She was the closest thing to a confidant as any person in his life, and he supposed it was because she knew, better than most, how to keep secrets. She did that well. But she could be a pain in the ass as easily.

She met his gaze with affection. Ollie's age was a mystery, but he guessed her to be closer to forty than thirty. She had an ageless face and not a strand of gray hair, which he supposed could be accounted for by the brassy auburn color that was her trademark.

"This is what comes of being a lone wolf, like you are, Cade. This is when you need your friends, not turnin' inward and givin' up."

"No sermons now, Ollie. I just need you to help them. Essie and the boy."

"Have I ever refused you anything?" Her cocoa-colored eyes softened as she watched him. "I do like her though. Your hostage girl."

"She's not my hostage. She never was."

"No, I guessed she wasn't. But I'd say she's falling in love with you."

He turned his head away and closed his eyes. He was tired. Bone tired and he ached all over. He couldn't think about his feelings for Essie now. Couldn't allow himself to remember her soft green eyes or the way she'd asked him to make love to her. If he did, he'd only end up blaming himself again, because it was—really, all of it—his fault. But mostly, what had happened to her.

"You rest, Cade," Ollie said, standing up. "I'll see you in the morning."

"You remember what I said," he warned.

"I'll remember."

CHAPTER 17

———— ◆ ————

Essie and Pink moved down the darkened streets of Billings, avoiding crowds near the local saloons and gambling palaces and places illuminated by streetlamps. Pink was not only acquainted with all the liveries in town, but he also claimed he knew most of the stablemen who operated them.

By the time the moon had risen in the sky, they'd checked all but the last with no luck at all. No sign of Lalo and they'd found no one who'd seen a boy fitting Little Wolf's description either.

Discouragement weighted her steps as they walked to the last place. She'd been so sure she'd been right. To fail was simply unacceptable. Yet it seemed that Little Wolf had vanished like smoke once he'd made it here. It seemed altogether likely that they'd merely passed through town on their way to some other destination. A mine, perhaps. Those mining camps nearby infamously employed children for slave wages to explore their most dangerous shafts where adults could not fit. Immigrant children and even those children of the Cheyenne who were no longer eligible for school. *God help him if they've taken him there.*

Finding him in one of those camps, scattered as they were throughout the southern part of Montana Territory, might take months if not years.

What else could those men possibly want with a boy like Little Wolf?

Pink took her arm. "This way." Steering her down a darkened alley, she thanked her lucky stars again that he was with her. She would have been a fool not to listen to Ollie on this. The streets of Billings at night were no place for a woman alone. Or, in her opinion, *anyone* alone.

Klingman's Stables sat at the far edge of town, near the cattle pens and the rail yards. In fact, it wasn't clear where the cattle pens ended and the stable paddocks began until she saw a row of hacks and wagons lined up against one fence line, and finally, a hand-lettered sign over an inconspicuous entryway.

Pink tugged at the door only to find it locked up tight. "Dad blast it," he muttered. "Must've closed for the night."

"Maybe we can sneak in the back through the fence and take a peek?"

"And get your fool head shot off?" He shook his head like she was daft.

"Good point," she agreed. "Does that mean someone is watching the place?"

"Retired for the night, and prob'ly not feelin' all that generous about bein' disturbed, I reckon. Might 'soon blow us to kingdom come for trespassing, as answer the door."

"I thought you said you knew him."

"I *do* know him. That's the problem. He's…ornery."

"Could you, for me, Pink? He's our last hope."

He considered, looking none too happy about it. "Why don't we come back in the morning?"

"If he was your boy, would you wait?"

With a sigh, he turned and raised a fist to the door. "That there's why I never had no children." He pounded on the door and they waited a minute. Two. He pounded again.

"We're closed!" came a shout from behind the door.

"It's me! Pink! Open up, Hiram. I need a favor."

"And I need my bones to quit aching," Hiram complained. "But nobody's makin' that happen. So go away."

"We're looking for a horse, Hiram. A small paint. Brought in the last two or three days or so. Seen one like that?"

"No!"

Essie's face fell as she met Pink's look.

"You sure?" Pink shouted through the door again. "Mostly white with patches of—"

"Maybe," Hiram grumbled. "Lemme think a minute."

She and Pink waited while Hiram contemplated. Then they heard the heavy lock open.

"Well? What are you waitin' for? Come on in."

Hiram was a small, crooked man with shaggy gray hair and a belly from too much whiskey. He frowned up at her, then at Pink.

"Hiram Klingman? This here is Mrs. Sparks. Mrs. Sparks? Hiram."

"Don't like surprises," Hiram grumbled, half to himself, as he turned to make his way into the stables. "A man can't hardly have a moment's peace anymore."

They walked to the far back of the stable. When they reached the last stall, Lalo peered over the door and gave them a sniff.

"This the one you mean?"

Essie had never been so happy to see a horse in all her born days. "It's her! It's Lalo!" she cried. "I knew it. I knew I'd find you somewhere."

"Funny you'd ask about her. I had a bad feelin' about this one." Hiram scratched his ear. "Something about them two fellers made me itchy."

"They stole her, those men, from a boy," Essie said, petting the horse's velvet nose. "What can you tell me about them? Did you recognize them? Have you seen them before?"

"Horse thieves? Nope, can't say I have. But they paid me with a gold piece for her board."

"A gold piece. So they didn't try to sell her?"

"I wasn't buyin'. Like I said, something about them two. But I reckon they aim to sell her if they find a buyer."

"Did they mention where they were staying? Anything? What did they look like? Did you get their names?"

"That's a lot of questions, missy."

"They took that horse from a boy we're lookin' for," Pink told him. "He could be in real trouble. So anything you remember might help us find him."

Hiram erased the crankiness from his expression with an effort, tucking his fingers into the straps of his seen-better-days overalls. "I think they were brothers. I heard one of them call the other one...what was it? Payton, I think was the name he used. He was the tall one. The other one, a head shorter and thick as a board. But they were jangling a bag o' gold coins between them like they'd just struck it rich."

Essie slid a worried look at Pink. "Anything else you can remember? Any little thing?"

He thought for a minute. "Well, I'm not much for reading. But I did notice some kind of symbols on that little gold bag of theirs because they was unusual. I've seen 'em before on some hogsheads and crates gettin' offloaded at the rail yard. And if I ain't mistaken, those symbols were Chinese letters."

Little Wolf staggered through the opium room, carrying a covered bucket of offal, trying not to breathe. Naturally, that was impossible, so he inhaled some of the sweet-smelling smoke the men lying on the beds exhaled. Most of them looked asleep. Those who weren't were on top of a woman who stared with dead eyes at the ceiling as she let the man have sex with her.

Except for animals, he'd never before seen real sex, though he'd heard his parents beneath their buffalo robe when he'd been just a boy, and he'd learned young what that was. But that seemed nothing like what was happening here. His mother used to giggle and speak softly to his father and sometimes make noises of pleasure. If these girls made noises, they were noises of pain, grunting sounds as men forced themselves on them.

He'd walked past a room occupied by Shyen Zu and an older Chinese man who'd paid four bits for her time. That was two bits more than some of the other girls got, though she kept none of that money for herself.

Little Wolf had stopped outside her door and listened to the bed rock against the flimsy wall, to the sounds of the man grunting, to Shyen Zu's gasps of pain when he did something to her Little Wolf could not see. He'd had the impulse to break down the door at that terrible sound. To rescue her. But Chen Lee had walked by then and struck him with his cane for standing still. And, shamefully, he'd moved on.

Later, when he'd seen her, Shyen Zu's face was bruised and she wouldn't talk to him.

A fist of anger had boiled up in his chest for her. He wanted to kill Chen Lee and the man who'd hurt her.

With a start, he realized that the violence that had bubbled up in him, since that stay in the Wages of Sin, was relatively new. Never before that had he wanted to take another person's life. Never had he even wished another dead. But now he felt that part of him that once believed things could get better leaking away from him. Was this how it was to be a man? Was revenge a sacred duty in this world? Did a man have to kill to survive?

It was not the way of the Human Beings. At least, he didn't think so. Counting coup was true bravery, his father had told him. To get close enough to kill one's enemy, but only touch instead. That way, the enemy would know how close they came to death. And then they would have to live with that defeat.

But the old ways wouldn't work on men like Chen Lee, or the men who took him up in the mountains. Or Sergeant Laddner. Men like those did not understand about courage or honor.

Perhaps he didn't either. Now, all he cared about was getting out. Getting out with Shyen Zu.

So as he worked, he watched for opportunity. Like an eagle, hovering on the currents of air, he watched. Waiting.

Knowing he would find it.

As he set the half-full bucket down to tip another piss pot in, opportunity scurried across his line of vision with a flash of silver. The simple three-toothed comb bounced across the floor with a metallic *ping*, unnoticed by the girl from whom it had fallen.

He blinked at the thing, instantly categorizing its usefulness.

Glancing around to see if anyone was watching, he reached for the comb and stuffed it in his pocket before hurrying off to finish his job.

With an effort that cost him, Cade rolled toward the moonlight spilling through the barred window and gazed out at the stars. He could not see the valley from here, or the street, but he could hear the sound of people there, even at this late hour. And he could see the halo of the oil street lamps of Billings which had been, no doubt, lit by Boone Proctor, a kindly drunk who earned his meager living lighting and dampening the streetlamps.

But the stars…they blinked to life in the velvet wash of black above. Through the small window of his cell tonight, the sky felt boundless.

He felt small.

This country, the valley that surrounded Billings, was as much a part of him as the mountains they'd come down. It wasn't often he thought of the land here this way, but he loved it. This land was his history, muddled though it was, and in his heart he'd always imagined he would end up here one day, settled permanently.

And by permanent, he didn't mean in Boot Hill, the cemetery above the town, where more than a few men had ended their Montana dreams. But it looked like he might have miscalculated on that account as well.

He'd gone over options in his mind again and again tonight. If there were regrets to be had, losing Little Wolf and Essie were two. But he'd run flat out of options on both accounts now.

There was what he *should* do and what was best to do. Those two things were seemingly at odds with one another.

Something came back to him then. Something Three Bears, his grandfather, had told him once during one of his summer visits with the People.

He'd been almost thirteen then, that summer before his mother's death. The summer before his life changed unalterably. He'd been showing off for some girl, riding with the other boys in a dangerous way that ended with a collision and a broken arm for his friend, Running Fox.

It was not the way of the People to punish such foolish behavior. Instead, his grandfather took him for a long walk. He said nothing along the way, even when they reached the top of the rim rock. There, they sat for hours, listening to the wind blow in the grasses around them. They sat until his legs fell asleep and his back ached and Cade could no longer take the silence and he broke. He told his grandfather about wanting to impress the girl, about his jealousy of Running Fox who always caught the eye of the girls and always bested him in competitions. He'd told him that he'd known how he acted was wrong. That he should have been the one who broke his arm.

"Do you know why I brought you here?" his grandfather asked.

He didn't. Unless the silence itself was the punishment.

The old man ran his hand over the red soil and sifted it through his fingers. "You are a boy who lives in two worlds. Your father's world and the world of the Human Beings. The *vé'ho'e* world is not like ours. They forgot how to listen to the earth. They listen to each other, instead, and argue the right and wrong of things. They think they own the ground. They rip down the trees to make fields and take rocks from the holes they dig and use them for their money. They do not sit on the earth or sleep in the sacred circle. They no longer hear the wind in the grass, or, if they do, they cannot remember what it is saying.

"Your blood is both *vé'ho'e* and *Tsitsista*. One day, you will choose between those worlds. Perhaps you will remember this day when I crumbled the earth in my hands. You will think of the way of the Human Beings. When your path is uncertain, sit and listen to the earth. It will speak to you. Wait, in the quiet, until it does. Then you will know what is right. Then, choose without fear, because your path will be honorable."

Cade gathered a fistful of dirt from the jail floor and flung it toward the open window. He watched it sparkle and float in the moonlight before disappearing from sight.

Listen. Wait. You will know what is right.

Honorable.

Fight for my life? Or fight for theirs? Anything it takes to clear my name would smear Essie's. Or Little Wolf's.

It seemed useless to consider his growing feelings for Essie. She couldn't understand who or what he was— something in-between. It didn't stop him from wanting her. He ached with wanting her. He could still feel her heated kiss against his mouth. The soft give of her body against his.

"You talk about fear, as if I'm the only one who has something to lose here," Essie had said. *"But I think it's you who's afraid, Cade...so don't pretend that thinking of me as your hostage, to push me away, is for my sake. At least admit it's for yours."*

A wave of pain washed over him and he rolled onto his back. Nothing was clear to him anymore. Not honor or fear or...whatever he was feeling for the woman who'd given herself to him in that hot spring. But he would be damned if he would put her in more jeopardy.

He closed his eyes, knowing soon enough daylight would come. And he would take it in greedily, knowing his days were numbered.

CHAPTER 18

Ollie was waiting for them at the door when they returned to the sporting house.

"Well? I thought I left you two here with specific orders to stay put," she said before they could offer any excuses.

"Please don't blame Pink," Essie said. "I twisted his arm, and truthfully, he knew I'd just go on my own if he didn't help me."

"Damn fool girl," Ollie muttered. "I'm doin' my best to keep you safe."

When Essie explained where they'd been, Ollie was only slightly mollified. "It could'a waited until daylight."

"Maybe, but *I* couldn't. I think we know where Little Wolf is," Essie told her. "At least, generally speaking. I think those men might've traded him for that gold."

"Well, that is bad news," Ollie said, "because once that happens, it's the Devil's own work to get him out."

"So you've heard of this happening before? Of a boy being sold there?"

She nodded. "There's very little regulation down in the Chinese quarter, no oversight at all. They take care of their own and don't bother the townsfolk. They do things differently there. They keep girls in cribs and treat them like chattel."

"Why doesn't someone help them?" Essie asked.

Pink glanced at Ollie and she looked away. "Someone should. But women have few rights hereabouts, in case you hadn't noticed. China girls, even less. It's a fact of life."

Essie shook her head. "Only because we—all of us—allow it."

With a sharp look, Ollie studied her for a long time, contemplating what, Essie couldn't imagine. Finally, she rolled her eyes and said, "You're absolutely right. Pink, I have something to tell you. Essie, this is not for your ears. But if you happen to hear what I'm about to say, then we shall be agreed that I told you nothing."

Confused, Essie stared at her, a bad feeling crawling up her spine. "And what, exactly, am I not to hear?"

Ollie turned directly to Pink. "Pink, Cade's been arrested. He is in jail right now as we speak."

"What?" Essie gawped.

Ollie ignored her. "Those two men who were chasing him caught up with him in Coulson and trounced him pretty good."

"How bad is he?" Essie demanded.

Still talking to Pink, she said, "Doc's already seen him. No use anyone trying to see him tonight. Morning'll be soon enough. But they're chargin' him with horse thievery and kidnapping, as well as the murder of a certain teacher from the Industrial School who is apparently still missing—"

"They're what?" Wide-eyed, Essie could hardly believe what she was hearing.

"—and if they don't come to understand that she's alive and well—"

"Of course I'm alive and well."

"—or that the boy stole that horse, and not Cade, then they'll hang him for certain."

Hang him? Oh, dear God. "Stop talking as if I'm not in the room!"

"Now, Pink," Ollie continued, "since I promised that mule-headed friend of mine in jail that I would not impart any of this information to Mrs. Sparks, and that I'd make sure she was on a train east first thing in the morning—"

Essie scoffed and jammed her hands on her hips. "I most certainly will *not* be."

"—the only way she can hear about him is if you tell her, as you made no such promises to him. I will leave that in your capable hands."

Pink shook his head disbelievingly, then slowly turned to Essie. "Mrs. Sparks," he began. "It 'pears that Cade has been taken—"

"Oh, for heaven's sake! I don't need to hear it again. News like that is bad enough the first time." She turned back to the door. "I'm going right now to see him."

"He doesn't want you to know where he is."

"I don't care if he doesn't like it. I will not let him hang for something he didn't even do."

"So…he didn't take you?" Ollie asked, pinning her with a look.

"Well," she equivocated, "that…that's a complicated issue."

"I don't think they'll think it's complicated. Either he did or he didn't, Essie."

She pressed her hands together. Cade's life might all boil down to what she said about that first morning. What she was willing to say. "He didn't. I…I chose to go with him. On my own."

"That's not what they claim they saw. At least, that's the talk around town."

"They can say whatever they want. If *I* say he didn't kidnap me, then they can hardly say he did."

Ollie and Pink exchanged dark looks. "You know what that will mean for you, don't you, Essie?" she warned. "To claim you willingly ran off with a man like Cade?"

A man like Cade? She recalled all the times he'd saved her life, protected her, wrapped himself around her to keep her warm. She thought of the hot spring and the memory of him inside her sent a wave of longing through her. Did she know what running off with a man like Cade meant for her? "Can you imagine that I do not understand?" she asked

Ollie. "But I dare anyone to call me a liar."

"No one's callin' you anything, least of all me. I know the man Cade is. But there are a bunch of witnesses who'll say otherwise. Who'll claim he had a knife to your throat."

"Be that as it may. Let them say what they will. If I don't press charges, what can they do? And if they press me, let them explain shooting at us both on the way out. They could have easily killed me themselves. So if their great concern is for my well-being, let them explain that."

"They can do whatever they want, and usually do. And they can still hang him for stealing that horse—"

Pink interrupted. "I reckon if there's any horse thieves to be had, it was them that tried to sell that pony to Hiram. Find them, find your horse thieves."

"That might work. But the boy…" Ollie began.

"Yeah, about him." Pink grabbed Ollie's coat off the rack near the door. "They can't rightly claim it was the boy stole that horse without admittin' the low-down thing they done to him. We need to go find him before somethin' worse happens. And it might take more than us findin' him to get him out. It might take cash."

"*My* cash?" Ollie asked, but the question was rhetorical.

Essie shook her head at Pink. "Certainly selling a Cheyenne boy is illegal. Can't we just get the sheriff? Take him back? After all, slavery was—"

"You're talkin' about a Cheyenne boy," Pink told her. "And there's some things even the law won't step into out here. The Chinese world is one of 'em."

"What makes you think we can buy him back?" Ollie asked.

"If we can't, we'll take him," Essie vowed. "But I'll pay you back whatever it costs."

"Last I heard, you're fresh outta work."

Pink's gaze slid to Essie, one dark eyebrow raised.

"I have some money saved back at the school," she said, though it was all she had in the world. "It's not much, but it will be a start."

Ollie frowned with a sigh. "Keep your money. I'll bring

what I've got on hand. You know where to look for him?"

"We have a good idea." Holding the coat up for Ollie, Pink sent Essie a slow, certain smile.

It never hurt, Essie thought, to have a man who wore the name Pink so well on your side in a fight. "I have one stop to make first. After that, we'll go find the boy."

The silver comb bent easily in Little Wolf's hands in the darkened hole of a room in which Chen Lee kept him. With his fingers, he worked the teeth of the comb until one was separated from the others and bent at just the right angle.

Now, he fitted the tine of the comb into the lock of the manacle strapped around his leg and gave it a jiggle. Lock-picking was a trick many of the children had learned at the school. There was a root cellar they kept padlocked outside the kitchen and there never seemed to be enough to eat. Hunger drove them to invention, and when no one was looking, he and some of the other boys would sometimes pilfer apples and other food to distribute among the children. If the disappearing food was later discovered, it was assumed to be a shortage from the store. They never suspected the children of being clever enough to manage it. No one had found the courage to try the same thing on the padlock of Wages of Sin while someone was inside, though it would have been a better use of their skill than pilfering apples. But Wages was at the center of the courtyard and too hard to approach.

He put the place that had lived in his nightmares from his mind. He would never go back. If they caught him, he would find a way to escape again. But he wouldn't get caught. Tonight would be his last night in these chains, and Shyen Zu's as well.

He and Shyen Zu would run away together like Huckleberry Finn and Tom Sawyer, and maybe they'd even build a raft to float down the Yellowstone to his mother's camp. Or he would make her his wife so no man could ever hurt her again. Not that he wanted to take a wife to his blankets yet, but a Cheyenne boy could do worse than

Shyen Zu, the prettiest girl he'd ever seen.

The manacle made a click as he twisted the comb inside the lock and it fell open on his ankle. The metal clanged against the floor and he trapped it in his hand before it could make even more noise.

He released a breath and stretched out his leg. A raw, bruised spot on his ankle ached, but he ignored it, getting to his feet and hobbling toward the closed door. Pressing his back against it, he stopped to listen.

In the room next door, the bedstead banged against the wall and he heard the low, sharp demands of a man's voice. He didn't know the name of the girl in that room, but he had seen her, a sad-faced girl with blank eyes. Every now and then he saw her sip on the pipe in the smoke room with some man she was pleasuring. It was perhaps the only way to survive the life in this place for a girl like her.

The rhythm beat faster and faster, along with other noises coming from the rooms around him. The cacophony of sounds at night, he'd found, made sleeping impossible, but would likely cover his own escape if he was lucky.

Chen Lee hadn't locked his door, having chained him in place, but that was his mistake. He'd been here long enough to realize that the old man's belly had only one soft spot. A small window of time, every night, when most of the girls were working and he'd chained Little Wolf in his room, Chen Lee took the pipe himself. Not a lot and not enough to put him to sleep like it did his clients. But for a few minutes, his hawk-like eyes relaxed and he felt safe.

Little Wolf opened the door, peeked down the hall, then slipped out to find her.

A banging on the jailhouse door woke Cade from a fitful sleep. He jerked awake and instantly regretted it as pain knifed through him. It took him only moments to remember where he was and why. He lowered his head back down to the thin pillow. The heavy pulse in his ears made his head ache again.

From somewhere nearby, he heard the creak of a jail cell

door opening and the sheriff stumbling around, muttering in the dark. Earlier, the sheriff had kicked the drunk out who'd previously occupied that cell and had bunked down for the night here. Cade supposed the sheriff had reason to be cautious. He had a real "murderer" in his jail cell and sentiments in town were, no doubt, running hot against him. He guessed he should be grateful for the protection, but it didn't really matter now. They would have their pound of flesh one way or the other soon enough.

The banging started up again and, with his Colt drawn, the sheriff looked through the window at the person doing the banging. "I'll be," he muttered. He lit a lamp and unlocked the door.

Rolling a look in that direction, Cade's curiosity was piqued.

"Sheriff Sampson? My name is Essie Sparks and as you can see, I'm very much alive."

Cade's heart sank. *Oh, Essie…no.*

The tall man ran a hand down his face and stepped back from the door. "Ma'am? If you are, indeed, who you say you are, it's good to see you lookin' so…healthy. Come on inside. Ollie? Pink? I suppose you knew about this earlier?"

Ollie made no reply, she just glanced in Cade's direction with apology. Apparently, she'd no sooner left him than she broke her promise not to tell Essie about him. A girl he hardly recognized walked in after Ollie. No longer the ragged girl who'd survived four days in the mountains with him, Essie was so pretty it almost made his heart stop.

"I assume," Sampson continued, "I can get folks to vouch that you are who you say you are."

"Anyone at the school knows me." She lifted her gaze to Cade.

Her first good glimpse of him, as he rolled slowly to a sit, made her bite her lip and turn away. He could only imagine how he must look after getting worked over by Laddner.

She swallowed thickly before turning back to the sheriff. "There's been a misunderstanding."

"Well," Sampson said, "I can see you're breathin', which

is a clear improvement over the supposition we all had. Bein' taken by a renegade—"

"It *was* a renegade, a Crow, I think, but it wasn't this man. I've never seen this man before in my life."

Sampson wasn't fooled. "Is that so?"

He glanced back at Cade, who watched, feeling the weight of the lie on his shoulders.

"Yes. It is." She lifted her chin, her gaze straight and steady at the sheriff.

"You surprise me, Mrs. Sparks, you bein' a respectable widow woman and all. Teacher of children. I'm afraid that dog won't hunt."

His accusation seemed to throw her. "What do you mean? It's true."

"He's been identified by that scar on his cheek and by that Appaloosa that is well-known to be his. And not just by Mitchell Laddner, but by the Reverend Dooley himself." He lifted a wanted poster from his desk and handed it to her. It was a picture of Cade, right down to his silver-gray eyes.

"So now what do you have to say?" Sampson asked.

"Say nothing, Essie," Cade told her.

Eyes downcast, she looked young. Impossibly young, standing there trying to lie for him. And pretty. So pretty. Ollie had cleaned her up and put her in some yellow thing that made her look like a ray of sunshine, all tucked and cinched and proper. And her hair...she'd put her hair up away from her face. It made that sprinkle of freckles stand out on her suddenly flushed cheeks.

He drank in the sight of her, pinning her in his memory the way she looked right now. Because if she was lucky, Jedediah Sampson would let her get off with a warning because of her lie and by morning, she'd be on that train heading east.

"You're right," she said at last. "I was hoping not to have to reveal what really happened, for all of our sakes. And especially because...no crime occurred."

"Essie," he warned again. "Stop talking."

"The truth is he didn't kidnap me. I went willingly with him. In fact, I was…we were running off together."

With a groan, Cade dropped his head in his hands and dragged his fingers through his hair. "She's lying," he muttered. "You know she's lying."

"You're sayin' you ran off with him with a knife at your throat?"

Her fingers toyed with her gold locket. "Whatever they *think* they saw, there was…a lot of confusion that morning. A lot of chaos with gunfire, but Cade did nothing to hurt me," she said. "In fact, he saved my life several times."

"He did, did he? You mean while he was bein' chased down for kidnappin' you?"

"He was protecting me. From the beginning. They were shooting at me that morning as well, and doing nothing to make sure they didn't hit me. Cade was the only thing standing between me and their guns and he took a bullet in the leg for it. And if that's not enough, you should know that Mitchell Laddner intended to shoot me if he found me, sheriff. To put me down like a ruined dog after he saw me go off with Cade. It would be a mercy, he told his friend, Moran, having been tainted by contact with a Cheyenne. A mercy. Did he mention that to you? Did he mention that we overheard him say those very words as we were hiding from him at the buffalo jump?"

For the first time, the sheriff's expression shifted. "He did mention losing you two at the jump, but said nothing about—"

"Of course he didn't. But if he'd caught us, you can be sure I wouldn't be standing here telling you this now. He had his own plans for me, because I gave him the mitten back at the Industrial School—monster that he is. And he wanted Cade dead, as well, for something he witnessed years ago. I believe it involved Laddner's cold-blooded murder of an innocent Cheyenne woman and child in an unprovoked raid of a peaceful camp at the Powder River. So, yes, we ran for our lives from them, because they intended, wholeheartedly, to murder us both. And I suppose the only reason Cade is even alive now is because there was a reward offered. Am I right? God forbid, Laddner would miss the chance to cash in on Cade's demise."

"Jedediah, listen to her," Ollie implored. "There is no crime if there is no victim. She says she wasn't one. I know Cade, too. He's not the devil they're saying he is."

Sampson went silent, rounding his desk and glancing back at Cade. "No use ganging up on me. This whole thing smells like a two-day-old trout. And I ain't sure what to believe. On top of that, he claims you're lying, Mrs. Sparks," he said, glancing at Cade. "Anyway, it ain't up to me. A judge will decide what's what. And besides the fact, there's a horse thievin' charge attached as well. A nice paint pony from the school went missing. Not to mention the other ones got loose."

"I happen to know that paint horse they're looking for," Essie said, "is sitting in a stable down the street, boarded there by two drifters who clearly stole it themselves and tried to sell it to Hiram Klingman."

Cade lifted his head, the first inkling of hope fighting through his darkness. *They found the horse? What about the boy?*

"So how do you connect that to Cade, who wasn't even in town when those men brought that horse in?" Essie asked.

"Well," Sampson allowed with a shake of his head. He folded his arms across his massive chest. "I reckon I could ask how it is you know which horse got stole, if it wasn't Cade who took it. But I imagine you'd have an answer for me about it, am I right?"

Cade got slowly to his feet and wrapped his hands around the bars, hoping Essie would hear his thoughts: *Don't tell him about Little Wolf. Keep him out of this tangled mess.*

Looking the sheriff dead in the eye, all she said was, "I can show you where the horse is."

Essie flicked a look at Cade and sent him a secret smile as Sampson shuffled through a stack of wanted posters.

"There's two sides to every story," he said at last. "And

all of that will require some lookin' into. But you should know, ma'am, you ain't doin' yourself no favors with your tellin' of it. And I'm advising you now for your own good."

Seáa...you'd have better luck telling an owl to crow.

"I appreciate the warning," Essie told him, "but the opinions of people who care nothing for me matter even less to me. Now, if you don't mind, I'd like a private word with Cade."

"I suppose it's all right. Just for a minute though. You've got no guns on you, do you?"

She released a nervous breath and held her arms out. "No."

"All right, then."

Ollie and Pink reluctantly walked outside and the sheriff moved to the other side of his desk and shuffled papers.

"What do you think you're doing?" Cade demanded when she moved close enough to speak in a whisper.

"Saving your neck." She wrapped her fingers around his on the bars, her eyes brimming with moisture. "Cade, are you all right? You look terrible."

He tried for a smile, but didn't quite make it. "I've been better. I warned you to stay away from me. Now look what you've done."

"Yes. Look," she whispered back. "I knew I shouldn't have left you back there. Alone."

"I let my guard down. It was my own fault. What about the boy? Do you know where he is?"

"Not yet. But we think he might be somewhere in the Chinese quarter."

A bad feeling crawled up his throat. "How do you know?"

"The gold coins those two were tossing around for Hiram Klingman were in a bag marked with Chinese lettering. I think those two men...I think they might have sold him for money."

Cade felt the blood drain from his face. He cursed silently.

"But to whom," she said, "we just don't know. If we can

find those men—"

"Only the dodgiest of businesses would risk that kind of thing," he said, feeling suddenly lightheaded again. "And if I had to guess, I'd try the seedy little opium den down by the river, run by a weasel of a man named Chen Lee."

"You know him?"

"Of him. Worst-kept secret in Billings is his little drug and whoring operation. He brings them up by wagon from the riverfront brothels of San Francisco. They're no better than slaves there, muddle-headed by that opium the customers smoke. Rumor is Lee murders the girls who are no longer useful to him, though no one has actually caught him at it yet."

"Oh, no," she breathed. "Cade—"

His bruised fingers tightened on hers. "Find him quietly. Don't get the sheriff involved. I don't want the boy in the middle of this whole mess."

"All right. But what if we—"

"If all else fails, go to my father. Tell him the boy is White Owl's son. She was my mother's sister."

"But…how will I find him?"

"Ollie knows his spread. He won't do it for me, but he might for White Owl's sake. Now go. And don't come back here. You've done enough damage to yourself already."

Stubbornly, she pulled her fingers away from his and whispered, "Don't tell me what to do."

Ignoring her, he gripped the bars harder. "When you find him, *if* you find him, you give him to Ollie, then get on that train and get out of town. Make yourself a good life somewhere. You hear me? Don't look back."

Lowering her gaze, she sniffed and leaned closer. "You're right. It makes no sense for me to care what happens to you. I should just turn away and try to live what's left of my life with as much dignity as I can muster after this…this debacle. And in truth, what we know about each other could be fit inside a thimble. Except," she added, "for the things that really matter. Like the fact that I trust you. Like your compassion and your bravery."

He said nothing, but lowered his eyes now too, unable to look at her face. Knowing what he'd see there. She was ripping him apart.

"Time to go, Mrs. Sparks," the sheriff called over to her.

She turned back to Cade. "So, I'm going to go now. And I'm going to find the boy and after that? Well…you're just going to have to live with whatever happens."

She left him standing there, gripping the bars like a caged animal. Alone.

CHAPTER 19

Little Wolf found Shyen Zu in her room, curled up in the corner. He'd waited until he saw the old man who had just used her leave, straightening his baggy cotton clothing as he walked.

"Come with me," he whispered to her when he snuck into her room. "We're leaving this place."

Her eyes went wide as she looked up at him, the bruise on her cheek still ugly and purple. With a shake of her head, she refused him. "No go. You stay."

"No. Shyen Zu, you will *die* here. *I* will die here. We can't stay. Run away with me and I will protect you. I will take you to my mother and her people. They will help you."

She sliced a hand across her throat and shook her head again. "You *boy*. Chen Lee kill. Quick, quick. He own Shyen Zu."

"I will take his scalp if he tries." He produced the small knife he had pilfered from the opium cutting room. Chen Lee hadn't yet missed it.

Afraid, she got to her feet, staring at the weapon. With a quick, longing look out the barred window at the darkened street beyond, she considered her situation. Little Wolf watched a dozen different emotions flicker across her expression before she finally turned back to him. A small, first-time-ever smile hitched her mouth that made her even more beautiful. "*Shi,*" she whispered.

"Yes? That means yes?"

"Yes."

He grabbed her hand and tugged her toward the door. Then he pressed a finger against his lips. "Follow me."

Pink, Ollie and Essie crouched in the alley across from Chen Lee's Opium House, watching Chinese men go in and come out of the tent that sat in front of the hastily built two-story building. Overhead, the moon was less than a crescent, so except for the meager light spilling from the cribs and the glow from smoking tent, the street was very dark. The strange smells from the cooking pots and burning incense from the shacks nearby drifted to Essie on the night air.

At this end of town, the construction that marked this newest section of Magic City hadn't kept pace. Here, summer tents and shacks made of thrown-together wood dominated the landscape, but none of these would last through the cold Montana winters. Before the next moon passed, most of these would be replaced by sturdier buildings, or their owners would follow work south to a more habitable climate.

A shiver ran through Essie at the thought, wondering if she'd seen her last winter here as well.

"I say we just go in and get him," Pink said.

Ollie took him by the arm. "What if he's not in there?"

"Then we say sorry and move on. Like as not, the boy's asleep at this hour. We go room by room if need be."

"That should make Chen Lee happy," Essie said. "Did you not notice the rather large Chinese man standing guard outside the tent?"

"I ain't no wallflower myself, Mrs. Sparks, in case it escaped your notice," Pink offered.

Ollie looked at him sharply. "We should have come armed."

"And end up alongside Cade, in jail?" Essie said. "No. We do this without violence."

"Easier said than done, I think," said Ollie.

Another man stumbled out of the tent, in some sort of altercation with an older Chinese man with a long, gray queue. The first man stumbled backward, shoved by the older man who was yelling incomprehensibly.

At the same moment, Essie caught sight of a movement at the front door of the house. It was so dark, she could hardly make it out, but the movement resolved into two shadows. One about the size of the boy she'd known as Daniel.

As the old man literally kicked the other man down the street, the movement to his right caught his eye, too, and instantly, he forgot about the man and shouted something to the large guard, hurrying to his side.

The shadows began to run.

She, Ollie and Pink took off running simultaneously, but they weren't equal to the strides of Chen Lee's henchman, who caught the two before they could jump the barrier of the shanties in their way.

In the boy's hand, something metal flashed in the half moonlight. The guard shouted and easily disarmed him, then grabbed the girl by the hair and hauled her back against him. Brandishing the small knife, he pulled his arm back to swipe at Little Wolf.

"No!" Essie threw herself between him and the boy. "Stop! Don't you dare hurt this boy!"

Shock flattened the large man's expression and he froze in place, sending a look back at Chen Lee who was, even now, running their way with a furious look on his face.

The old man barged in front of his bodyguard, yanked the girl out of the guard's hands and pulled her behind him. She squeaked in pain, but did little to resist the man who dragged her by the hair like a rag doll.

"No!" Little Wolf scrambled away from Essie's protective stance. "Let her go!"

"Stay back, Daniel," Essie warned.

The huge guard threatened her and the boy again with his knife, but hesitated as Pink and Ollie rushed up beside them. Pink took two threatening steps toward the guard.

"Get yourself back, Biggety Bob, or I'll kill you my own self."

Chen snapped at the man in Chinese and the man lowered the knife. The guard, who clearly spoke no English, squinted menacingly at Pink but found himself forced to take a step back.

Turning to Essie, Chen said, "You go! I own!" He thumped his chest with his fist. He jerked the girl by the hair again to prove his point.

"Own him? I think not. I think whoever sold him to you made a terrible mistake."

"Own!" He grabbed a pouch of coins from his pocket and shook it at her. "Own!" He lifted the girl by the hair again. "Own!"

"We're leaving now," Essie told him. "With the boy. Who you *don't* own. C'mon, Daniel."

Ollie grabbed him by his other arm, but he broke free from them both. "Not without Shyen Zu!"

The young girl stared back at the boy with terror-struck eyes. She was just a child. She couldn't be more than fourteen or fifteen.

"I promised her," he pleaded. "I won't leave her behind."

This unexpected complication was much more than she had bargained for and Essie found herself actually debating whether to risk rescuing this girl too, or simply settling for the boy's safe return. But one look at the girl's desperate expression and she knew she had to at least try. A man like Chen Lee would not lightly forgive her attempt to run away and if the rumors were true, might even do worse than simply punish her.

In a fight, it wasn't clear Pink would prevail, unarmed, against a behemoth like Chen Lee's guard, but the old man apparently didn't like the numbers standing against him. Or, just as likely, he suddenly saw an opportunity to make money. A sly expression wizened his face. "You pay. For boy."

"No," Essie told him. "No money for the boy. You lose

whatever you illegally paid those men for him. Or I could send the sheriff your way. Pink? Go get Sheriff Sampson. We'll see what *he* has to say about buying free boys as slaves."

All the conniving leaked out of his expression and the older man threw his hand up to stop Pink. "*Bu*! No!" He spat on the ground between them. With a murderous look at the boy, he relented, muttering something to the guard. Jerking the girl around by the hair again, he started back to the brothel with her.

Essie glanced back at Ollie, who gave her a small nod. "I will pay you for the girl, though," Essie shouted after him. "One hundred dollars."

Chen Lee stopped and turned back to her. "*One*?" He let out a bark of laughter then sent another wad of spittle to the ground at his feet.

"Two, then." It was nearly all they'd brought with them, all Ollie was able to scrape up at such short notice. Essie held up two fingers to be clear.

With a nasty smile, he stroked the terrified girl's bruised cheek with his hand. He held up five fingers.

Essie shook her head. "Two fifty. That's my final offer. That's all I have." She gestured to Ollie, who handed her the money they'd brought. She fanned it out for Chen Lee to see that they were not holding back.

Considering, the old man narrowed his eyes. "This," he said, gesturing to the money, "and that." He pointed a gnarled finger at the gold locket at her throat.

Instinctively, she grabbed it, protecting it from the little weasel as Cade had so aptly named him. "No!"

"No sell." He motioned to the guard and dragged the girl toward the brothel. She let out a terrified whimper.

Pink was already turning his pockets inside out to look for money and Ollie grabbed Essie by the arm. "I'm afraid for her."

Essie swallowed hard. Though the locket was worth something, it certainly wasn't worth what he wanted for the girl. But that, she realized, wasn't the point. At all.

"Wait!"

Chen Lee stopped dead and turned back to look at her.

Lifting her arms, she unlocked the clasp on the locket and slipped the thing off. With a killing look at the old men, she raised a palm to stop him when he walked back and reached for the necklace.

Prying open the locket, she fingered up the glass cover and tipped the contents into her hand. Short wisps of Aaron's blond hair floated into her palm and she closed her fist around it. Snapping it shut, she threw the necklace at hm. "Take it," she told him. "It means nothing to me now."

He did, fingering the thing with a victorious smile. Ollie shoved the money she'd brought into his hands and he had the guard count it quickly before he released the girl, throwing her at them.

Shyen Zu stumbled to the ground and stayed there on all fours. Little Wolf dropped down beside her, wrapping an arm around her.

As he walked away, the old man laughed and shouted something in his language at them, slicing a hand across his throat.

Ollie had to restrain Pink, who jerked toward the old man with a murderous look. "What the hell did he just say?"

The trembling girl spoke haltingly. "He say, this my last day, anyway. Free money." She got to her feet. Little Wolf rose with her. "We go now! Quick, quick!"

Pink growled down low in his throat.

"Come on," Essie told them. "She's right."

Pink lifted the girl by the arm and pulled her up against his side, while keeping an eye on Chen Lee and his guard who watched them go.

The old man disappeared into his opium den, laughing.

"How did you find me?" the boy wanted to know.

"That's a long story, Daniel, which I will tell you. But now, we have to get you both somewhere safe."

Wide-eyed, he shouted, "I'm not going back. I won't go back to that school. You can't make me!"

"And I wouldn't take you there," she assured him. "Trust

me, Daniel. You'll never go back there."

"You could take them to my place," Ollie offered as they walked. "But it's not a good situation for the likes of them."

"You *did* see where they just came from," Essie said, pulling Little Wolf against her. He was shaking, too.

Ollie shrugged. "Point taken. But the farther away we can keep them from that bastard back there, the better I'd like it. I'd sooner trust a polecat than him."

"Where do you suggest?"

"This might sound crazy, but the boy is sorta kin to Cade's father."

"No. That doesn't sound crazy. Actually, Cade said his father might help the boy if we needed him. But aside from that, his father should know what's happened to his son."

"Black Thorn?" Little Wolf asked. "You know him? Where is he?"

"I'll tell you everything," Essie said gently. Though she had no desire to tell him that his mother was gone. That he was an orphan. That all of them were in trouble. "In a little while."

Mitchell Laddner sat with his back to a corner at the Cattle Baron's Saloon, nursing a near-empty shot of whiskey. He'd had three drinks already and Moran was flat-out drunk, yakking it up with the local riffraff at the bar.

After giving the situation a lot of thought, Laddner had decided there were two ways he could go. One was to wait until the end of the month for the circuit judge, with the hope that a guilty verdict would get him his reward money. That, however, would risk the judge finding Cade Newcastle innocent, or Sheriff Sampson claiming he and Moran weren't eligible for the money because they'd been paid to find the man by Reverend Dooley. This also gave Tom Newcastle's half-breed son time to flap his mouth about the unfortunate incident at Powder River. While he felt no personal guilt over the squaw and child he'd shot that day—after all, they were godless heathens—their deaths at his hand, once revealed, might color his chances for a future here in this burgeoning hub of commerce where opportunity practically grew on trees.

No, he preferred his second plan better and decided it would take very little to implement it. Not only that, he couldn't be blamed for whatever happened. All it would take was a word here, a well-placed comment there…and once done, no one could deny him the reward or his status as the man who'd given the town of Magic City a dose of justice.

At Ollie's place, Essie tended first to the wounds on Little Wolf's ankle and Shyen Zu's cheek. Pink drew a bath for each of them and Lucy was given the task of helping the girl.

When she was through, Lucy came downstairs, looking pale. "She's covered with bruises," she told Ollie. "Poor little thing. She's just a girl, but those eyes of hers are a hundred years old. She's had things done to her no child ought, my guess is. I gave her my bed and the poor dear fell right asleep, like she hasn't done it in years."

"She probably hasn't," Essie agreed. Tonight, she felt like she hadn't slept in years either. "And the boy?"

"Sleeping, too. They've both had it rough." She would talk to him in the morning. But she dreaded telling him the truth. Pacing near the window, she pressed her hands together. She felt like a spinning top whose parts were beginning to fly off in all directions.

"You look ready to fall down yourself," Ollie said.

"I can't sleep. I can't stop thinking about everything. About Cade. All of it."

"You're exhausted. A good night's sleep will—"

"No. It won't," she said, fighting back sudden tears. "What if they hang him?"

The woman's glance out the window said she worried about the same thing. "We'll fight it. That's all we can do."

"He didn't go there to take me. His reasons were good. Humane. And then…the whole thing all got balled up. But Ollie, I think…maybe I was wrong about how he felt about me. He told me to go. To get on that train tomorrow. Even if we fix this thing, I don't think he wants me."

"What you did back there at the jail was brave. Lying for Cade the way you did. And the boy. Time for you to hang on to that bravery now. My philosophy? Don't buy trouble. Cade is thinkin' of you. And from where he sits, that advice is the best he could give. But that's today. Tomorrow is still to come. Remember, he's been alone a long time. It's hard for a man like that to change." She patted Essie's hand. "You can regret a man like him, a man who can't see himself settling down, but I wouldn't."

Something bittersweet lit her eyes as she talked about Cade, and Essie knew that in her own way Ollie loved him, too.

She nodded and took a deep breath. "You're right. I'm done with regrets, anyway. I have enough of them to fill a bushel basket. I thank you for holding my hand tonight, Ollie. You're a peach and a friend."

"Sleep well, Essie."

Before she lay down on the bed Ollie had offered her, Essie walked outside onto the balcony overlooking the street. It was quiet except for a light breeze that tugged at her gown and the unruly curls that had strayed from her pinned-up hair. The moon, with its half-light, peeked through the clouds and after a moment, she pulled her hand from her pocket.

Unfolding her fist, she stretched it out over the balcony and watched the thin tufts of baby hair lift and fly away like dandelion seeds in the dark. Heartbreak tightened her throat. "Goodbye, sweet boy," she whispered. "It's time for you to go." But only the breeze answered back.

Sleep was elusive that night, as it had been since this whole ordeal began. But in the dark, she formulated a plan. It wasn't much of a plan, but it was all she had. So, in the morning, before the rest of the house arose, she left a note for Ollie and walked down to Klingman's Stables. There, she rented a rig, complete with directions from Mr.

Klingman himself to the Double Bar N ranch. It wasn't but a few miles out of town, he'd said, and she knew she could make it there and back by noon.

It took longer than she'd expected, and the poorly sprung rig managed to find every pothole and rut in the old dirt road leading there. But finally, she saw the long drive that led to a ranch house perched on a rocky rise. It overlooked acres and acres of cattle ranch, and each acre boasted dozens of head of cattle. Klingman had suggested that the ranch stretched north as far as the eye could see, but she couldn't conceive of one man owning that much land.

As she turned into the drive, two men rode toward her up the drive on horseback. Cowboys, they were clearly posted to watch for visitors, invited or not.

She pulled the rig to a stop as they met her.

"Ma'am?" said the one with the battered gray hat. His face was sunburned, but as he took off his hat, a white strip of flesh belied his coloring. "You here for the barbeque, ma'am?"

"The what?"

"The barbeque. It's a little early, but I don't think Mr. Newcastle will mind. Already a few people here."

"Then I'm in the right place. But I'm not here for a barbeque," she told him. "My name is Essie Sparks and I came to speak with Mr. Newcastle. I have other business with him."

The two men exchanged looks. "He know you're coming?" asked the second.

"No," she said, "but it's quite urgent that I speak with him."

"Very well. You can follow us. We'll take you in."

"Thank you." She gave the reins a slap and followed them to the house.

The place was lovely, if rustic, inside, furnished with things no doubt shipped from far away. Oriental rugs paved the planked floor, rugged upholstery graced the seating area and the tables were made of fine cherry wood. And paintings of ships and boats and some southern sea that looked impossibly blue graced the walls. Nothing about this place spoke of his Cheyenne wife or son, and it made her wonder.

She wandered around the room, staring at the collections of things: deer antlers mounted on the wall; shelves of leather-bound books—a surprise; even a collection of G. Donovan's romantic novels, "Adventures in the West." She'd grown up loving them. She picked one up and opened it, scanning the page. A smile curved her mouth. Yes, even this one she'd read.

"You can't know how exciting it is for me to see someone holding one of my books as if they actually want to read it."

Essie turned in surprise to find a beautiful woman standing in the doorway, smiling at her. She was older, and her blond hair was tinged with gray, but that did nothing to diminish her vibrant smile or the twinkle in her blue eyes that matched her pretty cornflower blue dress.

"I'm sorry," Essie said, putting the book down. "I didn't mean to pry—I was just—I've read this whole series." She stuck out her hand. "I'm Essie Sparks. And you're…Mrs. Newcastle?"

A laugh bubbled from her. "Oh, heavens, no! Tom is just a good friend of ours. An *old* friend. My name's Grace. Grace Donovan. My husband Reese and I are here visiting from the East for the week with our son, Lucas. He's starting medical school in the fall and this is his western tour, so to speak."

Essie blinked. "Donovan?" She looked back at the book. "Not G. Donovan?"

"I'm afraid so. Those books don't belong to me, but I wrote them. Oh, don't be impressed. I'm so happy to hear you've read them all. You know, Tom was a part of that first one. I called him by another name"—she winked— "but he knows who he is. It embarrasses him to no end. But that adventure was a long time ago."

"It's so nice to meet you, Mrs. Donovan. I don't think I've ever met a real author before."

"Oh, we're quite real. I hope you're here for the barbeque

because I'd love to show you off as a genuine reader!"

"No, actually, I'm not. I don't really even know Mr. Newcastle. I'm a friend of his son's."

Grace Donovan's face grew serious. "Oh, my." She leaned out the doorway to snag the arm of a man walking by. "Reese, darling, come and meet Miss Sparks. This is my husband, Reese Donovan. Reese? Miss Sparks."

Reese Donovan ducked into the room, looking like he might have walked off the pages of one of Grace Donovan's novels. He was tall, dark and every bit as handsome as she'd described him in "The Lady Takes A Hero."

He shook her hand gently. "Very nice to meet you. I'm sorry, but Tom just asked if I'd haul some dry ice from the ice cellar for him. I was just—"

"Miss Sparks is a friend of Tom's son, Reese. *A friend of Cade's.*"

That got his attention. "Oh. I see. That's…that's…that's good to hear. Tom will want to talk with you. Does he know you're here?"

"I don't know—"

A man with Cade's roguish good looks walked through the door then, like he'd just blown in off the prairie. His salt-and-pepper hair was awry and though his boots were wiped clean, his long duster was splashed with mud. He took the coat off as he walked and handed it to a man who had followed him in, who then disappeared with the coat.

This man was all muscle and business, despite the fact that he was probably in his forties, but instantly she realized that Cade came by his appeal honestly, through the man who shared his name.

He removed his hat and tossed it on the divan. "Miss Sparks, is it?" Charmingly, he took her gloved hand in his and bent over it with a polite bow. "I see you've met my friends, Reese and Grace Donovan."

"It's Mrs. Sparks, actually. I'm widowed. And, yes, we were just…chatting."

Grace looked uncomfortably at her husband. "Darling,

why don't we leave them to it? I'm sure they have a lot to discuss."

"I'm frankly not sure what your business is, Mrs. Sparks," Newcastle said. "I have a few dozen people coming for a barbeque this afternoon. Is there something I can do to—"

"Mrs. Sparks is a friend of Cade's, Tom," Grace interrupted.

If she'd poleaxed him with a two-by-four, she couldn't have drawn a stronger reaction. He went pale and statue-quiet. "My *son*, Cade?"

Essie moistened her suddenly dry lips. "Yes."

Dropping her hand, he glanced at the Donovans, who looked suddenly uncomfortable. "Would you excuse us?" Grace said. "There are a million things left to do and…we'll leave you two to talk."

After they closed the door, Tom Newcastle walked to a table that held several crystal decanters and poured a drink. "I haven't seen my son in a long…a *very* long time. Can I offer you something? Tea? Coffee? Whiskey?"

"No, thank you."

He took a long, slow drink, draining his glass before he turned back to her. "What about him?"

"He needs you. And I'm here to ask you to come and help him."

It took her a while to explain the situation to him—the unvarnished truth about the kidnapping and the aftermath—but when she finished, he sat back with a lost expression, so different from the man who'd walked in the room earlier.

"One thing you didn't mention," Newcastle said at last, "was whether Cade asked for my help."

She twined her fingers together. "You know he didn't."

He nodded as if he most certainly expected that answer. "I guess you're aware that my son and I have a…difficult relationship. My fault, I fear. Nonetheless, I doubt he would welcome my help now."

"But he needs it, even so."

"And how do you think I could help him? Change things? The law will deal with him as it does everything in this territory. With a thimbleful of fairness and a modicum of justice. "

"And you're willing to accept those odds? For your son? I'm told you have a certain reputation here in Billings. People look up to you."

"That depends on your perspective, I suppose. And whether or not you're blood kin to me."

"He needs you behind him, Mr. Newcastle. I'm afraid for him. You can convince them. All they see is—"

"Who he's become?"

"No. They see what they want to see. Do you even know the man he's become? You'd like him, you know. He's a good man with a big heart."

"You're right. I wouldn't know. As I said, it's been a long time." Newcastle stood and walked to the grand windows that overlooked his domain. "Have you ever been at sea, Mrs. Sparks?"

She blinked at his change of subject. Glancing at the many paintings on the walls, she thought of Nathan. "No, I'm afraid I haven't."

"I used to live on a boat—a lifetime ago, down in the Gulf of Mexico. I was a privateer then. In charge of my destiny before I gave it all up to come here and seek another kind of fortune. For...*this*." He gestured outside his window. "The thing about the ocean," he went on, "is that you can rely on it to be...unreliable. You can prepare your boat, trim your sails, and even make sure every leak is plugged, but the sea will find her way in if you turn your back on her. It's much the same with children, I've learned, though I was apparently much better at sailing than at being a father to my only son. But one day, you think you've got everything under control and the next, you've lost your wife, made some terrible miscalculation and your precious vessel sinks. Or your son walks away. Forever."

"Forever hasn't happened yet." Essie stood and moved beside him. "And if he's stayed away, it's only because he doesn't know how to come back. Just as you don't know how to go to him."

"You're very young, Mrs. Sparks."

"Not so *very* young, Mr. Newcastle."

"And you're in love with him. Or am I wrong?"

Essie's lips parted as she pondered her answer. *Yes. I think I am.* "Are you going to help him?"

Those same gray eyes as the man she'd left in that jail cell studied her now. "Tell him that if he wants my help, he should send word for me. Otherwise, I'll only make matters worse for him."

"But—"

"I appreciate your coming all the way out here. It was very nice to meet you, Mrs. Sparks." Newcastle bowed slightly with a nod of his head. "Now I'm afraid I've got a barbeque to manage. My man, John, will see you out."

Magically, John, the coat-man, appeared at the door as if he'd had an ear pressed against it.

She stared at Newcastle for a long beat, unsure what to say to change his mind. "Standing on principle is a dangerous thing, especially when it comes to matters of the heart. It's true that the ocean can swamp your hopes and your dreams, but the heart is one place the sea can't invade, regardless how far you swim into it. Pride will only hold you afloat for so long."

Even the stubborn set of his jaw was familiar. "I can have one of my men accompany you back to town if—"

"That won't be necessary. Good day, Mr. Newcastle."

His hand was shaking as he turned to pour another whiskey. "Mrs. Sparks."

CHAPTER 20

In his cell, Cade sat with his back against the brick wall, listening to a growing commotion outside in the street. At first, he'd thought it was just the noise of commerce, but soon shouts moved in the direction of the jail and Sheriff Sampson swung out of his chair and pulled his shotgun off the wall. He checked the load, then pulled his Winchester Repeater off the wall for his other hand.

Cade got slowly to his feet, still bent over from the kicking he'd taken to the ribs. "What is it?" he asked Sampson.

"You don't want to know," he replied.

Sweat instantly beaded on Cade's upper lip. *A lynch mob.* Word had spread about his capture, and likely the false rumor of Essie's murder, too. Daylight had brought out the vultures and they were here to see a show.

"They'll have to walk over me to get you. I can promise you that won't happen unless I'm dead," Sampson told him before opening the door and pulling it shut tight behind him.

Cade climbed up on his cot to look out the small barred window. Even from there, he could see the crowd spilling around the side of the building. All of them against one man. A dead man's odds.

He had nothing to protect himself with. No weapon. Only

a locked cell that wouldn't hold them back a minute once they got the key. Some with guns were brandishing them at the sheriff.

Oddly, he thought of Essie. He wanted to see her one last time. Tell her...tell her how he felt. But maybe it was just as well. This wasn't something he wanted her to witness, a mob stretching his neck.

A calmness came over him out of nowhere.

No, not out of nowhere. Out of his thoughts of her. He'd done a lot wrong in his life, but taking her wasn't one of those things. And now that he knew what had come of it with her, he'd do it again. Maybe without the knife at her throat, though. Definitely without the knife.

Outside the door, Jedediah Sampson surveyed the gathering crowd and raised his hands to calm things down. But nobody could hear him over the din of the shouting for the half-breed's death. So he fired a shot into the air and that got their attention.

"You are leavin' here disappointed today," he told them. "There ain't gonna be any hangin' here today. Or tomorrow either."

The crowd swelled and surged toward the front stoop of the jail. "Stop right where you are!" he ordered, pointing the shotgun at the two closest men. "Before I add you to the list of idiots who've tried and failed to back me down."

Tyvan Root stepped forward. As one of Magic City's main builders, he had the ear of many in a town that had been raised practically overnight. Men who'd come West to be shed of things like law and order.

"You, Tyvan?" Sampson scoffed. "You surprise me."

"I got a wife and daughters, too, Jed. I'm in agreement with the majority here. We can't let this pass or it will start all over again. Renegades stealing our women? Where does it stop, I ask you? It stops when we stop it with a rope and a noose, that's where! They need an example of what happens when they step out of line!"

"And lynching is far less than he deserves!"

"Murderer!"

"Rapist!"

Shouts of agreement surged through the crowd of mostly men. A few women hovered at the back, wide-eyed at the spectacle. Sampson spotted Jacob Moran in the crowd, red faced and being jostled by the others. And there, at the back, silent but righteous, stood the good Reverend Dooley, checking his timepiece. To his left, he spotted Mitchell Laddner, enjoying the chaos he'd no doubt churned up. He'd lay good odds on Laddner being the instigator of this.

Jedediah kept two guns aimed on the crowd. "First off, the claim that the prisoner killed that girl is false. Nobody's dead. Mrs. Sparks is as alive as me, and I talked to her yesterday, right here in my office."

"That's a bald-face lie!" another man shouted. "We hear she's butchered up there in the mountains. Raped and butchered. That's what we heard."

"We heard they found her scalp on a Cheyenne lance, stuck up on the buffalo jump. And that there was more of 'em besides that one you got locked up!"

"It's a damned renegade uprising!" a skinny man at the front shouted. "We won't have it!"

Jed fired a shot into the air. "Settle down! All of you! Where'd you get your information? I suppose it was from Sergeant Laddner over there? Yeah, *him*, right behind you, Orem."

Laddner shrugged, glancing around him. "I'm not the one who needs to defend myself, sheriff. I'm the one who brought that heathen in. Besides, these folks here make up their own minds, isn't that right?"

The crowd concurred.

"I can't whip up a whole crowd. They did that all on their own, in the name of justice."

"Yeah?" Sampson said. "Let me tell you all something. This man and Jacob Moran, they got their own reasons for wanting this case settled sooner than later. They're hungry for the reward money and they're usin' you to try to get it. *I'm* telling you Mrs. Sparks is alive and well, and she claims there was no kidnapping and no rape. As for the horse thievin' charge—"

"You claim! Well, where is she?" somebody shouted. "Anybody seen her?"

"I have!"

Sampson turned to spot Ollie Warren pushing her way through the crowd. "I've seen her. And he's telling you the truth."

Ollie had some standing in town, despite her occupation, or maybe because of it. In a population of nearly all men, most of them had at least paid a visit to her establishment.

"Where is she then, Ollie?"

Ollie pushed her way to stand up on the stoop beside Jedediah. "For God's sake, you fools! She spent the night at my place, right as rain. She's…well, I don't know exactly where she is this morning, but I can promise you that she—"

A disbelieving murmur surged through the crowd.

"You're just protecting a murderer, Ollie!"

"No! *Boys*. That's Cade Newcastle sittin' in that jail cell. He's no savage. No murderer. You all know him. He's worked for you, Joey Navrone, cuttin' trees. And you, Cyrus Tomkins. He hauled goods from here to Helena for you for a whole summer. And you, Monty. He worked side by side with your son two winters ago, hauling feed to your cattle during that blizzard."

"That's the past," Cyrus Tomkins shouted. "He's been livin' as a Cheyenne for more'n a year and their savagery must'a rubbed off on him."

The sound of a few more rifles cocking resonated through the crowd.

Jedediah swung his guns toward the sound as the crowd jostled forward. "Anybody here wants into that jail has got to go through me! Now go home. All of you and—"

At the front of the crowd, a shove from behind knocked a man stumbling forward and a gunshot tore through the air! Jedediah Sampson spun around with a grunt of pain and collided with the wall.

Ollie screamed.

* * *

On her way back into town, Essie heard the noise before she saw the crowd surging around the jail. The gunshot, like the cracking of May ice, echoed down the corridor of buildings. And a woman's scream.

Oh, no! No!

Essie slapped the reins across the back of the horse and urged him to a run. She pulled up at the edge of the crowd as she caught sight of a few men shoving their way into the jail, past the fallen sheriff. Ollie was there, too, trying to help Jedediah, but was powerless to stop them.

They had Cade handcuffed and out of his cell and were already dragging him outside by the time she'd pushed through the crowd. Jumping onto the walkway, she screamed Ollie's name.

"Essie! Thank God!" Ollie yelled.

Cade caught sight of her, his face still a mass of bruises, and the look in his eyes futile.

"Stop it!" Essie cried, pummeling with her fist the man who had Cade by the arm. "Leave him alone!"

"Tell 'em who you are!" Ollie shouted.

But she picked up the sheriff's fallen rifle and fired a round at the sky instead. The sound stopped them momentarily and the crowd went quiet. She swung the rifle at the two men who held Cade. "I'm Essie Sparks and this man is innocent. I am not dead, as you can all plainly see. Let him go or I swear there will be a killing here today, but it won't be him. I will shoot one of you holding him, or maybe a few of you if need be."

"How do we know you're who you say you are?" someone shouted at her.

Essie shook her head. "You, who were so ready to avenge my death don't even know what I look like?" Her gaze scanned the crowd of men, who stared at her now as if they were seeing a ghost. "Well, ask that man over there. Reverend Dooley. He knows me. After all, it was him that sent Mitchell Laddner after us to kill us both."

Murmurs rose from the crowd. Dooley looked aghast and

blustered, "That's a lie!"

"Is it?" she shouted back. "Or maybe you just looked the other way, while Laddner did your dirty work. Like he always did at the school with those children you buried in those graves out back. The unmarked ones, filled with children you've neglected or brutalized in your hateful little Wages of Sin box, or the ones you simply allowed to die of broken hearts."

Heads turned Dooley's way and he puffed up like a ripe pine cone. Laddner edged backward in the crowd now, calmly trying to make himself invisible.

"Oh, and let's not forget where the pious Sergeant Laddner learned his trade. Murdering innocent women and children at the Powder River Massacre and probably others like it. How does that sit with your opinion of him now?" she asked the crowd. "Oh yes, they were only Cheyenne. Does that make a difference to you?"

"She's a damned liar!" he shouted, but now all eyes were suddenly on him.

"No. I'm not. There was a witness to that murder. It was this man," she said, pointing to Cade. "Cade 'Black Thorn' Newcastle. That's right. He saw the whole thing that morning, when he was hardly more than a boy. Maybe that's why Sergeant Laddner is so intent on seeing him dead. Too late now, eh, sergeant? Your secret's out. What was it you said about glass houses? Something about rocks?"

A few of the men near Laddner turned all their attention to him, shoving him rudely toward the back of the crowd.

"And the rest of you," she went on. "Shame on you! For letting a man like him bend you to his will. I won't change your mind here today about the Cheyenne, about who and what they are—though they were kind to me, up in those mountains. They gave me shelter and the benefit of the doubt, which is more than I deserved after all they've suffered and which is more than I can say for any of you here today. If I say this man—this good man—didn't kidnap me or rape me, or steal a horse, then my word is all you have. And the word of anyone else here, who merely thinks they know what happened, means nothing."

She cocked the rifle in her hands again and swung it toward the crowd, who flinched and backed up a step.

"If you hate him because his blood isn't as white as yours, then look to yourselves, all of you. Immigrants, half of you. Blood mixed from a dozen different cultures and countries. I defy any of you to say your blood is pure *anything*. And if any of you—any one of you—is *half* the man he is, then you will walk away from this lynch mob because you know it's wrong. And if you think that loving this man has ruined me, then I'm sorry for you. I would run away with him a hundred times again for the chance to be with him."

Cade lifted his head, watching her scan the sea of faces out there, his chest swelling with some emotion he hardly recognized. Not gratitude. Nothing that simple. He loved this woman. This brave, crazy woman. And no matter what the outcome, he was glad he'd lived long enough to witness her standing up here against all these men. For him.

At the back of the crowd, he saw a rider and a wagon full of men pull to a stop. For a moment, he didn't recognize the man shoving through the crowd toward him. He was older than he'd been the last time they'd locked eyes on one another. That last day he'd called him his son. But time had not diminished Tom Newcastle one bit. And as he moved through the crowd, his eyes met Cade's with a mixture of dread and hope.

He'd brought half his ranch with him and all of them were armed to the teeth. In the wagon with them was a blond-haired woman he didn't recognize who was standing and waving her arms at him in apparent solidarity.

Cade threw a look at Essie and put two and two together. She'd gone to his father. This couldn't have happened any other way.

Tom Newcastle barged through the morass of men and stepped up beside him. He strong-armed Cade from the two men holding him and kicked them off the stoop like naughty children. Two of his armed men joined him on the stoop and the others pointed their guns at the crowd along with Essie. "Now you've all had your say. But this is my boy. My son. And nobody's gonna hang him. You two," he said to his men, "get Cade inside. And help the sheriff inside, too. Who's the damned fool that shot him?"

The damned fool had apparently vanished in the thick crowd, but several men up front claimed it had been accidental.

"This whole thing's accidental," he said, reaching out to take the rifle from Essie's hands. She relinquished it reluctantly. "One big accidental mess. You'd better hope that man is all right, or I'll come looking for you personally." He stared at the crowd, picking out faces he recognized. "You all know me. We've been friends for years. But today, I'm ashamed to call you that. I expected more from you than turning into a thug-mob against my son. When my boy's name is cleared—and it will be cleared—I expect each and every one of you fools to come to my home and apologize to his face. And to this young lady who stood up for him at her own peril. Now get! All of you! Go home to your family, if you're lucky enough to have one. Or say a prayer to the Maker that one day you'll be lucky enough to have a son like mine."

Shamed, they did as he asked, but more than a few of them had words for both Reverend Dooley and Mitchell Laddner. But all that was out of Cade's earshot as his father's men helped him back inside the jail.

The others helped Sheriff Sampson into his chair. His wound was not serious, a through and through bullet to his upper shoulder, and someone sent for Doc Watley again.

Essie hurried to Cade's side as he was helped into a chair opposite Sampson. Her eyes were filled with tears and she just shook her head at him, unable to speak as one of the men with his father undid the cuffs on his hands.

"Cade? You okay?" the man asked. "I'm an old friend of your father's. Name's Reese Donovan. I sure am glad that mob didn't have their way with you."

Cade nodded, taking a mental inventory of his working

parts. "Thanks. I'm grateful to you all for saving my neck."

"This one did the saving," Reese told him, gesturing at Essie. "We were just the back-up plan."

His father came in beside the woman he'd seen standing in the wagon. She went immediately to Essie and put an arm around her. "There, now," she told her. "You just bawl your eyes out if you want, Essie. It's over now."

"I—" She dropped her face in her hands and to his surprise, did just that.

He reached out for her and pulled her up against him. "Shh. It's all right."

She nodded, looked up at him with moisture brimming in her eyes. "I thought they would kill you."

From his chair, the sheriff said, "I got nothin' to hold you on, Cade. I should've let you go last night, but that was my mistake." He gripped his bloody shoulder with one hand and looked up at Cade's father. "But as sheriff, it's my call. Tom, I'm releasing him to you. Since Mrs. Sparks is backing up his story and since that missin' horse showed up in town, clearly not by Cade's doing, the charges are hereby dropped. There will be no trial. He's free and clear. And when I get back on my feet, I'll make sure you get every one of those apologies you asked for out there. And Reverend Dooley and Laddner will have to answer for what's going on out at that school. I think we can make sure he isn't allowed to take out his bigotry on any more of the Cheyenne's children."

As Tom thanked the sheriff, Cade shielded his eyes one-handed in relief. That it was actually over was almost too much for him to take in. Pulling himself together, he released Essie with a squeeze, got to his feet and stood before his father.

Tom Newcastle had always been an imposing figure and that hadn't changed. But the man standing before him now looked nothing like the one who had taken that girl's side against him, all those years ago. He looked…nervous.

"Son?" Tom said. He put his hand out for Cade to shake.

Cade took it, and Tom clasped it in both of his, then

pulled Cade into his arms. It was a feeling so foreign to him that he froze for an instant before allowing it, before wrapping his arms around his old man as well. Tom buried his face in Cade's shoulder momentarily, then, with a self-conscious clap on his back, he bracketed his son by the shoulders, and pulled back to look at him. He took in the long hair, the broken cheek, the bloody clothes that had taken him down that mountain, and the man's eyes filled with tears.

"You all right now, son? You look like hell. And the best thing I've seen in a long time."

Cade nodded. "I'll live. Thank you…for coming and…for what you did out there."

"You can thank your girl, Essie, for that. She came to me and told me what had happened. You should hang onto that one, Cade. She's…a pearl."

He couldn't have agreed more. But his father wasn't finished talking.

He cleared his throat. "I…I should've come to you long ago. Mended the broken thing between us. I tried to find you a few times, but you didn't seem to want to be found. I should've tried harder. I don't know what the hell got in my way. Stubbornness, I guess. My pride. I suppose I just kept hoping you'd realize you'd misunderstood what happened between us all those years ago. Or forgive my damned temper for getting in the way when you needed me most. So I'm here, asking you to forgive me. To finally put that behind us? Dammit, I hope we can, Cade."

The others in the room pretended to be looking elsewhere as they spoke, but none were unaffected by Tom's obvious emotion, standing with his son again after so many years.

As he'd watched that crowd come for him, Cade had thought about his father, too. Thought about how his own stubborn will had gotten in the way all those lost years, too, and how pointless it had been to blame him for all that had gone wrong in his life. To get the chance to make it right now, Cade decided, was a gift. One he wasn't about to waste twice.

"We're both stubborn as cedar," Cade said, letting out a deep breath. "And it was as much my fault as yours. But yes. If we could, I'd like that. Very much."

Relief lightened Tom's expression. A big smile broke out on his face. "Get your things. We're all going back to our place."

Cade looked up suddenly. "But Little Wolf...what about—"

"We got him, Cade," Ollie said. "He's safe and back at my place. Along with a little bonus. I'll tell you about that later."

He swallowed with relief. "Thank God."

Tom said, "You come, too, Ollie. And, of course, Mrs. Sparks. I'd be honored if you'd come and stay at my place while you sort things out."

She hesitated, glancing at Cade. "I—"

"We need a minute," he told his father, who nodded and ushered everyone outside save the sheriff and Ollie who was tending his shoulder now.

Cade took her back to the open cell and pulled her inside. "This isn't the place where I should say what I'm about to say, but I don't want any misunderstandings between us—"

"Cade," she interrupted, "you don't have to say anything. I don't want you to feel obligated to say anything. What I did, I did because...well, because I had to. I thought the worst would be that I'd be ruined, like you said. That I'd be shunned by all those people out there. But that wasn't the worst. In fact, it didn't even matter to me. The worst would have been losing you. And I'm so glad it all worked out this way. But I already know how you feel. So please, don't say anything in the heat of the moment, feeling obliged to me or anything like that. I really...really couldn't bear it if you did."

"Are you done?"

She shook her head, but answered, "Yes."

"Good. Because now I'm going say what I'm going to say because I want to. Not because I have to, or because I'm obliged to you for saving my life, which I am. But here it is. I don't know what I did to deserve someone like you in my life. Someone as brave and fearless and beautiful as you, *Mo'onahe*. But I'm done being too foolish and stubborn to see how lucky I just got. I feel like I have a second chance and I don't want to waste it. So you would be doing me a great favor if you'd forget all I said to you last night about getting out of town on that train and going as far away from me as you can. Because if you did that, I'll just have to come and find you. And then we'd waste all that time."

She let out a breath of laughter. "Really?"

"I want you to stay. Stay and let me take back all that that happened between us at the beginning and prove I'm worthy of you."

"You don't have to prove anything to me, Cade. I know who you are. And I wouldn't take back a moment. Well," she quibbled, "falling in the river, maybe, and...the bear. And, oh, *shoes*." She grinned up at him.

He brushed the curls from her eyes with one finger. "I want you with me for the rest of my life, Essie. I want to sleep with you every night with my arms around you and wake up to you every morning. But I want to do it right. I'll never be like the other choices you might have. I'm half Cheyenne and I'll never deny that part of me."

"I would never ask you to."

He nodded. "I know. But if that means waiting for a while until you're sure you feel the same, then we'll take our time."

"Yes," she said, touching his cheek with the palm of her hand. "Let's take our time. In fact, let's take the rest of our lives. I don't care about what anyone else thinks. Only what's good for us. I've been married before, Cade. I wasn't looking for that. In fact, I never wanted it again. I was holding onto something that could never be again, but I finally let that go. I never thought...I never expected *you*. You're what I didn't even know I was looking for. Just you. So...yes. I'll stay. I'll stay. Because I've...I've fallen in love you, Cade." Her eyes glistened in the dim light of the jail cell and he brushed her cheek with his finger. "But you have to promise me one thing."

"Anything."

"No more grizzly bears. They are definitely off my list of things I ever want to see again."

"You have my word, *Mo'onahe*."

"Oh," she added with a sniff, touching the tender side of his face with a brush of her finger. "And call me that whenever you want."

He smiled back at her. "Until the grasses no longer grow on the prairies, *Mo'onahe*," he murmured, then dropped his mouth on hers and kissed her, deeply and true. And the kiss hurt his bruised mouth, but he didn't care. As he folded her in his arms, he gave up a silent prayer of thanks to the Great Spirit for sending her to him and for having the wisdom to steal her that day. But he guessed it was the other way around. She was the one who'd done the stealing and now he knew his heart would never be the same.

In the silence of that kiss, he heard the answer his grandfather told him he would if he only listened. *This is right*, the Earth whispered. *This is honorable. This is true.*

EPILOGUE

They told him it was because of him that they'd met and that today, three months later, on this cold November evening, they would be married.

Little Wolf watched with a secret smile from beside a fragrant, ribbon-tied evergreen bough as Essie and Black Thorn—Cade, as she always called him—exchanged their vows in the decorated great room of Tom Newcastle's home. His chest tightened as they smiled at one another in the candlelight that spilled from the antler chandelier above them.

He supposed each of them might have chosen a more peaceful way to begin a life together, but the Great Spirit had reasons of His own for sucking them down a whirlpool as discarded fragments only to spit them back up as a whole family: him and Shyen Zu, Essie and Cade.

They would not look like other families, which suited him fine. He had no desire to be like others. He wanted to be himself. Like Cade was.

Still, it felt strange to be surrounded by people who cared what happened to him after being alone so long. Aside from his new family, Ollie Warren, Pink and a few of Ollie's ladies were here for the wedding, too. Ollie and her girls had decorated the place with greens, and Pink had cooked the food that had been making his stomach growl for the past hour, laid out on the long table along the wall.

Walks Along Woman and Red Moon and several others of the tribe attended as well, with Red Moon reciting a Cheyenne prayer over them as they spoke their vows. And he'd heard that the Donovans, who couldn't be here, had generously sent them four train tickets to visit them in Front Royal, Virginia, when they could all find the time. The prospect of a train trip across the country to the East stirred his imagination. Perhaps it would be an adventure, like Huckleberry Finn's.

Or perhaps he shouldn't wish for another adventure quite on that scale.

A handful of Tom Newcastle's friends had come, too, the ones who hadn't shown up asking for Cade's death that day. Though they'd never caught those men who'd sold Little Wolf to Chen Lee, Mitchell Laddner was run out of town on a rail just shy of being tarred and feathered for his part in the abuse of children at the school. Reverend Dooley had been disgraced and immediately dismissed from the Industrial School, replaced by a new headmaster who had promptly dismantled the Wages of Sin and was changing things for the better there. Chen Lee had been arrested for the murders of his girls, to which Shyen Zu and Little Wolf had testified. His opium house was shuttered now and gone, which was, he supposed, the best he could hope for the girls Chen Lee had left behind.

Now, Shyen Zu appeared beside him, in a creamy-colored dress Essie had gotten her for the wedding, and she nudged him in the ribs. "What you forget? Quick, quick, little brother."

He frowned and glanced up to find most of the room staring at him. Cade was gesturing to Essie's finger.

Little Wolf practically jumped, realizing he'd forgotten the only job he'd been given here today. He pulled the gold ring from his pocket and handed it to Cade.

Sliding it onto Essie's finger, Cade spoke the last of his vows and the two of them kissed as the preacher pronounced them married. The room broke into applause.

But no one could have looked more tickled than Tom Newcastle himself. He nodded at the small band he'd hired, who struck up a dance for Essie and Cade.

It was no secret that Cade couldn't dance, but Essie didn't seem to mind. Instead, after a few minutes of shuffling together on the dance floor, she leaned close and whispered something in his ear.

He stopped trying to dance and pulled her back to look at her with a shocked expression on his face. Though there was too much noise to hear his words, Little Wolf saw the word "*Baby*?" form on his lips. Essie nodded with a secret smile of her own. Cade swept her into his arms again in front of the whole crowd, none of whom had any idea that their family was about to grow yet again.

Tom Newcastle stood beside him with a cup of punch, which Little Wolf was quite certain was spiked, and cleared his throat.

"What do you think of this whole shebang, Little Wolf?"

"They're very happy. And I am, too."

Tom nodded with a smile.

Little Wolf smiled up at him. "Should I call you grandfather now?"

"Do I look old enough to be a grandfather?" Tom spread his arms wide. Indeed, he did not, in his finely cut black suit and string tie. His eyes twinkled in the candlelight. "But for you and Shyen Zu, I'll make an exception and consider myself lucky."

But Little Wolf knew better. He was the lucky one here. And that luck had only just begun to unfold before him.

In another life, Barbara Ankrum was a successful commercial actress in Hollywood, going on auditions while she and her husband raised their two children. At some point, on the way to an audition apparently, it occurred to her that in order to get her creative life in hand, she ought to write a novel. This epiphany sprang directly from her love of romance novels and an obsession with all things Western. After selling the first book, a Western historical, she left casting directors behind and never looked back.

Barbara's bestselling books have been twice nominated for Romance Writers of America's prestigious RITA award and have won numerous other awards. She also writes contemporaries for Harlequin Intrigue under her own name and for Harlequin Blaze under the pseudonym, Carrie Hudson. After all these years, she still believes in happy endings and feels very lucky to be able to do what she does. The kids are grown now, but Barbara and her husband still live in Southern California with their two cats and a scruffy, unrepentant dog who will, no doubt, find her way into one of Barbara's books soon.

You can contact Barbara through her website at www.barbaraankrum.com

CPSIA information can be obtained
at www.ICGtesting.com
Printed in the USA
LVOW12s0510040717
540204LV00001B/26/P